D1523949

CAT COUNTRY

這自然是追想當時的情形。在當時，腦子已震昏。震昏的腦子也許會發生許多不相聯貫的思念，已經都想不起了；祇有這些——怎樣回去，和怎樣活着——似乎腦子完全清醒之後還記得很眞切，像被海潮打上岸來的兩塊木板，船已全沈了。

Cat Country

A SATIRICAL NOVEL

OF CHINA IN THE 1930'S

BY (LAO SHE) Shu, Sh'ing-ch'un

TRANSLATED BY WILLIAM A. LYELL, JR.

OHIO STATE UNIVERSITY PRESS

貓 城 記

√PZ
3
.S5619
.Cat

Copyright © 1970
by the Ohio State University Press

All Rights Reserved

Printed in the United States of America

Standard Book Number: 8142-0013-3

Library of Congress Catalogue Card Number: 78-83144

CONTENTS

PREFACE

The present translation was done from the edition of Lao She's *Mao-ch'eng Chi* that was issued as number fourteen of the *Ch'en Kuang Encyclopedia of Literature* by the Ch'en Kuang Publishing Company, Shanghai, 1949.

The asterisked footnotes in certain chapters have been inserted by the translator in order to familiarize the general reader with the various aspects of Chinese society that Lao She is satirizing; chapter titles have been added for the convenience of those readers who, having finished the novel, might like to locate a specific passage quickly.

I should like to express my gratitude to my wife, Ruth, for her encouragement and help in this project. Thanks are also due to Mr. Don Marion for his close proofreading of the first draft. I am indebted to my colleagues in the East Asian Division for the help and advice they gave me while I was preparing this translation. Finally, I am grateful to Mr. Weldon Kefauver and Mrs. Jean F. Kuenn of the Ohio State University Press for their advice on format and style and for all their various efforts in seeing the book through to publication.

WILLIAM A. LYELL, JR.

Translator's Introduction

As yet there is scant reliable information on the life of the author of *Cat Country* (*Mao-ch'eng Chi*); the little that is available, however, affords us tantalizingly interesting glimpses into a full and colorful life. With the caveat that the following pages are not at all intended in the spirit of a definitive study, the translator would like to share with the reader facts and interpretations in three interrelated areas of interest: I, Lao She, the Man; II, Lao She, the Writer; and III, Lao She and *Cat Country*.

I. LAO SHE, THE MAN

Lao She is the nom de plume of Shu Ch'ing-ch'un (1898–1966). His family belonged to the Manchu race that had controlled China since 1644 and would continue to rule it until the establishment of the Republic in 1912; at the time of his birth in 1898, however, the Shus lived in rather straitened circumstances in a not-so-prosperous section of Peking. The family was reduced to virtual poverty when Lao She's father, an imperial guard, died in the fighting that took place when the Allied Powers occupied Peking in the wake of the Boxer Uprising of 1900.*

The noted linguist, Lo Ch'ang-p'ei (1899–1958), was one of Lao She's lifelong friends. Lo, also of Manchu origin, remembers Lao She during their primary school days as a lad who was open, strong, and possessed of a great reserve of inner strength. He was, according to Lo's reminiscences, a tough little fellow who could take it: if a teacher beat him with a classroom pointer, the pointer would break before Lao She did. Nor would he shed a single tear, utter a cry, or in any other way beg for mercy.†

In his teens he worked his way through normal school, where he established a good academic record and even found time to make speeches and participate in debates; upon graduation, he was rewarded for his diligence with the principalship of a primary school. Lao She acquitted himself so well in this post that after a few years he was sent south to Kiangsu and Chekiang provinces to inspect the schools there, a high responsibility indeed for someone who was still little more than a boy.‡

Upon returning to Peking he was promoted to Education Advancement Officer (*Ch'üan-hsüeh-yüan*), a post

* Shu Chün-ch'eng, "Reminiscences of My Uncle (*Yi Shu-fu*)," *Central Daily News* (*Chung-yang Jih-pao*) (Taipei), Oct. 13, 1966, in the Supplement (*Fu-k'an*).

† Lo Ch'ang-p'ei, *Chung-kuo-jen yü Chung-kuo-wen* (*Chinese People and Letters*), (Hong Kong: Lung Men Bookstore, 1966), p. 96.

‡ Ibid., p. 96. See also Shu, "Reminiscences."

that most people considered an enviable one. The tough and highly independent Lao She, however, soon arrived at such an unfavorable estimate of China's modernized educational institutions that he decided he could no longer in good conscience remain in this post. (Disenchantment with educational modernization is a dominant motif in his works; Chapters 17 and 18 of *Cat Country* develop this theme at great length.) He thereupon resigned the office and taught for half a year at the Nankai High School in Tientsin before returning to Peking to take a post as secretary with the Peking Education League (*Pei-ching Chiao-yü Hui*). While with the league he concurrently taught Chinese at the Peking First Middle School. His combined income, however, was not one third of what it had been as an Education Advancement Officer: clearly, the change had been motivated by principle. During this same period the apparently indefatigable young Lao She also studied at Yenching University and managed to pinch pennies hard enough to support himself and his mother.*

During this period he was so pressed for money that his friend Lo Ch'ang-p'ei offered him a loan to help see him through the severe Peking winter. Lao She declined, saying that the cold winter winds were good for him and would "blow his bones hard" (in other words, "toughen him up"). By way of the last straw, Lao She picked this time to fall in love. When he shared the secret of his passion with Lo Ch'ang-p'ei, the latter rashly took it

* Ibid., pp. 96–97. See also Zbigniew Slupski, *The Evolution of a Modern Chinese Writer,* (Prague: Czechoslovak Academy of Science, 1966), p. 82.

upon himself to serve as go-between, an office for which apparently he was eminently unsuited, for the whole affair terminated rather melodramatically when the girl's father went off to become a Buddhist monk, and his daughter, the object of Lao She's youthful ardor, became a novice who finally accompanied the old man on his spiritual journey. Mr. Lo felt unconscionably guilty about the whole thing until years later when he felt that he had made up for this romantic debacle by introducing his old friend to Hu Chieh-ch'ing, the woman who eventually became Lao She's wife.*

As a young man in his mid-twenties, Lao She left China in 1924 and sailed to England where he taught Chinese in the School of Oriental Studies at London University. He was not to go back to his native land until six years later in 1930.† During the interim, Shu Ch'ing-ch'un, the unknown young Manchu, was to become Lao She the celebrated novelist. A half-year or so after his arrival in London, the novelty of being in a foreign land began to wear off and he began to feel terribly homesick for the familiar sights and sounds of China. Images of the familiar haunts of his native land shifted back and forth in the depths of his consciousness, forcing themselves to the surface whenever he dropped his guard. For instance, though he had mapped out a program of reading to improve his grasp of the English language, the old familiar images of China made it difficult to concentrate. No sooner would the words of

* Lo, *Chung-kuo-jen*, pp. 97–98.

† Ting Yi, *A Short History of Modern Chinese Literature* (Peking: Foreign Languages Press, 1959), p. 173.

Charles Dickens's *Nicholas Nickleby* or *The Pickwick Papers* succeed in conjuring up a new image on the surface of his imagination than one of the old, familiar images of a scene back in China would surge up and bump its newer competitor aside. It then occurred to Lao She that since novels are built of such images, he might as well try his hand at translating the abundant images of his own imagination into words and thus fashion a novel.*

The result was *The Philosophy of Lao Chang* (*Lao Chang te Che-hsüeh*). It took him a year to complete, and then on the advice of the Chinese writer Lo Hua-sheng (nom de plume of Hsü Ti-shan, 1893–1941), who was in London at that time, he sent it off to *The Short Story* (*Hsiao-shuo Yueh-pao*), which published it serially beginning with the July, 1926, number.† Back in China his friends Pai Ti-chou and Lo Ch'ang-p'ei handled the manuscript. Lo, thinking himself insufficiently qualified as literary critic, turned the manuscript over to the already-famous Lu Hsün (1881–1936) for an opinion. The latter acknowledged that the book was rich in Peking local color, but opined that with regard to technique there were places in it that could stand improvement. Though acknowledging his own inadequacy as a critic, Lo Ch'ang-pei, himself, objected by mail to his old friend that the whole thing was lacking in any philosophic foundation; Lao She countered in his return letter by asking what philosophic foundation there was to

* Lao She, *Lao-niu P'o-ch'e* (*An Old Ox and a Broken-down Cart*) (Hong Kong: Universe Bookstore, 1961), pp. 3–4.

† C. T. Hsia, *A History of Modern Chinese Fiction: 1917–1957* (New Haven: Yale University Press, 1961), p. 166.

Dickens' work. Despite the reservations of Lu and Lo, however, upon publication *The Philosophy of Lao Chang* was an immediate success, for it brought to modern Chinese literature—a literature that had itself only been born a few years previously with the publication of Lu Hsün's colloquial short story "Diary of a Madman" in 1918—an element that had been hitherto sorely lacking, and that element was *humor.* For whatever its defects, *The Philosophy of Lao Chang* was uproariously funny. It was further graced by vivid descriptive passages, sharp satire, and a fluent and racy handling of the Peking dialect.*

The Czech critic Zbigniew Slupski has said that while the story outline and plot of *The Philosophy of Lao Chang* were borrowed from *Nicholas Nickleby,* the techniques employed in the telling of the tale are clearly under the influence of the traditional Chinese storyteller.† Indeed, Lao She had been familiar with the art of the storyteller since his childhood in Peking, when he and Lo Ch'ang-p'ei used to misappropriate their school snack allowances to go to teashops and listen to the professional Peking raconteurs.‡ Many of the narrative devices of Dickens must have looked familiar to the young Lao She; others, of course, were new, and no doubt he learned from them. He could not, however, have either learned or imitated had he not been a mem-

* Lo, *Chung-kuo-jen,* pp. 98–99.

† Slupski, *The Evolution of a Modern Chinese Writer,* p. 32.

‡ See Lao She's short story "Crooktail (*Wai-mao-er*)" where he describes going to the story-teller's as a boy. Lo Ch'ang-p'ei has attested to the historicity of the opening of the story. See Lo, *Chung-kuo-jen,* p. 96.

ber of the storyteller's fraternity to begin with. Some critics have claimed that he was in part corrupted by Dickens, for like him, Lao She developed great skill in creating individual scenes, but was somewhat inept at grouping them together into the coherent wholes of novels. However, it is much more likely that this defect was picked up at home, for the structure of the traditional Chinese novel is also episodic and notoriously loose.*

His second novel, *Chao Tzu-yüeh* (*Master Chao Says*), also showed a similar Dickensian influence. He himself viewed the work as the tail end of *The Philosophy of Lao Chang*. Like the latter, *Chao Tzu-yüeh* was also set against the background of Peking and provided the reader with a satirical look at education, this time through the lives of modern students.

During his protracted stay in England, Lao She was much impressed with the question of comparative personality. What were the English like? What were the Chinese like? Cyril Birch has pointed out that Lao She "envied the English their civic pride and sense of responsibility; irresponsibility and self-interest became indeed his favorite targets of satire." † Concern with this kind of question produced the last of the three novels he wrote during his English sojourn, *The Two Ma's* (*Erh*

* The Mainland critic, Wang Yao, sees the influence of traditional Chinese fiction in the loose and episodic structure of Lao She's early works. See Wang Yao, *Chung-kuo Hsin Wen-hsüeh Shih-kao* (*A Draft History of Modern Chinese Literature*) (Shanghai: New Literature Press, 1953), I, 231.

† Cyril Birch, "Lao She: The Humourist in his Humour," *The China Quarterly*, no. 8 (Oct.–Dec., 1961), p. 47. I am indebted to Mr. Birch for the translation "reverie leaves" for *mi-yeh*.

Ma). Rather different from his first two works, *The Two Ma's* was a study in culture conflict (English and Chinese) and in generation conflict (the elder Ma versus the younger Ma). Assessments of how successful he was in comparing Chinese and Englishmen thrown together in the hurly-burly of London life have varied. Zbigniew Slupski, for instance, has pointed out in his recent study of the early works of Lao She that in *The Two Ma's* Chinese come off so badly that "the author justified thus, to some extent, the scorn of the English for the Chinese." * This somewhat ambivalent attitude toward being Chinese is strongly reflected again in *Cat Country.*

After leaving London he toured the continent for three months, spending most of the time in Paris. He fell in love with the city and would have stayed longer had he been successful in finding some kind of job to make ends meet. Forced to bid a reluctant farewell to France, he booked third-class passage to Singapore (he had just enough money to get that far). Here he welcomed the opportunity to get a firsthand look at South East Asia, a land that he had come to know, in part, through the works of Joseph Conrad. Lao She was a great admirer of Conrad; however, he was irked by the fact that Conrad's heroes were invariably white men while Asians appeared only in secondary roles at best and, at worst, were used merely for local color. He had also found it noteworthy that Conrad often treated Southeast Asia as the white man's poison: incapable of conquering the lush landscape of the South Seas, the Caucasian was often en-

* Zbigniew Slupski, "The Work of Lao She during the First Phase of his Career," *Studies in Modern Chinese Literature,* ed. Jaroslav Průšek (Berlin: Akademie-Verlag, 1964), p. 91.

gulfed by it. Lao She thought that he would write an entirely different kind of Southeast Asian tale, a tale in which Chinese would appear as the heroes, in which Chinese, buoyed up by their natural optimism, would confront the lush though lugubrious backdrops of Southeast Asian landscapes and conquer them! It was a historical commonplace that Chinese had played a leading, if not indispensable, role in the development of Southeast Asia: they had flattened its densest forests; they had cultivated its wildest ground; they had survived its nameless diseases. They had prevailed! To our young and confident author their struggle appeared as a veritable gold mine of material.*

However, to do an adequate job of refining this ore into fiction, he would have to have learned the Chinese dialects spoken in Fukien and Kwangtung, for it was from these provinces that most of the Chinese settlers in Southeast Asia had come. Furthermore, in Malaya, a good grasp of Malayan would have been necessary. Three new languages! All of this involved a far greater expenditure of time than he had forseen. Moreover the only job he had been able to get upon his arrival in Singapore was as a teacher—a job that would tie him to the city, far removed from the back country into which many of the Chinese settlers had penetrated.†

Somewhat discouraged by so many negative considerations, he lowered his sights a bit and decided to content himself with writing about the children with whom he daily came into contact. The result was *Little Po's Birth-*

* Lao She, *Lao-niu,* pp. 23–27.

† Ibid., p. 25.

day (*Hsiao-p'o te Sheng-jih*), a short novel in which he explored both the complexities and the simplicities of childhood.* He, himself, was especially pleased that in this novel his control of the colloquial language had progressed so far that he had been able to communicate everything he wanted to say, using only the simple language of children.†

Returning to China in 1931, he taught for three years in Cheloo University at Tsinan and then for one year at Shantung University.‡ While teaching at Tsinan, he came into contact with many people who had taken part in the "May 3rd Incident" of 1928 during which Japanese forces had attacked Tsinan in an effort to coerce the Nationalist Government into accepting certain political demands. He decided to center a novel on the incident and wrote *Ta-ming Lake* (*Ta-ming Hu*). The manuscript was lost in a fire occasioned by still another Japanese incident in 1932. Rather than rewrite it, he salvaged enough from it for a short story, "Crescent Moon (*Yüeh-ya-er*)," § a lugubrious account of the moral and physical deterioration of a prostitute that seems strangely out of place in the works of a humorist.

At about this time (the early 1930's), he apparently began to feel somewhat embarrassed about being a mere humorist, for it was a time when the Japanese had occupied Manchuria and obviously intended to conquer all of China late or soon. He was, in effect, confronted

* Ibid., pp. 26–27.

† Ibid., p. 29.

‡ Hsia, *A History,* p. 167.

§ Slupski, "The Work of Lao She," p. 91.

with an identity crisis, and for the next few years he was to waver between the roles of humorist and preacher. One moment he would be found on the sidelines of society good-naturedly pointing out the hilarious contradictions in it for the pleasure of passersby, but the next, one would find him mounted on a soapbox in the midst of the melee exhorting his fellow countrymen to reform. In the novel here translated as *Cat Country* (written in 1932) we shall find him on the soapbox more often than on the sidelines.

Disappointed with the never-published *Ta-ming Lake* as well as with *Cat Country*, in his next novel, *Divorce* (*Li-hun*), Lao She returned to the comfortable sights and sounds of Peking for setting, and backed away from the unsure terrain of satire onto the more certain ground of humor for style. He followed this with *Heavensent* (*Niu T'ien-tz'u Chuan*), a comic novel about the life of a foundling, growing to manhood in the home of his foster parents. C. T. Hsia has noted that *Heavensent* is in many ways modeled upon Fielding's *Tom Jones*,* another indication of the strong influence of English literature on Lao She.

Toward the mid-1930's he became increasingly convinced that he could not serve two masters and resolved to give up teaching so that he might fully devote himself to literature; he had become convinced that a writer ought to be nurtured by the society at large and not such a limited part of it as a university community.† Then in

* C. T. Hsia, *A History*, p. 180.

† Lo, Chung-kuo-jen, 101. See also Slupski, *The Evolution of a Modern Writer*, pp. 88–90.

1937, the year that Japan invaded China, his most successful novel was published, *Rickshaw Boy* (*Lo-t'o Hsiang-tzu*), a novel which was translated into English by Evan King and became an American best-seller shortly after its appearance in 1945. The setting was Peking; the hero, a young, strong, individualistic rickshaw boy who in the arrogance of his youth was convinced that he could stand up to anything that society could throw at him, but was in the end overwhelmed by that very society—a denouement that signaled at once Lao She's loss of faith in the power of individual effort to reform society and his awakening to the need for collective effort.* The success of the novel lies partially in the happy fact that in this work he managed to reconcile the antagonistic roles of humorist and preacher, and to find a middle ground between the two extremes from which he could utilize his humor to carry a very serious message while at the same time producing a very solid piece of fiction. One wonders whether he might not have continued to develop in this direction had the war not intervened. *Rickshaw Boy* was his finest novel and he seemed to have finally arrived as a mature writer. The War of Resistance (*K'ang-chan* 1937–45) against Japan, however, thrust a new role upon Lao She: patriotic propagandist. He was chosen president of the Chinese Writers' Antiaggression Association and retained that position throughout the war.†

In his role as president of the association, he was

* Evan King's translation fails to show this, since Mr. King took it upon himself to change the ending to a happy one.

† C. T. Hsia, *A Short History,* p. 366.

indefatigable in organizing writers and forging literature into a weapon against Japan. He also found time to write short stories, plays, a long ballad (some 40,000 words), and a patriotic novel, *Cremation* (*Huo-tsang*).* During the war years he also did much to promote the various traditional forms of popular theater, and in the wartime capital of Chungking he, himself, often used to mount the stage to show his own proficiency at both *hsiang-sheng* (a burlesque type humor, presented by a straight-man and comedian) and *ku-shu* ("drum singing," storytelling in song and recitative accompanied by a drum).†

After Japan's defeat, he began publishing the trilogy *Four Generations Under One Roof* (*Ssu-shih T'ung-t'ang*), a study of Peking during the years of the Japanese occupation. The first two volumes, *Bewilderment* (*Huang-huo*) and *Ignominy* (*T'ou-sheng*), were published in 1946; the third volume, *Famine* (*Chi-huang*), was published serially in *Fiction Monthly* during 1950. Ida Pruitt abridged the trilogy and translated it into a single volume, which she titled *Yellow Storm*.‡

At the close of World War II, the State Department invited him to come to the United States under its cultural cooperation program. He remained on a protracted lecture tour, returning to China in 1949 after the establishment of the People's Republic. Following his return

* Jos. Schyns et al., *1,500 Modern Chinese Novels and Plays* (Hong Kong: Lung Men Bookstore, 1966), p. 85.

† Hsü Chien-wen, "The Rise and Fall of Lao She, Part II," *Central Daily News* (*Chung-yang Jih-pao*) (Taipei), Oct. 23, 1960, in the Supplement (*Fu-k'an*).

‡ C. T. Hsia, *A History*, p. 369.

to the Mainland, he underwent a period of self-examination and self-criticism, and seemed entirely successful in making the transition to becoming a productive member of the new society.*

During the 1950's he began producing plays, stories, articles on the art of writing, and rose to become chairman of the Peking branch of the All-China Federation of Writers and Artists. Ideologically, however, his pre-1949 works were, for the most part, judged unacceptable by the new arbiters of literary taste. It was objected that in most of them his sense of justice as well as his compassion for the oppressed were both weakened by his humor, and he, himself, had once admitted as much. Furthermore, in direct opposition to prevailing party dictates as to what literature should be, too many of his works ended in gloom rather than the aura of revolutionary hope. Despite all this, however, he was given points for his poverty in youth, his love of the oppressed, his love of China, and his tireless efforts in remoulding himself; he was even honored with the title of "People's Artist." †

During the 1960's, however, there were increasing indications that he was in trouble. In September of 1966 the Red Guards even accused him of being anti-Mao and anti-Party. Then, on October 2, the *Central Daily News* in Taipei reported that due to harassment by Red Guards, Lao She had leapt from a building to his death. If this indeed be true, then there was a final macabre

* Birch, "Lao She," pp. 55–59.

† Ting Yi, *A Short History of Modern Chinese Literature,* pp. 172–75.

fitness about the way he died, for he had been a longtime critic of students and had (as is shown quite plainly in *Cat Country*) always been aware of the bursts of ignorant fury of which they were capable.* And yet, no matter what the circumstances of his passing, he did, after all, die in the bosom of his native and beloved Peking.

II. LAO SHE, THE WRITER

There are some men who prefer books to people, who would rather ponder a great idea than sip a cup of good tea. Books and ideas belong in universities; they are the things of intellectuals. Tea and people are more often associated with the storyteller's shop; they belong there, for they are the things of the common man. Lao She was a man who preferred tea and people to ideas and books. He was a storyteller, not an intellectual. And yet he often seemed hounded by a gnawing doubt that being a mere "storyteller" was somehow not enough, a vague feeling that he too ought to be an intellectual. At such times, as we have seen in the first section of this intro-

* The *New York Times* carried an AP release to the same effect on October 2, 1966. Another article in the *Central Daily News* two years later (April 11, 1968) quoted the wife of the noted Chinese violinist Ma Ssu-ts'ung as stating that she knew the true facts surrounding Lao She's demise because her relatives lived on the same *hut'ung* in Peking. According to her account, the Red Guards went to Lao She's home looking for trouble, and the old author, furious at their arrogance, struck out at them, whereupon they beat him to death. See "The Tragic Tale of the Literary and Artistic World on Mainland China" (*"Ta-lu Wen-yi-chieh te Pei-ts'an Ku-shih"*), an interview with Ma Ssu-ts'ung and his wife recorded by Huang Chao-heng.

duction, he would forsake his role as humorous teller of tales and begin to act strangely like an intellectual, analyzing and preaching.

Traditionally, Chinese society viewed fiction disdainfully as little more than a frivolous pastime. In the twentieth century, however, Chinese students returned from sojourns in Japan, America, and Europe with new notions about the value of fiction and the mission of the serious novelist. Around the close of World War I such students initiated a literary revolution, creating a new literature whose language was modeled on spoken Chinese (rather than the classical diction of standard Confucian texts) and whose content belonged to the new China of the twentieth century. At this point some of the aura of moral importance that had once belonged exclusively to the philosophic and historical classics of the Confucian tradition was now lent to the novel and short story. In concrete terms this meant that in the present century those members of the intellectual elite who would once have concerned themselves exclusively with the commentarial traditions of the classics had now taken up fiction as a respectable vocation for an educated man; it did not mean, however, that ordinary storytellers had suddenly become respectable intellectuals. Fiction did not suddenly become prestigious because society's attitude toward it had changed; it became prestigious now because intellectuals either wrote it themselves or patronized those who did.

Lao She, by virtue of background as well as temperament, was basically a writer and not an intellectual. Much of the conflict that he experienced between the roles of humorist and preacher stemmed from the fact that given the society in which he lived, and given the monumental problems that faced China in the twentieth century, he felt somewhat guilty at not being an intellectual who could analyze problems and then exhort his fellow countrymen in the direction of this or that solution. In an era of turmoil was it enough to be a mere entertainer?

Since he was never really one of them, it is not surprising that Lao She often felt a degree of hostility against the intellectuals. We find evidence of this antipathy in Chapter 19 ("Of Scholars Old and New") of *Cat Country*. Similarly, in a number of his short stories and novels he directs his humor against those people who have received a modern education and have thereby become "civilized" (*wen-ming-hua*). In this aversion to "civilization" and sophistication one is made vaguely aware of Lao She's own lower-class background. Both by class and temperament he belonged with the storytellers much more than with the college professors. He, himself, must have felt some of this when he gave up his career in college teaching.

Lao She was born and raised in Peking, and in China there is something as special about Pekingers as there is about New Yorkers in the United States or Parisians in France. Throughout his life, Lao She seems always to have felt most comfortable when writing about his beloved city. One is tempted to speculate that, no matter what the circumstances of his death may have been, it must have been a source of comfort to his departed spirit to have died in his much-loved Peking. In *Rickshaw Boy* he described her charms in early summer in the following words:

> The first wave of heat in the opening of summer had acted like a divine charm, bringing out everywhere the fascination of the ancient city of Peking; in due season, regardless of suffering, calamity, or death, she had chosen to display her powers, hypnotizing the hearts of a million people and leaving them in a dream-like trance, able only to sing poems in her praise. She was filthy; she was beautiful; she was senile and decadent; she was lively and smiling; she was disparate and confused; she was at peace and in leisure; she was Peking, immense, inimitable, and much to be loved.*

The most immediate association that the majority of Chinese readers make with the name Lao She is "Peking dialect." His passion for the language of his beloved city was fully as intense as his ardor for its walls, streets, and shops. However, his devotion to what some have called "Peking cockney" makes his work difficult going for Chinese readers who are not familiar with the dialect.

Lao She had an ear for language and thoroughly delighted in attempting to reproduce even its most subtle nuances on the written page. Of all the writers of the 1920's and 1930's, he was perhaps the most successful in recording the melodies and rhythms of the spoken language on the written page. This is so much the case that some of his sentences that are somewhat ambiguous when seen on the printed page become immediately clear when read aloud with the proper intonation. The prose of a short story like "Black and White Li" (*Hei Pai Li*), for instance, is so alive with the subtle overtones of

* Evan King, trans., *Rickshaw Boy* (New York: Reynal & Hitchcock, 1945), p. 370.

the living human voice that the Chinese ideographs fairly jump off the page and begin talking to you. This is something that only someone thoroughly familiar with the living art of the storyteller could have achieved.

As a craftsman, Lao She took a lifelong interest in the technical aspects of writing. He first revealed the extent of this interest to the general reading public in 1937 with the publication of *An Old Ox and a Broken-down Cart* (*Lao-niu P'o-ch'e*), a thin volume of monographs in which he discusses his early experiences as a writer and holds forth in a series of short essays on such subjects as humor, the description of scenery, the delineation of characters, style, etc. In this work, although he cites a number of the traditional works of Chinese vernacular fiction as examples, he more often discusses foreign models; apparently his experiences in England were still very close to him. Since the earliest influences are often the most decisive, it would be well perhaps to single out some of those that he touches on in *An Old Ox*.

As we have seen in the first section of this introduction, he was heavily influenced by Charles Dickens. In reading through the essays in *An Old Ox*, we discover that he was also familiar with the works of such diverse writers as Thackery, Walpole, Hardy, H. G. Wells, D. H. Lawrence, and Edgar Alan Poe.*

He also dipped into writers who would today be considered somewhat obscure. He was, for instance, so impressed with the short story, "The Misanthrope," by John Davys Beresford, that he wrote a Chinese version of it which he titled, after the nickname of its protago-

* Lao She, *Lao-niu*, pp. 71–94, passim.

nist, "Crooktail (*Wai-mao-er*)." * This is, so far as I know, the only story that Lao She ever did in direct imitation. During the 1930's he had expanded his creative horizon to include the short story as well as the novel. He found it a much more difficult form than he had imagined and became immediately fascinated with short-story technique. In this regard, it is significant perhaps that he should have decided to translate "The Misanthrope" into a Chinese setting, for the plot of the story is centered on a gimmick: the hermit protagonist of "The Misanthrope" has a peculiar ability to see people as they really are, morally speaking, whenever he looks at them back over his shoulder. There can be little doubt, I think, that it was precisely this gimmick that fascinated Lao She, the craftsman; he must have seen great dramatic possibility in it. As a matter of fact—in my judgment, at any rate—in working out the ramifications of this idea in "Crooktail," Lao She showed more imagination than had Beresford in the original. It is another indication of his devotion to the *craft* of fiction; he was always intrigued by the technical intricacies of style and structure, and wanted to know what made stories work.

The intensity of his concern with the craft of writing is quite understandable when one remembers that he was one of the pioneers in the creation of modern Chinese fiction. The whole movement toward the crea-

* Ibid., p. 57. The story is here identified as "The Hermit" and the author given as F. D. Beresford. I assume that "The Hermit" identification may have been due to a lapse of memory on the part of Lao She, and the "F. D." for "J. D." may well have been a printer's error. According to Lo Ch'ang-p'ei, the character, Crooktail, is—in his little boy phase at any rate—based upon Lo. See Lo, *Chung-kuo-jen,* p. 99.

tion of a new and modern colloquial literature was not yet a decade old when he started to write. To be sure, many of his models could be taken from the traditional vernacular literature of the past, but there were also pathways that he sought to explore where the traditional craft of fiction had left no signposts; hence he was greatly interested in the techniques employed by English writers.

He especially admired D. H. Lawrence and Joseph Conrad, for instance, for their ability to take characters and scenery and juxtapose them in such a way that an intimate relationship would obtain between the two. Writing in 1937 about his early experiences as a writer, Lao She singled out for special approval Lawrence's description of a funeral in *The White Peacock.*

> Again a loud cry from the hill-top. The woman has followed thus far, the big, shapeless woman, and she cries with loud cries after the white coffin as it descends the hill, and the children that cling to her skirts, weep aloud, and are not to be hushed by the other woman, who bends over them, but does not form one of the group. How the crying frightens the birds and the rabbits. . . .*

Lao She found it especially noteworthy that Lawrence had combined people and background by having the woman's crying frighten the birds.† Similarly, he was greatly impressed with Marlow's description of the sea in Conrad's short novel, *Youth:*

* D. H. Lawrence, *The White Peacock* (Carbondale and Edwardsville: Southern Illinois University Press, 1966), pp. 171–72.

† Lao She, *Lao-niu,* p. 84.

> "Ah! The good old-time—the good old time. Youth and the sea. Glamour and the sea! The good strong sea, the salt, bitter sea, that could whisper to you and roar at you and knock your breath out of you." *

Lao She particularly admired this passage for its fusion of man and nature, of actor and backdrop. He felt that traditional Chinese fiction was often faulted by a failure to integrate characters and scenery. Many of the traditional novels carried the narration along in vernacular prose, but inserted stretches of verse when describing scenery † with the result that the protagonists often played out their parts against a static backdrop that had been limned in by verse. The result was a disjointed lack of continuity between characters and setting. Lao She complained that even the beautiful eighteenth-century novel *Hung Lou Meng* (*Dream of the Red Chamber*) was not free from this shortcoming. He also confesses that in his early works he himself had not mastered the art of description, but would often avail himself of the enormous stock of four-character clichés available in the classical language. When his friend Pai Ti-chou objected to the resulting mixture of colloquial and classical diction in his first two novels, Lao She had countered that

* Joseph Conrad, *Youth: A Narrative* (Garden City, N.Y.: Doubleday Anchor Books, 1959), p. 65.

† The contemporary critic, C. T. Hsia, has pointed out that the eighteenth-century novel *The Scholars* (*Ju-lin Wai-shih*) was the first major vernacular novel to integrate descriptive passages with the narrative text in colloquial prose rather than resorting to the time-honored device of inserting verse descriptions. See C. T. Hsia, *The Classic Chinese Novel* (New York and London: Columbia University Press, 1968), p. 204.

by larding the colloquial with classical phrases, he was raising its level. Later, after having realized that he had really used the four-character clichés of the classical language merely because they were ready-made and provided a quick and easy way to get through the descriptive parts of a story, he then made a positive effort to avoid this shortcoming and employed the colloquial language for descriptive passages.*

As translator, perhaps I might point out that Lao She's rather professional interest in writing descriptive passages is not altogether an unmixed blessing, for occasionally it leads him to create imagery so complex that it develops a momentum of its own and then, in Frankenstein fashion, carries the author away to the frontiers of ambiguity. The description of the crowd in Chapter 11 ("The Capital of Cat Country") of the present work is a good case in point. On the other hand, he often comes up with a splendid passage like the one in Chapter 7 ("A Land of Peeping Toms") where he describes a Martian sunrise.

We occasionally encounter a compulsive punster, but a bird like Lao She is a bit more exotic: he was a compulsive "metaphor-ster." Much of his prose is just chock-full of similes and metaphors. This is not so true of the present novel as it is of some of his other works, but, even so, the sensitive reader of *Cat Country* will probably soon become aware of this penchant. His metaphors and similes are delightful most of the time, but occasionally they fall flat. I imagine that if one were walking downtown with him and spotted a bowlegged

* Lao She, *Lao-niu,* p. 17.

girl on the other side of the street, Lao She could immediately produce a string of uproariously entertaining similes and metaphors describing the unfortunate girl's shortcoming. It was a peculiar talent that he had and one that he developed with practice.

His technical interest in the art of telling a story continued throughout his entire life; he was a devoted lover of the craft. The first work in which he discussed the technique of fiction was *An Old Ox and a Broken-down Cart,* published in 1937; then in 1964 (some twenty-seven years, two wars, and a revolution later) he published a second collection of essays on writing, *The Language Must Be Beautiful* (*Ch'u-k'ou Ch'eng-chang*).* In tone, it is entirely different from his first work; the essays and speeches included in it were composed under the stress of varying forms of political pressures and shifting orthodoxies, and they were written by a new (i.e., ideologically retrained) Lao She; and yet despite all that, behind its prose one still recognizes the familiar silhouette of the old Peking storyteller. One finds him still grappling with the old problems—use of dialogue, description of scenery, use of metaphor, character delineation, etc.

A typical Lao She novel is characterized by a loose and episodic structure.† A certain informal and ram-

* Lao She, *Ch'u-k'ou Ch'eng-ch'ang* (Peking: Writers' Press, 1964). I have followed Slupski in translating the title of this work. See Slupski, *The Evolution,* p. 118.

† Like many of his contemporaries he published most often on a serial basis in periodicals that paid by the word and this may do as much to explain his fondness for episodic writing as the influence of Dickens or the traditional Chinese novel.

bling quality that is characteristic of much of his work often causes the reader to be conscious of the storyteller behind the prose. In many of his works, much in the fashion of the traditional teashop storyteller, he will unceremoniously interrupt the narrative continuity of his tale in order to address his reader-audience directly with a critical aside on this or that character or event. Some modern Chinese readers, conversant with, and influenced by, the techniques of Western literature, find this teashop atavism objectionable; to object to it, however, is to demand that Lao She not be Lao She. One can well imagine that his own answer to such an objection might well be: "If you don't like it, go to another shop where the tea is stronger and the stories better—if you can find one."

After becoming familiar with his works, a reader of Lao She is not only aware that he has to do with a storyteller but can even begin to make out the vague outlines of that storyteller's personality behind the prose: an open, witty, straightforward, and masculine northerner. He is a rather attractive person, this storyteller, and one often gets the impression that he would make a good friend, would be the kind of person that one would like to be around.

The attentive reader will also note that this teller of tales can talk entertainingly about almost anything—except women and love. He was, by his own testimony, never able to write very well about females and never felt very comfortable in their presence.* As a mature writer, he felt that one of the major weaknesses of his

* Lao She, *Lao-niu*, p. 14.

work was his inability to handle successfully the theme of love between the sexes.* Like many of the heroes in Chinese knight-errant fiction, he seems to have felt that too keen an interest in the opposite sex was a mark of effeminacy. (A masculine northerner would readily assume that there must be something "sissy-ish" about a man who likes to be around women all the time.) Though women were not subjects he relished, he did write exceedingly well about old women. The description of Madam Ambassador in Chapter 15 of *Cat Country* is a good example.†

In sum, Lao She was an enormously talented enter-

* Ibid., p. 22.

† His attitude toward women may have had much to do with the powerful figure of his own mother. As we have seen, from an early age, he was financially responsible for her; in fact, his relatively late marriage (in his thirty-fourth year) was partially due to the weight of this responsibility. In general he seems to have been a devoted son; however, his relationship to his mother was not always one of pure filial obedience. His nephew, Shu Chün-ch'eng, relates that when Lao She returned from England, he had converted away from his mother's pious Buddhist faith to Roman Catholicism. He was apparently a dedicated convert, for once while his mother was taking her midday nap, he destroyed her wooden image of Kuan Yin (the Buddhist Goddess of Mercy) and threw away the offerings that she had arranged in front of the little wooden statue. Upon waking, the old lady was so incensed that she drove her son from the house with repeated blows. Relatives and friends arranged a truce on the condition that Lao She apologize and make restitution by replacing the small wooden statue of Kuan Yin that he had destroyed. He agreed. Instead of buying another Kuan Yin, however, he purchased a small statue of the Virgin Mary which so closely resembled Kuan Yin that the pious old lady happily burned incense and recited sutras before it without a second thought. Eventually, however, Lao She was so moved by the piety of his mother's faith that he renounced his Catholicism and returned to Buddha. See Shu, "Reminiscences."

tainer. He was not, either by nature or training, an intellectual. As we have seen, in his works, he was occasionally tempted to forsake the storyteller's teashop for the political activist's soapbox; but perhaps even this temptation can be traced back to the brotherhood of nimble tongues and inventive minds, for the traditional storytellers themselves—ever maintaining a sense of distance between themselves and the tales that they were telling—always felt free to address the audience directly when occasion demanded in order to approve a loyal minister or condemn an unfilial son.

Beyond everything else, however, the thing that most endeared Lao She to the hearts of his Chinese readers was his racy Peking dialect and rich, northern sense of humor. These are the hallmarks of his talent; these are the things he could not have "learned" either from native or foreign models. They are the essence of Lao She the writer. Apart from his lifelong dedication to the craft of writing—and his amazing productivity—they are perhaps the qualities for which he will be most remembered.

III. LAO SHE AND "CAT COUNTRY"

Written in the early 1930's, *Cat Country* is a satire on the China of that period. What kind of China was it that Lao She returned to? In other words, what kind of China was Lao She satirizing in *Cat Country?*

After the Nationalist occupation of Peking in June of 1928, the nation was nominally wrested from the control of the warlords and unified under the direction of the Nationalist Party; however, this new unity was more apparent than real. Then in 1931, there occurred the Nine-Eighteen Incident: on the eighteenth of September (the ninth month) Japanese troops, on dubious pretext, occupied Mukden in Manchuria. They rapidly seized other strategic centers, and then early in 1932 split Manchuria off from China by establishing the puppet state of Manchoukuo; neither China nor the League of Nations seemed able to do anything to stem the tide of Japanese aggression.

On the twenty-eighth of the first month of 1932 there occurred the One–Twenty-eight Incident. Ostensibly the issue was trade. In protest over Japanese aggression in Manchuria, the Chinese had organized anti-Japanese boycotts. Friction in Shanghai led the Japanese to demand that the authorities in that city dissolve all boycott associations. Before the demands could be negotiated, Japanese marines, on January 28, occupied the Chapei section of the city. Hostilities did not end until early in March; during the interim, a large area was laid waste, and a number of lives were lost. The galleys of one of Lao She's novels, *Hsiao P'o's Birthday,* and the manuscript of another, *Ta-ming Lake,* were lost; the fighting also resulted in the closing-down of the *Short Story Monthly,* the periodical in which all of his works had hitherto first appeared. All of these incidents were intimately related to the writing of *Cat Country.*

> After *The Short Story Monthly* ceased publication, the only decent literary periodical being published in the wake of the Shanghai incident was the *Contemporary Magazine* under the editorship of Shih Chih-ts'un. Mr. Shih asked me to do a long story for his magazine and I agreed. This was the first time that I

> had done a manuscript for a magazine other than *The Short Story Monthly.* What I wrote this time was *Cat Country.*[*]

In the same passage, he goes on to tell us that, apart from the request of Shih Chih-ts'un, his own motivation for writing the novel was disappointment in national affairs and indignation over China's military failures.

Lao She, himself, considered *Cat Country* a failure. He held that writing it had been a mistake because the style of the work was in direct conflict with his own basic personality structure. *Cat Country* was an attempt at satire, but Lao She felt that he, himself, was constitutionally a humorist and not a satirist. In an essay titled "On Humor," he distinguished satire and humor in terms of personality types rather than literary genres.

> Above all, humor is a frame of mind. We all know people who are overly sensitive and always approach things with a surcharge of emotion, never willing to make allowances for others. . . . A person with a sense of humor is not at all like this . . . he sees the flaws in mankind and wants to point them out to others; however, he does not stop at merely spotting these flaws, but goes on to positively *accept* them. And thus everyone has something funny about him, the humorist himself being no exception; if we take this to an even higher plane, then the fact that man is limited to a hundred years of life at most and yet would like to live forever, is in and of itself an extremely funny contradiction given in the very nature of human existence itself. Thus our laughter carries with it an element of sympathy, and at this point

[*] Lao She, *Lao-niu,* p. 39.

> humor ceases being merely funny and enters the realm of profundity.*

And what of satire? Again in Lao She's own words:

> Satire must be humorous, but it is more biting than humor . . . [Satire] doesn't make us laugh comfortably, but rather makes us smile coldly, and when we have finished smiling, then (considering our own conduct) it causes us to blush. . . . A humorist is warmhearted; the heart of the satirist is cold.†

It is apparent that for Lao She, the satirist takes a toughminded view of things, whereas the humorist is a bit more tenderhearted. In political terms, one might say that the humorist is a "gradualist," the satirist an "extremist." Indeed much of the criticism leveled against Lao She on the mainland has come close to saying precisely this.

Since he thought himself more suited to humor than satire, it is understandable that he should have considered his venture into the realm of satire a flop. In "How I Came to Write *Cat Country*," he states:

> As I see it, *Cat Country* is a failure. It is a book that mercilessly exposes how very mediocre my brain really is. When I had written half of it, I wanted to beat a retreat, but the hard facts of life would not grant me such an easy out. Consequently, I forced myself to continue patching it together until I had reached the end. Some people think that it is really worthy of praise simply because it is not my usual

* Ibid., pp. 71–72.

† Ibid., pp. 74–75.

> humorous self—much the same way that any kind of performance by Mei Lan-fang in a male role would be worthy of praise.* People who feel this way are really simply sick and tired of my humor. It's not that they are praising *Cat Country* because they have found something good in it; it's rather a case of when you've eaten steamed bread rolls (*man-t'ou*) for too long, you eventually get so sick of them that you'll consider a bowl of tough rice as really quite tasty. . . .†

Lao She felt that he was, by temperament, not the satirist and that in trying to write a satire, he himself was changing roles as would Mei Lan-fang in playing a male lead (*fan-ch'uan*). He felt that he lacked the depth and insight requisite to good satire. Again in his own words:

> What I thought [about the situation in China at the time I wrote *Cat Country*] was what most ordinary people were thinking and there was really no need to say it since everyone knew it anyway. . . . I simply gave a straight-forward presentation of what was common knowledge at the time and then dignified the whole thing by calling it "satire." I guess I must have gotten carried away. In my hands "satire" became "preaching," and the more I preached the more sickening it became. A man who takes it upon himself to preach to people is either exceedingly intelligent, or an utter numbskull. Now I know that I'm not the

* Mei Lan-fang, the most famous Chinese opera star of this century, sang female roles. Occasionally—more or less for the fun of it—opera companies put on *fan-ch'uan* or topsy-turvy productions in which the performers take roles opposite to ones that they normally play.

† Lao She, *Lao-niu,* pp. 39–40.

> brightest man in the world, but I'm not willing to admit that I'm an utter ass either. And yet, since in fact I *did* write *Cat Country,* what can I say? *

We know by his own testimony that the reason he became an "ass" was disappointment in domestic affairs and indignation over China's military failures in the early thirties. In "How I Came to Write *Cat Country,*" he tells us that his disappointment moved him to exhort, or if you will, to preach; however, he notes that this kind of preaching and exhortation is the piddling virtue of a woman, something of which any masculine northerner ought properly to be ashamed.

Lao She is justly famous for his metaphors. The following one, though somewhat obscure, does afford us further insight into why he wrote *Cat Country.*

> An absolutely brainless man might find some nourishment in a dunghill; a brainy man wouldn't pay any attention to the dunghill in the first place. But it takes a half-brainy half-brainless clod like myself to come up with the idea of *improving* and *preserving* the dunghill. Such a man goes over and preaches at the flies that have gathered atop the turds, saying: "Hey, come on! Let's keep this place in better shape! It's not very sanitary you know!" I took a beating because I allowed external stimuli to get the better of my emotions, and thus make me forget for a while that besides "feelings" I also had a "brain" that I could have used. And thus it was that I was moved to go over and preach at the flies.†

* Ibid., p. 41.

† Ibid., p. 42.

In the same essay he goes on to tell us that in writing *Cat Country* he purposely avoided being funny, with the result that the novel does not even have humor to recommend it.

> Friends often exhort me not to be so humorous in my writing. I appreciate their intentions, for I myself realize that because of my humor, I often slip into being obnoxious. But after . . . failures [like *Cat Country*], I realize that it is most difficult to change a dog into a cat.*

If *Cat Country* is such an out-and-out flop, why should one read it in the first place? Well, to begin with, *Cat Country* is better than Lao She would have us believe. There is some spritely as well as tedious writing in it. Like most of Lao She's novels, it is uneven in quality. In addition to literary value, however, it possesses a great deal of worth as social documentation on China in the early thirties.

In *Cat Country* one will see reflected a China threatened by invasion from without, and yet engaged in an apparently senseless civil war within (Nationalist against Communist and warlord against warlord), a China floundering in a chaos of "-isms," each of which claims to be the panacea for her ills, a China whose younger and more progressive citizens are trying desperately to reform and modernize her against the deeply rooted conservatism of their elders.

Against so many problems, so many warlords and corrupt bureaucrats, against so much inertia, Lao She

* Ibid., p. 43.

sees little hope. Unlike his famous contemporary Lu Hsün, he was unable to place his faith in youth. In *Cat Country* he has nothing but satirical scorn for the modernized high school and university students with their privileged positions and almost endless series of student movements. He gives equally short shrift to the modern young scholars, fresh back from the sojourns in Europe and America, and bringing home with them little more than foreign mannerisms and a taste for expensive foreign products.

In *Cat Country* we will see no way out of the morass of difficulties in which the cat-people find themselves bogged down, for Lao She himself saw no solution. He was, as he himself has noted, preaching. He was the prophet of doom, telling his people that unless they modernized, became more moral and upright, and put aside their petty differences to stand united against the Japanese threat from the north, then China as a nation and civilization would be totally destroyed in the near future.

Lao She had originally become famous in China for humor and for his fluent and faithful recording of the wit and rhythms of Peking Chinese, a medium of expression carrying with it all the connotations of beauty, wit, and prestige that are enjoyed by Parisian French. Since such was his primary claim to fame, it is little wonder that in writing *Cat Country* he felt rather uncomfortable in the role of doomsday prophet; and it may well be—as he himself suggests—that his satirical analysis of Chinese society was neither very witty nor creative. It is likely, however, that it faithfully reflects what a good number of people felt and thought about China at that time. For as Lao She himself has said: "What I thought was what most ordinary people were thinking and there was really no need to say it since everyone knew it anyway." Everyone may hay have known it, but you will find little of it in the books written on the history of the times. One must go to literature to learn how it feels to live in a certain period and to share the humanity of those people who lived it.

CAT COUNTRY

1 *The Crash*

The aircraft was a total loss. And as for my friend, a man who had been my childhood schoolmate and a man who had just piloted me through space for the better part of a month—there wasn't a single bone of him left in one piece.

And how was it with me? Well, I still seemed to be alive, but God only knows how it happened that I too hadn't died in the crash. At any rate, things were what they were and there was no point in crying over spilt milk.

Our goal had been Mars. According to my late friend's calculations, we were already in the Martian atmospheric envelope before the accident occurred; if he was right, then I must indeed have landed on the planet Mars! The soul of my dead friend ought to be at rest, for to be the first Chinese on Mars was really something worth dying for! But how could I be sure that I was *really* on Mars? I ended up by deciding that, barring evidence to the contrary, I'd have to assume that I was on Mars, even if I wasn't; I had no way of proving it one way or the other. Of course, it ought to have been possible to determine my location from the stars, but unfortunately my knowledge of astronomy was as developed as my knowledge of hieroglyphics. My friend could have determined our location without the slightest hesitation, but my friend . . . my friend, my poor childhood friend!

Since the aircraft was a total loss, how would I get back to Earth? I'd better not think about it! All I had to my name was the clothing on my back (so ripped and torn that it looked like shredded confetti) and whatever food happened to be left in my stomach. I didn't even know how I was to survive *here,* much less how I was to get back to Earth! Ignorant of both the languages and geography of this strange planet, I began to wonder if there were any creatures here similar to human beings. I had as many questions as. . . . But there was no point in thinking about them. "A castaway on the planet Mars" —wasn't there some comfort to be derived from a title like that? There was certainly no point in letting worry eat away at whatever courage I had left.

All of this, of course, is a distant recollection of my situation as it was then. At the time I was in a state of shock and it may well be that my traumatized brain produced a good many other disconnected thoughts, however, I can't remember what they were now. All I can remember is that I was concerned with how I would get back to Earth and how I would survive; these two thoughts, like boards washed up on a beach as the only trace of a sunken ship, are the only two that remained with me after the experience.

After I had come to my senses, the first thing I

thought of doing was devising some way of burying the pile of bone and flesh that had been my friend. I couldn't bring myself to look at the plane, for, in its own way, it too had been a good friend: it had brought us both here, faithful machine. My two friends were both dead and I was the only one left alive. I began to feel that their misfortune was all my fault. The two skilled members of our expedition had both died and I, the unskilled third, was the only survivor; the luck of an idiot—what painful comfort! I knew that I could bury my schoolmate single-handedly, but I wouldn't be able to cover up the plane; therefore, I didn't have the heart to look at it.

I should have gone to dig the grave right away, but I didn't. I just stared vacantly at my new environment through a veil of tears. Why didn't I immediately clasp my friend's bones to my breast and have a good cry? Why didn't I start digging right away? Why? Why? Perhaps it was because of the state that I was in, a state somewhat like that of a man who has just awakened from a dream. Perhaps I shouldn't be held responsible for all my actions at such a time. In retrospect, this is probably the most reasonable and charitable explanation that I can give of my failure to bury him immediately.

I continued to stare vacantly at my surroundings. It's strange, but even now I can remember very clearly everything that I saw. Whenever I feel like it, I can close my eyes and recapture those scenes. They stand before me in full color. Even the shadow lines where one color fades into another still stand out clearly. Those images are engraved upon my mind as indelibly as the mental pictures that I retain of going, as a little boy, with my mother to my father's grave to tidy things up and sacrifice to his spirit.

I really can't say what I especially noticed at the time, for I directed equally to everything around me a "disinterested attention," if that phrase means anything. I was like a bush in the rain, whose movement is entirely dependent on the drops: if a drop falls on a leaf, then that leaf moves.

I saw a grey sky. It was not a cloudy sky, but rather a grey-colored atmosphere. One couldn't say that the light of the sun was weak, because I felt very hot; however, its light was not in direct proportion to its thermal power. It was simply hot, but not at all bright. The grey atmosphere that surrounded me was so heavy, hot, dense, and stifling that I could almost reach out and grab it. The weight of the atmosphere could not have been due to dust in the air, for things could be seen very clearly in the distance. It wasn't at all like it is back in Peking when we have dust storms of wind-blown sand. It was rather that the light of the sun was diminished upon first entering this grey world; what was left of it was then evenly distributed so that every place received some of the light, thus creating a silver-grey world. It was a bit like the summer drought in North China when a layer of useless grey clouds floats in the sky, shading the light of the sun without at all reducing the extremely high temperature; however, the grey atmosphere here was much darker and heavier so that the weighty ashen clouds seemed glued to one's face. A model for this universe would be a beancurd parlor back home filled with hot fumes in the night, lit by a single oil lamp scattering rays of ghastly light through the mist. In sum the atmosphere made me feel very ill at ease; even the few small mountains in the distance were grey, distinguished from the sky only by their darker hue. Because there was some sunlight, the grey of the mountains was speckled with a bland shade of red, making them look somewhat like the necks of pheasants. A country of grey—I remember that that's what I thought at the time, although I really didn't know whether there were any "countries" there or not.

As I drew my line of sight back from the horizon, I noticed a plain and it too was grey. There were no trees, no houses, no fields. It was flat . . . flat . . . flat . . . boringly flat. A carpet of grass hugged the ground; its leaves were very large, but none of the stalks were upright. Since the ground was obviously fertile, why, I wondered, was no one cultivating it?

Not far from where I stood a number of hawk-like birds took off, all grey except for white tails. The white of their tails did bring a note of change to the monotony of this all-grey universe, but it was powerless to lighten the foggy and depressing atmosphere. The tails of the birds reminded me of slips of paper money (the kind we burn for the dead back home) floating in a dark and gloomy sky.

The hawk-like birds flew over in my direction and started watching and waiting. Suddenly my heart gave a start. They weren't watching me; they were watching my dead friend! Watching that pile of. . . . In the distance I saw a few more of them take off. I became excited and instinctively began feeling around on the ground, foolishly hoping to find a shovel or a spade. I couldn't even find so much as a stick. I went over to the plane to see what I could find. If I had a piece of steel,

I'd be able to dig out some kind of grave. But the birds were already circling overhead. I couldn't take time to look up at them again, but I could feel that they were getting lower and lower. Their cry, a long and piercing cry, now sounded directly over my head. I reached the plane and, having no time to select carefully, I grabbed at it, catch-as-catch-can. I had no idea what part it was I had gotten hold of, but at any rate I tore at it like a madman. One of the birds landed. I screamed at him as loud as I could. His sharp wings were trembling in the air and his feet were just about to touch down when, startled by my cry, he hooked up his tail again and flew off. But this one had no sooner taken off than two or three others came clucking down like magpies after food. The cries of the birds still on wing were long and drawn out, as if they were importuning their brethren on the ground to wait for them. Finally they all came down with one great *whoosh.* I started tearing at the plane again and noticed that the palm of my hand was sticky with blood, but I wasn't conscious of any pain. I kept on trying to tear something off the wrecked craft; but it was useless. At last, I rushed them and started kicking and screaming. They spread their wings and started falling back in all four directions in order to avoid me, but it was apparent that they had no intention of taking off. One of them was already perched on that heap of. . . . He was already beginning to peck!

So furious that I could feel the blood rising in my eyes, I rushed him. I intended to grab him in my bare hands; but as soon as I made a pass at him, the rest of them surrounded me and began attacking from all four sides. I kicked and flailed in all directions; they fell back again helter-skelter, cackling with wings spread wide. As soon as I had kicked out in any direction and returned my leg to its original position, the one that I had kicked at would close in on me again, eyes blazing with fury. And now the more they attacked, the bolder they got; they no longer fell back after having closed in for the attack. Now they began pecking at my feet.

Suddenly I remembered that I had a revolver stuck inside my belt. I had just straightened up and started to feel for my gun when—I don't know when they had come—I noticed that there was a group of men standing seven or eight paces in front of me. As soon as I focused in on them, I saw clearly that they all had the faces of cats!

2 *China Was Never Like This—Or Was It?*

Should I pull out my revolver or wait? Either course of action involved a variety of considerations. During the minute it took me to make up my mind, the calmer I tried to make myself, the more excited I became. Finally, I put down the gun, and smiled at myself. This Mars adventure was something that I had ardently sought out on my own, and if this pride of cat-men killed me, I'd have only myself to blame. Besides, their malevolence was, as yet, only an assumption on my part; how could I be sure that they weren't really kind and benevolent people? It didn't make much sense to pull a pistol before I found out. Good intentions always make a man courageous; and now, filled with benevolent intent, I was not the least bit afraid of them. Whatever was coming, for better or for worse, I'd let it take its natural course; at any rate, if there was to be any violence, I would not be the one to initiate it.

Seeing that I hadn't moved, they shifted forward a couple of paces. Their movements were slow, but determined, like the advance of a cat who has spotted a mouse. The birds all took off now, and from every beak there hung a piece of. . . . I closed my eyes!

Before I had opened my eyes again—and I had closed them for only a tiny fraction of a second—my arms were pinned to my sides. I hadn't anticipated that the cat-people would be quite as quick and agile as that, for I hadn't heard the sound of a single step.

Had refusing to draw my revolver been a mistake then? No! For at least *my* conscience was clear on this point. Reflecting that sudden disasters are the food and drink of an adventurous life, my mind began to calm itself and I no longer felt like opening my eyes. It wasn't that I was trying to gain an advantage by feigning weakness; it was just that my mind was genuinely calm. Rather than relaxing their grip a bit because I wasn't putting up any resistance, they began pinning my arms tighter and tighter! I thought to myself: "What a suspicious bunch of characters these cat-men are!" This sense of my own psychological superiority inflated my pride, and I became even more determined not to match strength with them. There were four or five hands on each of my arms, soft, but tight, and possessed of a certain elasticity. It would be more accurate to say that my arms were "squeezed" to my sides rather than pinned. It felt as though there were so many bands of leather digging into my flesh.

To struggle would have been useless. I saw clearly now that if I tried to break free, their hands would puncture the skin and rip into my flesh. So that's the kind of people they were—people who would sneak up, capture someone, and then maliciously inflict physical cruelty upon him regardless of whether he resisted or not! As though the infliction of physical pain could diminish a man's heroic stature! Shameless! At this juncture I really began to regret not having drawn my revolver. In dealing with this kind of people—if my judgment of them was accurate—one ought to operate on the principle that "getting in the first blow is half the battle." I am sure that a single blast from my revolver would have sent them all running, if only I had used it. But the situation was what it was and no amount of regret would improve it. Since I had set a trap for myself with my own righteousness, why not see it through and die in the afterglow of that righteousness?

Opening my eyes, I discovered that they were all standing behind me, as though they had arranged it beforehand so that even if I did open my eyes I wouldn't be able to see any of them. Before I realized it, their sneaky way of doing things had caused me to conceive a hatred of them. I wasn't afraid to die, but I couldn't help thinking to myself: "Since I've already fallen into your clutches, if you want to kill me, why do you have to be so sneaky about it?" Before I knew what I was doing, I said out loud, "Why do you have to be so . . . ?" I didn't finish my question, for I realized that they wouldn't be able to understand my language anyway. The only effect that my words produced was a tightening of their grip on my arms. "Even if they did understand my language, I'd probably still be wasting my time," I thought. I didn't give them the satisfaction of turning my head around to look; let them do what they would! But I did wish that they'd tie me up in ropes, for neither my flesh nor my spirit could stand that soft, tight, hot, and hateful grip of theirs.

There were even more birds overhead now, wings spread straight out, and heads all crooked down as they watched for a chance to come swooping down to enjoy the body of my childhood schoolmate and friend!

What was that bunch of clods behind me up to? I couldn't stand this "soft-kill" of theirs! I kept looking at the birds overhead, cruel birds who could in the space of a few minutes completely devour my friend. Would they really be able to finish a man as quickly as that? If so, then perhaps they really couldn't be considered cruel. I even began to envy my late friend: at least he had had a quick death, a clean and comfortable death. Compared to the way that I was getting it on the installment plan, he was infinitely more fortunate.

There were a number of times when I felt like saying, "Hurry up and get it over with," but each time, as the words reached my lips, I swallowed them back again. Although I knew nothing about the character and habits of cat-people, I felt that in the few minutes I had been with them I had already intuitively discovered that they were the cruelest beings in the whole universe; cruel people never understand the concept of "getting things over with"; to them, sawing away slowly at a man is a kind of pleasure. What good would it do to say anything? I was fully prepared for them to stick pins into the soft flesh under my fingernails and pour kerosene into my nose, that is if there were such things as pins and kerosene on Mars.

I began to shed tears, not because I was afraid, but rather because I began longing for home. Glorious China! Great homeland where there's no cruelty or torture and kites never devour corpses! I was afraid that I should never again see that glorious piece of land, should never again enjoy a rational human existence. Even if I were able to preserve my life on Mars, I was afraid that even Martian "enjoyment" would just turn out to be another kind of pain.

Now there were several pairs of hands on my legs too. The cat-men didn't make a single sound, but I could feel their warm breath on my legs and back. It was a loathsome feeling, as though some giant snake had coiled around me.

Clank! The sound was as clear and crisp as though it had occurred in the midst of years of silence. Even today from time to time, I still hear that sound. Fetters had been placed on my ankles! I had expected them to do something like that. They had made the fetters so tight that my ankles immediately went numb.

What crime was I guilty of? What were their intentions? I couldn't figure any of it out. There was really no need to think about it either; since, in the society of the cat-faced people, even intellect was lacking, one could not reasonably expect to fathom their actions on the basis of the ordinary springs of an equally lacking human emotion. Trying to understand them rationally would be a waste of time.

Now they had the handcuffs on too; but unexpectedly, they didn't take their hands off my arms and legs. Excessive caution—and extreme cruelty is a natural outgrowth of that kind of caution—is an important part of a life of darkness; thus my hope that they might take their clammy hands off me once they had me safely in handcuffs and fetters, had been extravagant.

Now there were two clammy hands on my neck too.

They were afraid that I was going to turn around and look at them! As a matter of fact, I didn't have the slightest intention of giving them that satisfaction, for a man—no matter how low he may have sunk—always has some degree of self-respect. Grabbing me by the neck like that! They were really too low for words! Perhaps it was a logical consequence of their excessive caution, or perhaps they held several glittering knives behind my head which they didn't want me to see.

"Shouldn't we be going somewhere now?" I thought. No sooner had I thought this than they—almost as if to show me that they too could do things quickly when they had to be—kicked me in the leg. That kick was my marching order. My ankles had already been choked numb and the kick caused me to stumble forward involuntarily, making their hands, which seemed like hooks that were soft and hard at the same time, dig into my ribs. Behind me I heard a hissing sound something like the noise that a cat makes to scare his enemy as he prepares for a fight. There were several sounds like that in succession. I concluded that it was probably the way that the cat-people laughed. It was, no doubt, an expression of their pleasure in tormenting me. My body was soon a mass of sweat.

If they were really in a hurry, they could carry me easily enough, and that would suit me to a tee; for I was really incapable of any more walking. This, of course, was precisely the reason that they insisted on my walking—that is, if it's not an insult to the word "reason" to use it in such a context.

By now there was so much perspiration that I couldn't open my eyes, and my hands were handcuffed uselessly behind my back. I couldn't even shake my head to throw off the beads of sweat, for they still had a firm choke-hold on my neck! I walked erect. No. You really couldn't call it "walking," but I can't find another word capable of depicting a movement which was a combination of twisting, turning, stumbling, and jumping all rolled into one.

After we had only moved off a few paces, I heard—fortunately they hadn't stopped up my ears—that flock of birds descend with a great *whoosh;* it sounded like a group of soldiers making a banzai charge on the battle-field. Obviously they had all gone down to get a share of . . . I began to hate myself. If I had only acted a little sooner perhaps I should already have my friend buried by now. Why had I wasted so much time staring like an idiot at my new environment! "My friend! Even if I don't die, by the time I am able to find this place again, I probably won't even be able to find a scrap of you left! All of the sweet and beautiful reminiscences of an entire lifetime will never be able to make up for the bitter shame of this one memory. Whenever I think of it in the future, I shall always consider myself the most worthless of all human beings."

It was something like having a nightmare: although I was suffering great physical pain, I was still able to think of other things. All of my thoughts were centered on my late friend. When I closed my eyes I could still see those birds pecking at his dead flesh and could feel them pecking at my own living heart. Where were we going? In my present situation, even if I had been able to force my eyes open, I really wouldn't have been able to look at anything, much less remember the landmarks clearly enough to make my escape later. Was I walking, or jumping, or rolling? Only the cat-people could have answered that one. My mind was not on any of this; it was as though my body no longer belonged to me. I was only conscious of sweat pouring off my head. There was just a tiny bit of consciousness left in me; I was like a man who has been wounded but has not yet passed out. Everything had gone hazy and I couldn't tell where my body began or ended, but was only conscious of sweat leaving it at various points. It seemed that my life was no longer in my own hands, and yet I did not feel that I was suffering.

Everything went blank. Then, after a while, the darkness passed, and I forced my eyes open the way a man does waking up from a drunken sleep. I became conscious of an excruciating pain in my ankles. Instinctively I started to feel for them, but discovered that my wrists were still handcuffed. It was only at this point that things began to come slowly into focus before my eyes, although I had already had my eyes open for some time. I was on a small boat, but had no idea as to when or how I had gotten there. I must have been on the boat for a long time, for my ankles had regained their feeling so that now I was acutely conscious of the pain occasioned in them by the leg-irons. I tried turning my head. Those clammy hands weren't on my neck any longer! I turned around and looked, but there was nothing behind me. Above was a silver-grey sky and below, a warm-sticky river of deep leaden hues. It made no sound but seemed to be flowing very rapidly; I was out in the middle of it going downstream.

3 *How Do You Get Out of Here?*

I didn't have time to worry about the danger that I was in; at a time like that, the idea of "danger" doesn't even occur in a man's mind. Heat, hunger, thirst, and pain—none of these matched in intensity the feeling that I had of utter exhaustion. (I had just finished a plane trip that had lasted over half a month.) I couldn't sleep on my back because the handcuffs prevented me from getting my spine down flat, but somehow or other I managed to work my way into a lying position on one side and went to sleep like that. I entrusted my life to the mercies of this steamy, oily river, and simply concentrated on getting to sleep; for in the situation that I was in there was little point in hoping for sweet dreams or any other embellishments.

When I woke up again, I found myself propped into a sitting position in the corner of a small room. No, it really wasn't a small room either; it was more like a little cave. There were no windows and no doors. Four wall-like pieces of something or other surrounded a bit of ground from which the grass hadn't even been weeded out. The roof was a small bit of gunmetal-grey sky. My hands were free, but now there was a thick rope around my waist. One end was tied round my waist and I couldn't see the other. Maybe it was tied to something on the other side of the wall. Perhaps since I'd descended from the sky, they thought that it would be a good idea to anchor me to the ground. How odd! The pistol was still in my shirt!

What did they have in mind? Kidnapping? Demanding a ransom of Earth? No, they'd never go to all that trouble. Maybe they thought that they had captured a monster? Perhaps they planned to train me and then put me on display at the local zoo. Or perhaps they planned to send me to a biological institute as a specimen for dissection; that would make more sense. I smiled at my own imagination. I really seemed to be going a bit mad. I was exceedingly thirsty. Why hadn't they taken my pistol away? I felt both surprised and comforted by their failure, but neither of those feelings added any saliva to a dry mouth. I looked all about, and just as I stood on the edge of despair, I spotted a lifesaver!

In the corner parallel to the one that I was sitting in, there stood a stone jar. Could it be . . . ? My instinct told me not to waste time wondering, but simply get over there and see. (Instinct is really more intelligent than intellect.) But my ankles were still fettered. Perhaps I could hop across. Gritting my teeth against the pain, I tried to stand, but couldn't. After several attempts, I discovered that my legs would no longer obey my orders. All right, I'd sit down then. I was so thirsty that I thought my dried-out trunk would begin to split apart. My physical needs had stripped me of all my usual vanity and I decided that perhaps I could crawl! The little room wasn't very wide, and if I got down on my belly, I'd probably be within a few inches of my goal. Just by stretching out my hand, I'd be able to attain the highest hope that my life had ever known—that precious jar! But before I could get down flat, the rope around my waist warned me that it would not permit it. If I insisted on going forward, the rope would leave me hanging in mid-air. It was hopeless.

But the fire in my mouth caused me to use my wits again: feet foremost, I advanced flat on my back, like a beetle that has been turned upside down and can't right itself again. Although the rope was very tight, by using all my strength I should be able to force it up over my rib cage. (At first I had considered trying the same trick head first, but decided not to because my hips were broader than my rib cage and would not have allowed me to force the rope very far in that direction.) If I distributed the rope evenly over my rib cage, I might be able to reach the jar with my feet. Even though the rope might rip and tear my skin, it would still be preferable to dying of thirst. I made my move, the skin on my chest did start to break, but I couldn't afford to worry about it. I just kept struggling toward the jar. I was in great pain, but I didn't have time to let it concern me. I continued struggling forward, and finally my feet actually reached their treasured destination!

Although I could reach the jar by straightening out my feet, the leg-irons were so tight that I couldn't spread my legs apart far enough to grab hold of it. By curling my legs up slightly, I was able to take enough pressure off my ankles to enable me to spread the tips of my feet a bit, but then, of course, I could no longer reach far enough to do any good. It was hopeless.

The only thing I could do was lie there and gaze helplessly at the sky. Without thinking, I pulled out my pistol. Dying of thirst, I gazed at that graceful and handy little instrument. I closed my eyes and placed its shiny little mouth against my temple. A single movement of my hand and I should never be thirsty again. Just at that point an idea suddenly dawned on me! I bolted upright and turned round toward the corner of the wall; I aimed carefully at the rope. Bang! Bang! The heavy rope was partially torn and badly singed. Like a madman, I tore at it with my hands and chewed with my teeth. Finally, I succeeded in breaking the rope apart! In my delirious joy I completely forgot that my feet were still fettered; I got up quickly and fell just as quickly to the ground. Taking advantage of the position that I had fallen in, I crawled towards the stone jar. I took it in both hands. There was something bright and shiny inside. It was water! Perhaps it was water, or perhaps it was. . . . This was no time to hesitate. It was very difficult to handle the heavy jar, but I succeeded in getting a mouthful. It was quite cool and, of course, to me it was tastier than any nectar of the gods. It came to me, as though I had discovered some kind of truth or other about human life, that diligence is usually rewarded in the end. There wasn't much water in the jar to begin with, and before long there wasn't a single drop left.

I held that precious jar in my arms like a baby. And now that I was feeling a bit better, I started indulging in fantasies again. If I could get back to Earth, I would certainly take this jar back with me. But was there really any hope of getting back to Earth? I went blank and stared idiotically, for who knows how long, at the mouth of the jar.

The short, sharp, cries of a flock of birds flying overhead awoke me from my reverie. Looking up, I saw that a strand of light-peach colored evening clouds had arisen in the sky. The natural grey of the sky wasn't completely out-tinted by this new hue, but the sky did appear somewhat higher and clearer, and the top of the wall that surrounded me was edged with a line of fairly strong light. "It will be dark before long," I thought.

What ought I to do?

None of the plans that I might have put into practice had I still been on Earth seemed appropriate here. Since I had absolutely no conception as to the nature of my enemy, how could I decide on a course of action? Even Robinson Crusoe hadn't faced this kind of difficulty. At least, he had been completely on his own, but I had the cat-people to deal with. I had to devise a way of escaping from them; and yet I knew nothing of their history and background. I had to do something. What would it be?

Well, the first thing would be to get rid of the leg-irons. Up to this point I had not yet looked at them to see what they were made of, because I assumed that leg-irons would be made of iron. Now that I took time to examine them, I discovered that they weren't made of iron! They were made of some greyish-white material. Now I knew why they hadn't confiscated my pistol: there was no iron or steel on Mars, and the overly cautious cat-people had feared that some danger would descend upon them if they touched something unfamiliar. They hadn't dared confiscate my gun. I felt the fetters with my hands. Although they weren't of iron or steel, they were hard. I tried, without luck, to tear them apart with my bare hands. "What can they be made of?" A blend of curiosity and the exigencies of escape were present in my question. I rapped them with the muzzle of my gun and produced a metallic sound, but it didn't sound like iron. Silver? Lead? If it were something softer than iron, then perhaps I could use something to grind it through. Perhaps I could smash that stone jar and use one of the splinters to. . . . At this point I had completely forgotten about my plan to take the jar back to Earth with me. I picked it up, intending to smash it against the wall. But I didn't dare. What if I were to attract the attention of someone on the other side of the wall? I thought that there certainly must be someone out there guarding me. No. That couldn't be, for there had been no reaction to the two shots that I had fired just now. When I had fired the gun, I wasn't scared. But now, in retrospect, I fearfully imagined what would have happened if a bunch of cat-people had come rushing in after I fired those shots. But since, in fact, they hadn't come in, what was I being so timid about? I threw the jar against the wall, but only succeeded in chipping off one small splinter. But precisely because it was small, it was also sharp. I set to work.

Perhaps it is true that you can grind a column of steel into an embroidery needle if you're only willing to put enough work into it, but to hope to saw or grind one's way through a pair of fetters in a very short time was, I'm afraid, a bit too optimistic. "Experience" is, for the most part, the offspring of "error." All right! Then I'd simply go on erring in an optimistic frame of mind. Experiences that I had brought here from Earth didn't seem to have much value anyway. I ground away at it for a very long time but didn't even succeed in marking up the surface; it was as though I were grinding a diamond with a piece of stone.

I began feeling about in the rags that were hanging from my body. I felt in my shoes and even my hair on the off chance that I might discover something that would be of service to me in my predicament. It seemed that I had already become a beast without reason. What was this? There was still a box of matches in the pants pocket that was dangling from my belt, and it was a *steel* box of matches at that. If I hadn't made my careful search, I certainly would never have thought of it. Since I don't smoke in the first place, I don't make a habit of carrying matches. Why did I have them on me now? I couldn't figure it out. Wait a minute! I remembered. A friend had given them to me. He had heard that I was going off on a distant exploration and had come to the airfield to see me off. Saying that he had nothing that was really worth giving to me, he had stuffed the little box into my watchpocket. "It's a small box and I trust it won't add too much weight to the aircraft." I still remembered his words. It seemed to be something that had happened years and years ago. Half a month of space travel is not a thing that calms and sharpens the mind.

I idly fingered the box as I reminisced over the events of half a month ago. Since there was no hope immediately before me, I contented myself with recapturing periods of past felicity. Strange, how life can find comfort in a number of directions.

It began to grow dark, and I began to feel hungry. I lit a match, intending to look about for something to eat. It burned out and I lit another. As much for fun as anything else, I placed the tiny flame of the match against the leg-irons. Suddenly. PSSHHHH!!! The flame travelled around the iron as fast as the flying brush of a skilled calligrapher might describe a circle on a piece of paper. There was nothing left on my ankle but white ashes. A nauseous odor drilled into my nostrils and made me throw up. So the cat-people knew how to make things of synthetics. I hadn't expected that!

4 *What Strange Men These Cat-Men Be**

Since I still wasn't at liberty to come and go as I pleased, what was the good of having freed my hands and feet? However, I wasn't going to let thoughts like that get me down in the dumps. Reflecting that at least I had no obligation to the cat-people that required me to stand guard over this little enclosure, I packed away my gun and matches and, holding on the rope, began to climb the wall. When my head was over the top, I faced a huge sheet of dark grey: it wasn't like the blackness of night, but was rather like a thick, pure, fog. I pulled myself over the top and jumped down. Where would I go? Once I was outside, I lost eight tenths of the courage that I had had inside. There were no people, no lights, and no sounds. In the distance—perhaps it wasn't too far, for I couldn't estimate distances very well in this grey atmosphere—there seemed to be a forest. Did I

* The cat-people—like his fellow Chinese, the author would have us believe—do things very slowly. For ages untold, both the individual time of their lives and the collective time of their history have been similarly snail-paced.

dare enter the forest? What kinds of wild animals might lurk there? I raised my head and looked at the stars. I could only make out a few of the larger ones which gave off a bit of feeble red light in the grey sky.

I was thirsty again, and this time I was hungry too. My lack of know-how and experience precluded the possibility of a night hunt, even if I had been able to overcome my adversion to treating birds and beasts as enemies. Fortunately, Mars wasn't chilly; you could probably go nude here day and night and still not catch cold. Leaning against the base of the wall, I sat down and stared alternately at the few stars I could see and the distant forest. I didn't dare think of anything, for sometimes even the silliest of thoughts can move a man to tears: it is much more difficult to bear loneliness than to stand up under pain.

Sitting this way for a while, I gradually lost the strength to hold my eyes open, and yet I didn't dare make so bold as to go to sleep. I'd close my eyes for a while and then, with an almost subconscious start, open them, and then close them again. Once it seemed as though I saw a dark shadow, but when I tried to make it out clearly, there was nothing to be seen. For a second I thought that I had seen a ghost and reprimanded myself for such foolish notions. I closed my eyes again. But no sooner were they closed than a certain uneasiness prompted me to open them. Huh? It seemed that I had seen a dark shadow again, but no sooner had I set eyes on it than it disappeared. My hair began to stand on end. Going to Mars for the ghost-hunting to be had there —that had not been part of my plan. I didn't dare close my eyes any more.

Nothing happened for a long time. I pretended to close my eyes, leaving them open just a crack. There it was! That dark shadow again!

I wasn't afraid. This was certainly no ghost, but a cat-man. The cat-people's vision must have been highly developed, for apparently they could see my eyes open and close from a great distance. Tense and excited to the point where my breathing had almost stopped, I waited. When he got right up to me I'd be able to take care of him, whoever he was. I seemed to feel quite superior to cat-people, although I couldn't have explained why. Was it perhaps just because I had a gun? What a childish reason to feel superior!

Apparently time had no value here, for it seemed as though several centuries passed before he got very close to me. It seemed to take him anywhere from a quarter of an hour to an hour for each pace. It was as though each of his steps carried with it the accumulated caution that he had inherited from an entire history. He'd hazard a step to one side, and then the other; he'd bend down and then slowly stand up again; he'd twist to the left, retreat to the rear, and then fall prone on the ground like a snowflake. He'd crawl forward a bit and then arch his waist, moving like a young cat practicing hunting mice at night. Fascinating!

If I so much as opened an eye, much less moved, he might very well, with a single bolt, run outside the very bounds of space itself. I didn't move, but I did keep my eyes open a very tiny crack to see what he was up to after all. I could tell that rather than *his* having any hostile intentions, he was afraid that *I* might harm *him.* He certainly couldn't have intended to murder me, for he had come alone and weaponless. How could I make him understand that I had no intention of harming him either? I decided that the best thing would be simply not to move; for then, at the very least, I wouldn't scare him away.

He got closer and closer. Finally I was even able to sense his body warmth. He inclined his body away from me like a relay runner standing ready to receive the stick from his teammate. He waved his hand back and forth across my face, but when I nodded my head ever so slightly, he pulled it back again lightning speed. He maintained his on-the-mark position, but he didn't run. He was watching me. I nodded gently again. He still didn't move. I raised my hands v-e-r-y slowly, palms up for him to see. He seemed able to understand this hand-talk, for now *he* nodded too. He even drew back the leg that he had held poised in the direction of possible retreat. Still keeping my palms up, I bent my fingers slightly as a sign of greeting. He nodded at me again and I began to sit up straighter to get a better look at him. Apparently, he had no intention of taking flight now. After having whiled away the time in this exceedingly painful and ludicrous manner for at least half an hour, I stood up.

If whiling away the time is equivalent to working, then the cat-people are great workers. What I am trying to say is that after I stood up, we went on whiling away the time like that for God knows how long. We used hand gestures; nodded our heads; screwed up our mouths; twitched our noses; and brought practically every muscle in our bodies into play—all to show that neither of us had hostile intent toward the other. We could have gone on like that for at least another hour, perhaps even a week for that matter, if dark shadows hadn't appeared in the distance. He saw them first. By the time that I made them out, he had already begun to run away four or five paces in the opposite direction. And now as he ran, he motioned for me to go with him, and I did.

The cat-people run silently and fast. I tried to keep up, but I was just too hungry and thirsty. Before we had run very far, little stars began to appear before my eyes. However, I seemed to realize intuitively that if the cat-people in pursuit ever caught up with us, it was certain that there wouldn't be any great advantage in it for either my friend or myself. Besides, I felt that it would be well to stick by this new friend, for he might prove very useful to me in my Martian adventure. The cat-people behind us must have been catching up, for my friend put on even more speed. I kept up for a bit more, but then I couldn't take it any more. I thought my heart was going to jump out of my mouth. There were some sounds behind us, sharp wailing sounds. The cat-people must have been very worked up about something, for I had already discovered that ordinarily they were quite quiet. I thought that my only hope would be to hit the dirt, for if I went on running, my life might well end in a mouthful of blood at the very next step.

With the last ounce of strength that I had left I pulled out my pistol, threw myself to the ground and wildly fired off a shot. Without even having been conscious of the explosion of the shell, I passed out. When I opened my eyes again: a room, grey color, a circle of red light, the earth . . . the aircraft, a pool of blood, a rope . . . I closed my eyes.

It was only several days later that I learned that my cat-friend had dragged me back to his home like a dead dog after I had passed out. Had he not told me, I should have never known how I got there. (The ground on Mars is so beautifully soft that not a single place on my body had been torn open, by all that dragging!) The cat-people in pursuit of us had been so frightened by the shot that I had got off that they probably hadn't stopped running for three days. This little gun—and only twelve rounds of ammunition—had made me a famous hero all over Mars!

5 *When in Rome . . .*

I slept right through and, had I not been awakened by a fly biting me, I might have gone on sleeping like that for eternity. You will have to excuse me for using the word "fly," for I really don't know what they were called. In appearance, they were like beautiful little green butterflies; but in action, they were many times worse than flies. There were millions of them, and every time I raised my hand, it was as though I had occasioned a flurry of little green leaves.

Since I had slept on the ground the whole night, I was very stiff. I decided that in the cat-language there was probably no word for "bed." Brushing flies away with one hand and rubbing my stiff body with the other, I surveyed my new environment. There was nothing to be seen in the room; apparently it was used as a bedroom, but since the ground served as the bed the most important part of a *bed*room was missing. I was hoping that I might find a basin so that I could wash up. I had been salted in my own sweat for half a day and a full night; but there was no wash basin to be seen. Since there was nothing else to engage my attention, I began inspecting the walls and roof. Both were made of mud. There was no decoration of any kind. Four walls surrounding a foul smell—that was the room. There was a hole in the wall a bit over three feet tall; this apparently served as door, window, or anything that you wanted to use it for.

It was a miracle that my gun hadn't been taken away by the cat-people or lost on the road. I packed it away and clambered out through the little hole. Now I realized that it wasn't a window; windows would have been useless, for the room was situated in the midst of a dense forest (it was probably the same forest that I had seen last night) and the leaves on the trees were so thick that the strongest rays of sunlight wouldn't have been able to penetrate, even if the sun hadn't been hidden by the grey atmosphere. No wonder the cat-people had such good night-vision! It wasn't cool in the forest either; it was moist and steamy. Despite the lack of sun, it seemed as though there was warm air wrapped inside the grey atmosphere. There was no wind. I looked all around hoping that I could find a spring or stream to bathe in, but met with no success. I encountered nothing but thick leaves, moist air, and a foul smell.

Then I discovered my cat-friend perched in a tree! He must have been watching me for a long time. But when I caught sight of him, he went digging into the leaves to hide himself. That irked me a bit. Was that any way to treat a guest? Just give him a stinking room and not be concerned about his thirst or anything else? I considered myself as his "guest," for coming here had certainly not been my idea; he had invited me. However that might be, I realized that I would get nowhere with him by standing on ceremony. I marched discourteously over to the tree where he was hiding. He responded by retreating out to the end of a branch; I climbed up into the tree, grabbed hold of the branch and began shaking it as hard as I could. He made a sound that I didn't understand, but I stopped shaking the branch anyway. I jumped down and waited for him. He seemed to realize that there was no escape. Ears back against his head like a tomcat who has just lost a fight, he came slowly down.

I pointed to my mouth, stretched my neck, and opened and closed my lips several times to signal him that I was hungry and thirsty. He understood and pointed to the tree. I thought that he meant for me to eat the fruit. I shrewdly deduced that perhaps cat-people didn't eat wheat or rice as a staple. But there was no fruit on the trees. He climbed back up into the tree and very carefully plucked four or five leaves. He put one in his mouth and put the rest on the ground; he pointed at me and then at the leaves.

Feeding me like a sheep—that was more than I could take! When I didn't go over to take any of his leaves, the expression on his face became extremely unpleasant; he seemed to be angry too. Naturally I couldn't fathom the reason for his anger any more than he had probably been able to figure out the reason for mine. I realized that if we went on getting on each other's nerves like this, no possible good could come of it and, moreover, it was pointless. If we kept this up, neither one of us would ever understand the other.

Still, I really couldn't bring myself to go over and pick

up and eat the leaves that he'd dropped so cavalierly at his feet. I gestured to him to hand some of the leaves to me. He didn't seem to understand. My anger began to change to wonder. Could it be that the rule set down by our ancient Chinese sages proscribing physical contact between members of the opposite sex when things are given or received—could it be that the same rule was practiced here on Mars too? Could it be that on Mars, males were also required to observe this rule amongst themselves? I couldn't say. Uh-huh, it just might be that they did observe the same rule at that. (This surmise was, in fact, accurate, as I proved to myself after a few more days residence on the planet.) All right then, it would be ridiculous to get into a squabble just because of failure to understand each other. I picked up one of the leaves and wiped my hands off on it. Actually my hands were too dirty to be cleaned by wiping, for several places had been torn open on the broken ribs of the aircraft and were still covered with dried blood. But habits are not easily broken, and I tried to wipe them off anyway.

I took a bite from one of the leaves. It was quite tasty and there was a lot of juice in it. Due to my inexperience in eating leaves I let a bit of the juice drip out from the corners of my mouth. My cat-friend's hands and feet began to twitch as though he were preparing to run over and catch the few precious drops that I was losing. These leaves must be very valuable indeed, I thought to myself. But since the forest was so large why should he have grudged a few measly leaves? Forget it. There were enough odd things going on without worrying about that. After having eaten two of the leaves in a row, my head began to feel a bit dizzy, and yet it wasn't at all an unpleasant sensation. Not only did I feel that precious juice enter my stomach, but I was also conscious of an anesthetic effect that it communicated to every part of my body; however, it did not make me very numb at first. My stomach began to feel full and languorous, and my brain too became a bit sluggish as though I should like to doze off but couldn't. It was almost as though I were benumbed and excited at the same time—the kind of feeling that one gets when slightly high. I was still holding onto a piece of leaf, and my hand had that loose and comfortable feeling that one experiences just after waking up. I didn't have the strength to lift it any more. In my heart I felt like laughing, but I couldn't have told you whether or not that feeling had been transmitted to my face. I leaned against a large tree and closed my eyes for a while. Then after a very short interval, I shook my head lightly once or twice and the feeling of intoxication was past. And now every last pore in my body felt relaxed and happy enough to laugh, if pores could laugh. I no longer felt the least bit hungry or thirsty, nor did I any longer mind the dirt on my body. The mud, blood, and sweat that clung to my flesh all gave me a delicious feeling, and I felt that I should be perfectly happy if I never took another bath as long as I lived.*

The forest appeared much greener than it had before

* To a Chinese reader these leaves would, of course, bring to mind opium. It was probably not the West that first brought opium to China, but Western powers *were* responsible for its massive importation into China in the nineteenth century despite Chinese prohibitions against it.

and the grey atmosphere that surrounded me seemed just right, neither too hot nor too cold. There was even a general, poetic beauty in the green trees and grey atmosphere; and if one sniffed carefully, one could tell that it really wasn't at all a foul odor that was wrapped in the dank air so much as it was a very rich and fragrant sweetness, something like that given off by a very ripe musk melon! "Happiness" is insufficient to describe my state of mind at the time. "Ecstasy" on top of "ecstasy" would be more like it. Those two leaves had given my mind a grey kind of strength and had blended my whole being into the grey atmosphere, had made me one with it, like a fish thrown into water.

I squatted down next to the tree. I had never before liked to squat, but now it was the only position that I found relaxing. I began to take a closer inventory of my cat-friend, and didn't find him nearly as revolting as I had previously; in fact, I began to feel that he was really quite likeable.

By cat-people, I don't mean to call to mind the image of a large feline walking upright and wearing clothes. My friend wore no clothes. I smiled and pulled off the few tattered remnants of shirt that still covered my own chest. Since it wasn't cold anyway, what sense did it make to wear such a tattered shirt? However, I did keep my trousers on. This wasn't out of prudishness, but out of the desire to keep a belt to hang my pistol on. Of course, I could have gone nude and still worn the belt, but I couldn't bring myself to part with that box of matches. I'd have to keep my pants so that I'd have a watch pocket to keep that box in just in case they should ever put me in those inflammable leg-irons again. I took off my boots and threw them to one side too.

To backtrack for a bit, my cat-friend didn't wear any clothes. His waist was long and narrow. His hands and feet were very short, and his fingers and toes were also quite stubby. (No wonder these cat-people ran so fast, but worked so slowly. I remembered how clumsy they had been in putting the leg-irons on me.) His neck was so long that he was able to bend his head down his back. Above two exceedingly round eyes set low on a very large face, he showed a great forehead. It was covered with a fine fur that joined directly to the equally fine and delicate hair on his head. The nose and mouth ran together much the way that the nose and mouth of a pig do. The ears were set on top of the skull and were quite small. The entire body was covered with a glistening coat of fine fur. Close up, it looked grey; but at a distance, there was a touch of green flashing in it that reminded one of grey English camlets. His trunk was round and seemed made for rolling. On his chest he sported four pairs of small breasts forming eight little black dots. I have no way of knowing what his internal structure was like.

His movements were the strangest thing about him. As I saw it, there was speed in his inertia and inertia in his speed—an odd combination that made it impossible for one to guess his intentions and merely gave the impression that he was unusually mistrustful. His hands and feet were never at rest and he was fully as dexterous with his feet as he was with his hands. In fact, he seemed to use his hands and feet more than any other of his organs. He'd feel, first to one side, and then to the other. No, it wasn't really "feeling" so much as it was "probing," the way that an ant uses his antennae.

But what, after all, did my cat-friend have in mind by bringing me here and feeding me these leaves? Without thinking, I was just on the verge of asking him. But how could I ask? We didn't speak the same language.

6 *Felinese and Other Things**

In the space of three or four months I had mastered "Felinese." Malayan can be learned within half a year, but Felinese is much simpler. By manipulating four or five hundred words back and forth, you can express anything you want to. Of course there are some complicated things and some complex ideas that can not be expressed very clearly in this way, but the cat-people have a way around that: they simply don't talk about such things. There aren't many adjectives or adverbs, and nouns are not abundant either. Anything that vaguely resembles a reverie tree is a reverie tree: you have the big-reverie-tree, the little-reverie-tree, the round-reverie-tree, the pointed-reverie-tree, the foreign-

* The Chinese language has often been criticized—perhaps unjustly—for its imprecision in expression. In modern China many reformers sought to do away with the cumbersome Chinese characters altogether, arguing that the learning of them placed an unnecessary burden on the student. Many felt that the high rate of illiteracy in China was largely due to the needless difficulty of the written language.

reverie-tree, and the big-foreign-reverie-tree. As a matter of fact, none of these trees are actually related to each other, and it is only the treasured leaf of the true-reverie-tree that can inebriate a man. They didn't go in much for pronouns, and relative pronouns were non-existent. In sum, it was an exceedingly childish language. Actually, all you had to do was remember a few nouns and you knew enough to carry on a conversation, for you could use gestures for most of the verbs anyway. They had written words too, funny things that looked like tiny towers or pagodas and were extremely difficult to recognize; an ordinary cat-person could only remember ten or so at the most.

Scorpion—such was my cat-friend's name—recognized quite a few of the words and could even compose poetry! You can write a cat-poem by piling up a number of nice-sounding nouns; you don't have to throw in any content at all.

Precious leaves
Precious flowers
Precious cats
Precious bellies

This is a fragment from Scorpion's "Feelings I Had Upon Reading Our History." And the cat-people *did* have history—twenty thousand years of it!

Once I was able to talk, I began to understand my host. Scorpion was an important person in Cat Country. He was landlord, politician, poet, and military officer all rolled into one. He was a landlord by virtue of owning a large stand of reverie trees. (Reverie leaves were the cat-people's staple of staples, and the reason that he had taken me in was intimately related to this food.) He started talking and took out several slabs of history to corroborate what he was about to say. The books were all made of stone and each slab was two feet square and half an inch thick; each of these "pages" contained ten or so very complicated words.

According to him, five hundred years ago the cat-people planted and harvested crops and had never heard of reverie leaves. Then one day a foreigner brought some of the leaves to Cat Country. At first only the upper classes could afford to eat them, but then they began to import the trees and everybody became addicted. Before fifty years were out, non-eaters were the exceptions. Eating the reverie leaves was an exceedingly carefree and convenient way to live. There was only one thing wrong with it: although the leaves seemed to do wonders for stimulating one's spirits, they had exactly the opposite effect on the hands and feet. Farmers no longer planted their crops and laborers no longer tended to their tasks. Everyone became idle. At this point the government issued an order prohibiting the eating of reverie leaves. On noon of the first day that the order was issued, the queen was in such pain from withdrawal symptoms that she thrice slapped the king across his royal mouth—Scorpion moved aside another slab of the history—and the king was, himself, in such pain that his only reaction was to weep. That very afternoon another order was issued making reverie leaves the "National Dish." Scorpion commented that in the entire history of the cat-people, there was no other act as honorable and humane as this one.

During the four hundred years after reverie leaves

were made the "National Dish," Cat Country's civilization progressed several times faster than it had before. (For instance, among twenty thousand years' of poets, not one had ever before used the expression "precious belly.")

But this is not to say that there were no social and political upheavals. Three hundred years back, the cultivation of reverie trees had been widespread; but the more leaves that the people ate, the lazier they became and gradually they even became too slothful to plant the trees. It just so happened that precisely at this point, they encountered a flood year—Scorpion's grey face seemed to turn pale as he spoke, for the cat-people were terrified of water—and many of the reverie trees had washed away. The cat-people could have gone without another food, but they could not do without reverie leaves. Now that they were hard up for leaves, they couldn't afford to be indolent anymore, and all over the country people began stealing. The government decided that there were simply too many robberies being perpetrated and issued a most humane order: from now on stealing reverie leaves would not be considered as a criminal act. Thus the last three hundred years of their history had become known as The Age of Plunder. There was really nothing wrong with that, for stealing is an act that most fully expresses a man's freedom; and "freedom" had, throughout their entire history, always been the highest ideal of the cat-people.*

* The word for "freedom" in Felinese is not at all like the one we use in Chinese. By "freedom" the cat-people mean "taking advantage of others; non-cooperation; creating disturbances." The rule that they have about non-contact between the sexes probably

"In that case, why is it that you still plant the trees?" I asked this in Felinese. In its true Felinese form, the question goes like this: "In that case (one expresses this by a twist of the neck), why is it that (you express this by rolling the pupils of your eyes twice) you (one simply points at the other person) still tree trees (the listener will understand the first "tree" as a verb)?" There no way of expressing the "still" of my original question. When I finished my question, Scorpion closed his mouth for a bit. The cat-people normally go around with their mouths open, since they don't use their noses too much for breathing. Thus, a closing of the mouth is used to indicate either gratification or deep thought.

His answer was that at present there were only a few dozen people who planted trees and all of them were very powerful politicians, military officers, poets, and landlords all rolled into one. They had to plant the trees, for if they didn't, they would lose all of their power. To be in government you needed reverie leaves, for without them, you'd never get to see the emperor. To be a military officer you needed reverie leaves as rations for the troops. You needed them to be a poet too, for reverie leaves can make you daydream. In sum, reverie leaves were omnipotent and once you had them, you could tyrannize your way through the world. "Tyrannize" was one of the most exalted words in the vocabulary of the upper class cat-people.

The most important task for Scorpion and the other

---

comes from this too. For since a "free" man will not allow others to touch him, when two people meet, they neither shake hands nor kiss, but simply twist their heads a bit to the rear as a sign of respect. (Author's note to the original text.)

landlords was to devise ways of protecting the reverie leaves. They had soldiers, but they couldn't possibly use them, for the Cat Country army so prides itself on "freedom" that when they have a good supply of reverie leaves to eat, they simply won't obey orders. Furthermore, their own soldiers often robbed them. According to cat-people's way of looking at things—one could tell this from the tone of Scorpion's voice—this was something to be expected. Then who, after all, did protect the reverie leaves? Simple—foreigners. Every landlord had to support a few foreigners as guardians. The awe that the cat-people had for foreigners was one of the distinguishing characteristics of their nature. Because of their love of "freedom" they couldn't put five of their own soldiers together for more than three days without one of them being murdered and, consequently, fighting a foreign army was a virtual impossibility. With apparent satisfaction, Scorpion added: "Our ability to murder each other grows stronger every day; and the new ways of mutual massacre that we have devised are almost as ingenious as the new devices that we have discovered for writing poetry."

"Killing has become a kind of art," I observed. Since there is no word in Felinese for "art," I used our Chinese word, *yishu;* I explained its meaning to him at great length, but he still didn't understand it. However, he did succeed in learning how to say this one Chinese word.

In ancient times they actually had fought foreign countries, and had even won on occasion, but within the last five hundred years—as a result of constantly massacring each other—they had completely erased from their minds the very concept of "fighting foreigners," and had devoted themselves exclusively to doing each other in: hence, their unusual awe of foreigners. If it weren't for the support of foreigners, their emperor wouldn't even be able to safeguard his own supply of reverie leaves.

Three years previously another plane had come, but the cat-people never found out where it had come from, but simply remembered it as a kind of large, featherless bird. Hence, when my plane arrived, they knew that another intruder was amongst them. They assumed that I was another Martian, for it had never occurred to them that there might be another planet besides Mars.

Scorpion and some of the other landlords had run to the spot where our plane had crashed, in the hopes of recruiting another foreigner to guard the reverie trees! The foreigners that they had originally invited in to do this job had, for some reason or other, all gone home; and now they were faced with the problem of recruiting new guardians.

They had agreed that once they had recruited me, they would take turns in using me, for recently they had experienced great difficulty in obtaining foreigners. They had originally planned on *asking* me if I would like to work for them. But then when they discovered I wasn't a cat-man, they couldn't decide how to handle me. Having never before seen a foreigner like me, they had been extremely frightened at first; but seeing that I behaved in such a docile manner, they had soon changed their plans from *asking* to *shanghaiing.* (These were the big shots of Cat Country, and therefore, not at all lacking in guile; moreover, when the occasion demanded, they could even bring themselves to take a few risks.)

CHAPTER SIX

Looking back on it, I realize that had I used force at the very outset, I certainly could have frightened them away. However, perhaps it was just as well that I had not, for though I could have frightened them away for the time being, they certainly wouldn't have been willing to leave such a scarce commodity alone for very long; besides I wouldn't have been able to find anything to eat anyway. But on the other hand, maybe letting them capture me had not been such a good idea after all; for once they had me in captivity, although they continued to fear me, they had ceased to respect me.

Seeing how tractable I was, it had occurred to all of them simultaneously that rather than taking turns with my services, it would be much more profitable to monopolize me. If one of them could make off with me; then there would be no need to discuss the terms of my servitude; all he'd have to do would be to give me enough to eat. At this point every one of them decided to go back on his word to the others and see if he couldn't make off with me himself at the earliest available opportunity. Breaking treaties and disregarding solemn agreements was, after all, a part of "freedom." I could tell that Scorpion thought that his success in finally making off with me was something to be very proud of.

After they had tied me up, and thrown me into that little boat, they had all taken a short-cut to that sky-topped little room to wait for the river to bring me to them. They, themselves, were so afraid of water that they didn't dare get in the boat with me. If the pilotless boat turned over on the way, then, of course, the fault would be with my own bad luck and have nothing to do with them. The room was not far from a stretch of sand;

since the river almost totally dried up by the time it reached that stretch of sand, they knew the boat would surely run aground at that spot.

Once having installed me in the little room, they had gone home for a meal of reverie leaves. They could not carry the precious leaf with them, for travelling about with a supply of reverie leaves would be very dangerous, indeed. For this reason, they seldom took long walks; the risk they had taken in coming out to the spot where I had crashed was a special exception.

Scorpion's stand of trees was closest to the little room; but it was still a long time before he came to visit me, for after a meal of reverie leaves, one must always nap a while. He knew that the others wouldn't be likely to come back before taking naps either, and given the head-start that the favorable location of his stand of trees would afford him, he fully expected to get there first and make off with me. But no sooner had he arrived than the others followed; he had been unprepared for that. "Fortunately, you scared them away with that *yishu.*" He pointed at my pistol as though he felt especially grateful to it. (After that he began calling anything that was difficult to describe an "*yishu.*") Now I began to understand everything that had happened to me since my arrival. I asked him: "What were those leg-irons made of?"

He shook his head and told me that all he knew about the material was that it had come from abroad. "We import a lot of foreign things because they're so convenient to use," he said, "but we'd never stoop to imitating them, for we are the most ancient of all the countries on Mars." He closed his mouth for a while and then observed: "When we go walking we always have to take handcuffs and leg-irons with us." Perhaps he was making a simple statement of fact, or perhaps he was pulling my leg—I couldn't tell.

I asked him where he stayed at night. That little sky-topped hole that I had occupied was the only structure that I had seen in the forest, and I was sure that he must go to some other place to sleep. He didn't seem interested in answering my question, but rather asked me if I'd give him a stick of *yishu* so that he might show it to the emperor. I gave him a match and broke off my questioning on his sleeping habits; for in a society where people emphasize "freedom" a great deal, everyone must have his own secrets.

I asked him if he had a family. He nodded his head. "After we've harvested the reverie leaves, you can go home with me and see for yourself."

I wondered what tasks he had in mind for me back at his home. "Where is your home?" I asked.

"In the capital where the emperor resides. There are lots of foreigners there; you'll be able to see your own friends."

"I am from Earth; I don't know any Martians."

"Well, you're a foreigner anyway, and all foreigners are friends."

There was no point in explaining things to him any further. I just hoped that we'd get the reverie leaf harvest in quickly so that I could go to the capital and have a look around.

7 *A Land of Peeping-Toms* *

My relationship to Scorpion, as I perceived it, could never be one of friendship. That's the way *I* saw it at any rate. Perhaps *he* was sincere in *wanting* to be my friend, but I simply couldn't bring myself to like him. For even if—and this was true of all the cat-people—he was sincere, then even his sincerity would be totally self-centered. For it seemed that the main reason that Scorpion made friends was in order to be able to use people for his own benefit. During the past three or four months, I had not, for a single day, put out of my mind the desire to go and bury the corpse of my old friend. But Scorpion availed himself of every means that he could devise in order to prevent me from doing so. This in itself was an indication of his selfishness; it also showed that the concept of "friendship" was totally foreign to the minds of the cat-people. I say he was selfish because it seemed that, to him, guarding the reverie trees was the only

* In Scorpion's opportunism and villainy we can discern the silhouette of the Chinese politician-warlord of the 1920's and 1930's.

thing that I had come to Mars to do. I say lacking in the concept of "friendship" because Scorpion forever reminded me: "He's dead. He's already dead. What's the point in going to him?"

He refused to give me directions for getting back to the place where my friend's body was, and he watched over me like a hawk to make sure I didn't try to find the way by myself. Actually if I took my time (all I'd have to do would be to follow along the bank of that river), I'd certainly be able to find that area again. But every time that I got more than half a mile out of the forest, he would be sure to pop up out of nowhere and block my path. He'd block me, but he wouldn't try to take me back by physical force. Instead, he'd tell me about a number of stories in which he figured as the victim, and make me feel sorry for him as though he had been an old widow relating her tale of woe. Sniveling and wiping the tears from his eyes he'd go on and on; and before I knew it, he'd manage to get me to completely forget my own troubles. Behind my back, no doubt, he pursed his lips and sniggered at me for being such a simpleton; but even realizing this, I still wasn't able to harden my heart against him. In fact, I almost began to admire him!

I didn't entirely believe all that he told me and decided to check things out for myself. But he'd already guarded against that, for he never allowed any of the other inhabitants of the reverie forest to get close to me. I saw them only from a distance, for whenever I dashed over in their direction, they would immediately disappear. This certainly must have been in compliance with orders issued by Scorpion.

I decided not to eat any more of the reverie leaves.

Scorpion's exhortation against such a course was exceedingly smooth, sincere, and devious: I couldn't stop eating them, for then I'd be thirsty and water wasn't easy to come by; moreover, if I did stop eating them, I'd have to bathe and what a bother that would be; we've had experience; you can't give up reverie leaves; other foods are too expensive, and not good to eat anyway; I'd just have to eat reverie leaves; there was a kind of poison in the atmosphere that would kill me if I stopped. However, in spite of all this, I still held fast to my decision not to eat them any more. Then he started sniveling and wiping his eyes again; I knew that this was his last resort. However, this time I couldn't afford to be soft, for I realized that Scorpion's plan was to have me eat reverie leaves until I became just like the cat-people. I just couldn't allow him to manipulate me at his own sweet will like that, and I had already made the mistake of being too easy-going with him anyway. I wanted to get back to a human kind of existence: I wanted to eat, drink, and bathe. I was not going to allow myself to metamorphise into something only *half*-alive like the cat-people. If by going without reverie leaves, I could live humanly and rationally as I had before, then even if I should only live a few weeks, it would still be worth it. Even if I were to be offered eight thousand years of the cat-people's half-dead existence, I should still refuse it. I explained this to Scorpion, but he was, of course, unable to understand. He probably concluded that my brain must be made of stone. But, come hell or high water, I had made up my mind on this point and I would not change.

After negotiating this point with him for three days

without arriving at any conclusion, I was forced to resort to my revolver. However, I had not forgotten the concept of fair play, and placing the revolver on the ground between us, I told Scorpion: "If you insist on my eating the reverie, then one of us has to die. Either I kill you or you kill me, I don't care which. You decide!" Scorpion ran six or seven yards in the other direction. He couldn't kill me. A gun in his hand wasn't even as useful as a straw in the hands of a foreigner; besides, what he wanted was *me,* and not my revolver.

We arrived at a compromise: I'd eat a reverie leaf every morning. "Only one leaf, only one little piece of our treasured leaf, in order to work as an antidote against the poisonous vapors in the air," said Scorpion. He had gotten me to put away the revolver and now sat across from me, pointing a short finger at me. He would provide me with an evening meal, but getting water would be difficult. I suggested that I go down to the river every morning for a bath and at the same time bring back a jar of water. He didn't approve. Why should I travel such a distance every day just to bathe? It was stupid, especially since I'd have to carry a jar all the way. Why not simply relax and eat reverie leaves instead? "There are good things right before your eyes, but you don't know how to enjoy them." I was positive he'd say something like this, but he didn't. Furthermore —and this was what he really had in mind—he'd have to accompany me. I said I didn't need his company. But he told me that he was afraid that I might try to run away and that's what he was most concerned with. Actually, if I planned on running away, I could do it whether he accompanied me or not, couldn't I? I asked him that question straight out, and he actually closed his mouth for a full ten minutes or so; I was afraid that I had scared him to death with my implied threat.

"There's really no need to accompany me. I've decided not to run away. I *swear* to you that I won't run away."

He shook his head lightly: "Taking oaths is something that only children do for fun."

I got hot under the collar. Insult me to my face, would he! I grabbed the fine hair on his head. (This was the first time that I had used force on him.) He hadn't expected it or he would have long since run far out of reach. His surprise at my reaction was probably genuine, for I later found out that what he said about taking oaths was true. He sacrificed some fine hair and perhaps a piece of scalp with it in order to break away from me. From a safe distance he explained that in the history of Cat Country, taking oaths had once been a common practice. However, within the last five hundred years there had been too many instances of people taking solemn oaths and then not paying any attention to them. Hence, except for the hell of it, no one took oaths any more. Although trustworthiness was not a bad thing in itself, still, actual experience had proved that it was inconvenient. Therefore the government reform that abolished the taking of oaths had actually been a forward step in progress. Scorpion kept feeling his scalp as he explained all this to me, but he didn't seem the least bit angry. Since no one ever honored them anyway, he said that children now treated taking oaths as a kind of game. I later discovered that this was, in fact, the truth.

"Whether or not you cat-people are trustworthy has nothing to do with me. My oaths are *real* oaths," I said very firmly. "I have absolutely no intention of running away. Whenever I decide to leave you, I shall first tell you to your face."

"You still don't want me to accompany you when you go to bathe then?"

"Do as you damn well please!" And that was that.

The supper wasn't bad; in fact the cat-men were really quite good at the culinary arts. The only thing was that there were too many green-flies on the food. I pulled up some grass, wove dish covers, and ordered the man who brought my food to cover it. But he didn't see things the way that I did, and even thought my request a bit ludicrous. Because of Scorpion's order, he didn't dare speak to me, but he did shake his head gently in negation. I knew that since uncleanliness was one of the glories of the glorious history of Cat Country, there was no way that I could reason with him. It was a shame, but I'd have to resort to force. Whenever a dish came uncovered, I'd tell Scorpion to go explain things to the servant. This was a great mistake, for there finally came a day when no food came at all. The next day when food *was* sent, there was not a single cover on anything, and everything was covered with a layer of green-flies.

Actually what had happened was this: because I had told Scorpion to go and "explain" things to the servant who brought the food, I had caused both Scorpion and the servant to lose their respect for me. For usually in such cases, it is the prerogative of the upperclass cat-men to strike the servant immediately; the servant considers this entirely proper and even expects it. Since I had not struck him immediately, he had lost all respect for me. But what was I to do? I didn't want to go around hitting people, for to me the concept of personal integrity is inviolable. But if I didn't hit him, not only would no one bring any food to me, but moreover I'd lose all my security on Mars. There was nothing that I could do; I'd simply have to sacrifice a piece—and I can honestly say it was a very small piece—of the cat-man's scalp. It worked. The covers were not left off any more. This almost made me cry, for what kind of historical progress was it that made one man forget the personal integrity of another?

Going to the river to take a morning bath was the first esthetic experience that I had had since my arrival on Mars. I'd go from the reverie forest to the beach every morning before the sun came out; it was only a little over a mile away, just far enough to make me perspire a bit and to loosen up my limbs. On the beach, I'd walk along in just enough water to cover the tops of my feet, splashing about and waiting for the sun to come out. The scenery before sunrise had a certain tranquil beauty about it: there was no mist in the grey sky as yet and some of the large stars were still visible.

Except for the gentle lapping of water on the sand, all was silence. When the sun came out I would go into the middle of the river. As I walked out, the water would gradually deepen, but it wasn't until I'd gone over half a mile that it would cover my chest. Then I would have a most enjoyable swim. I would usually swim about for half an hour or so, leaving only when I felt hungry. Then I'd go back in to the beach and dry myself in the sun. I would place my pistol, matchbox, and tattered pants on a great rock. Naked in this great, grey universe, I would feel totally carefree, the freest man in all creation. As the sun grew gradually hotter, fog would slowly rise from the river and I would feel a bit stifled; Scorpion was right, even if he hadn't said anything, I would still have sensed the poisonous miasma contained in the atmosphere. At this point it would probably be time to go back and eat that piece of reverie leaf.

But it was not possible for me to long preserve even this pleasure; again it was Scorpion who spoiled things. On about the seventh day after I had begun taking my baths, as soon as I arrived on the beach I saw some black shadows moving back and forth in the distance. I didn't pay any particular attention to them, but merely waited, as usual, for the pleasure of watching the beauty of the sunrise.

A grey-red color gradually rose in the east. After a bit, a number of thick clouds broke apart and transformed themselves into large, deep-purple flowers. Suddenly the sky lightened so that the stars were no longer visible. Then the deep-purple cloud-flowers joined together to form a horizontal layer, and the purple color changed to a deep orange touched with a very light streak of pale grey and acqua. They were bordered with a bright silver-grey. The horizontal layer began to split apart again and some large, black spots began to appear in the orange.

Golden rays began shining down so intensely that they were even able to show through from behind the black spots. And then from out of the clouds emerged a sphere of blood-red. It was not quite round and seemed to shudder a bit before settling down in the morning sky, and while this was going on, the broken clouds had shattered into tiny fragments, scattering golden fish scales across the sky. The river grew bright and began to give off a golden glow. The remnants of the morning clouds became thinner and more broken until, gradually, they disappeared, and there were only left in the sky a few threads of pale, peach-colored, silk. The sun climbed higher. The entire sky changed to a silver-grey, but in some places little touches of blue still showed through.

I had been so wrapped up in gazing at the sky that I had been oblivious to everything else, and when I turned around, I was quite surprised to discover a column of cat-men standing fifty yards or so back from the bank of the river. I didn't have the foggiest notion as to what they were up to. At first I assumed that it was some business that concerned only them, and I didn't pay any attention to it. I decided to simply go on with the business of taking my bath; however, as I walked along the bank toward a deeper part of the river, I noticed that the column of cat-men shifted its position too. As I dove into the water, I heard a cry of alarm. I bobbed up and down a few times and then swam to a shallow place where I could stand up to look. Another cry went up and the column retreated several paces. I realized what was going on: they had come to take in the spectacle of my bath!

If they had never seen anyone bathe before, I suppose there was no harm in their watching me. I knew that they hadn't come for the kicks to be had from seeing me in the nude, for the nude body is nothing new to the cat-people since they don't wear clothes anyway. Undoubtedly, they had come to see how I swam. Well then, should I continue with my swimming exhibition in order to broaden their horizons, or should I break off my morning dip? I couldn't make up my mind. At this juncture, I spotted Scorpion. He was closest to the bank, perhaps five or ten yards closer than any of the others. I realized that he was showing-off that he was not afraid of me. Jumping forward a few feet more, he waved to signal me to jump farther out into the river. On the basis of my three or four months' experience on Mars, I could tell that if I obeyed his signal, the end result would be to greatly bolster Scorpion's prestige. That was more than I could take. Ever since I can remember, I have always detested anyone who would rely on the prestige and power of a foreigner to hoodwink his own people. I walked in toward the beach, and Scorpion started walking forward again too. When I was fifteen or twenty yards from him, I picked up my revolver from the rock on which I had left it, and began closing in on him.

8 *The Profit Motive*

I seized Scorpion. He smiled. In fact I had never before seen him smile so assiduously. The madder I got, the more he smiled. It seemed that the cat-people kept their paltry stock of smiles solely in order to avoid beatings. I asked him what he meant by gathering all these cat-people to watch me bathe. He didn't say anything, but just kept on smiling as ingratiatingly as he could. I knew that he was up to something, but I was too sick of that wretched look of his to go to the bother of finding out what it was. I simply told him: "If you ever do anything like this again, watch out for your scalp!"

The next day I went to the river as usual. Before I had even arrived at the beach, I was conscious of a blackish mass in the distance. There were even more of them than yesterday! I decided to go along with my bath as if nothing had happened in order to see what they were up to; I could always give Scorpion a working over when I got back.

The sun came out. I stood in a shallow place, pretending to be totally wrapped-up in splashing in the water, but secretly watching the cat-people at the same time. Before long, Scorpion came along leading another cat-man who was carrying what appeared to be a pile of reverie leaves in both arms; they were stacked up hard against the bottom of his chin. Scorpion came first and the cat-man carrying the leaves followed him. I saw them walking along the line of cat-men; first Scorpion would put out his hand, and then the cat-man following him would extend his. I noticed that the stack of reverie leaves that he held in his arms was gradually diminishing. So that was it! Scorpion was taking advantage of the gathering to sell a few reverie leaves! He had, no doubt, jacked-up the price in honor of the occasion!

Now, basically I am a man who has *some* sense of humor; but a moment's anger will cause even a person like myself to go to extremes. I well knew how afraid of me (simply because I was a foreigner) the cat-men were. I also knew that this whole ridiculous spectacle was undoubtedly the handiwork of Scorpion alone, and it was by no means my original intention to cause this innocent group of spectators to suffer harm just in order to punish Scorpion. However, at the time, my fury caused me to forget all considerations of benevolence. I'd simply have to give Scorpion a taste of my strength; otherwise, I should never again be able to enjoy my morning exercise in peace. Now, if the cat-men had also wanted to come for a swim in the morning, then of course, there would be nothing that I could say: this river was not my exclusive possession. But to have one man swim while several hundred others stood around watching, and then to have someone come along and take advantage of the gathering to do business—well, that was more than I could take!

I decided not to grab Scorpion first, for I knew that he wouldn't tell me the truth anyway. The only way that I could get to the bottom of all this would be to capture one of the spectators. I started easing my way toward the river bank, keeping my back to them so as not to make them jumpy. Once I got to shore, it would be a matter of a hundred-yard dash and then I could catch one of them off-guard.

No sooner had I reached the bank and turned around, than I heard a most baleful cry—a cry even more pitiful than that made by a pig being slaughtered. My hundred-yard dash began. Ahead of me, it was as though an earthquake had suddenly occurred. Each one of the group seemed torn between the desire to scatter in order to escape with his own life and the contrary desire to group together with the others for security. Some ran; some fell; some forgot to run; and others went down and tried to crawl back up again. In the twinkling of an eye they were dispersed like autumn leaves scattered by the wind—a little pile here, a little pile there; one to the east, two to the west. They were running and screaming as though they were completely out of their minds, and by the time that my hundred-yard dash was over, there were only a few of them left at the finish line, lying scattered about the ground.

I grabbed one of them; but as soon as I looked, I saw that his eyes were closed and that he had stopped breathing. My regret at having killed him was much more intense than the panic of the calamity itself. I shouldn't have taken advantage of my superiority for killing; however, what was done, was done. Without thinking, I grabbed another. His leg was broken, but he was still alive. Thinking about it in retrospect, I'm really not proud of what I did that day; for I saw clearly that his leg was broken, and yet I went ahead and seized him for interrogation anyway. I well knew that one had already died of fright, and then cruelly went ahead to grab another one whom I might well scare to death too. If I can be excused for all of this on the grounds that I was acting "unconsciously" in the heat of the excitement, then the argument for the innate goodness of man won't hold water.*

To get a half-dead cat-man to speak—and to speak to a foreigner at that—is the most difficult thing imaginable. I knew that forcing him to talk would be no different from murdering him, for he would certainly die of fright in a very short time. Poor unfortunate! I let him go, and looked around again. The few that had fallen were all injured, of course, and were reduced to crawling on the ground. They were crawling very fast, but I didn't pursue them. Two of them were no longer moving at all.

I am not usually afraid of danger, but this time I felt that I had *really* stirred up a hornet's nest. Who could tell what odd kind of concoction the cat-people's law might turn out to be. Even though there might be a legal difference between murdering a man and scaring him to death, yet from the point of view of conscience, wasn't it the same thing after all? I couldn't decide what to do.

* Mencius (372–289 B.C.) argued that human nature is good and when it operates spontaneously or "unconsciously," it tends toward acts of benevolence.

Perhaps I'd go and hunt down Scorpion. After all, he'd gotten me into this mess in the first place and he certainly ought to have some way of getting me out of it. But even if I did find him, he wouldn't be likely to tell me the truth. Why not wait for *him* to come looking for *me?* Why not take advantage of this opportunity to find the aircraft and take care of my dead friend's body? Then if Scorpion ran into any danger in the reverie forest and came looking for me, I would be in a good position to interrogate him. For if he didn't tell the truth, I'd refuse to return. Extortion? Perhaps. But how else can you handle a man to whom trust means nothing and who doesn't consider lying as shameful?

I tucked my gun under my belt and with a heavy heart followed along the back of the river. The sun was very hot and I seemed to sense that I lacked something —of course, those goddamned reverie leaves! Without them I wouldn't be able to resist either the rays of the sun or the noxious mist that was rising from the river. "Cat Country will never produce a sage!" I said to myself. (I had to content myself with swearing at the cat-people in order to lighten my own sense of shame.) I thought of going over and taking the reverie leaves from the hands of those two dead cat-men. Was I really going to go so far as to rob the dead? After all, I could always go back to the reverie forest and break off a big branch; there would certainly be no one to stop me. But I didn't feel like walking that far. In the end, I actually wrested the leaves from the dead hands of the fallen cat-men! Half of one leaf had already been bitten away; I ate the other half and continued following my way along the river bank.

CHAPTER EIGHT

After walking for some time, I recognized a dark grey hill, a hill that I knew was not far from the spot where out plane had crashed. However, I didn't know how far the crash site was from the river or which side of the river it was on. It was really hot. I ate two more of the reverie leaves, but still didn't feel any cooler. Since there were no trees, there were no shady spots in which a man might rest; I decided to press on and find the aircraft no matter what the cost.

At just this juncture, someone called from behind. I recognized Scorpion's voice in the distance, but didn't stop. However, he was faster than me, and before long he had caught up. I thought of grabbing him by the scalp to shake the truth out of him, but when I saw the pathetic state that he was in, I didn't have the heart to lay a hand on him: his pig-mouth was swollen; a part of his skull was fractured; there were a number of scratches on his body; and he looked as though he had just been doused in something, for the fine hair was stuck to his skin. In sum, he looked like a drowned rat. Although I was the one who had scared a few of the cat-men to death, apparently he had been the one who had gotten the beating. It occurred to me that although the cat-men didn't dare take on foreigners, they were most courageous in laying into each other. Their disputes were, of course, none of my business; and yet, in spite of myself, I began to identify with, and even feel some sympathy for my terrified, injured, and defeated friend. Scorpion opened his mouth several times before he managed to get a word out. "Hurry back! The reverie forest is being plundered!"

I laughed. Whatever sympathy I may have felt for

him had been obliterated by his words. If he had taken a beating and had come to ask me to avenge him, then although it wouldn't be the most admirable thing in the world to do—still, looking at it from a Chinese point of view, I would have followed him back immediately.* But the reverie forest being plundered? Who wanted to be the running-dog of this capitalist anyway? If it was being plundered, let it be plundered. That had nothing to do with me.

"Hurry back! The reverie forest is being plundered!" The pupils almost popped right out of Scorpion's eyes. It seemed that the reverie forest was everything and that his life was nothing by comparison.

I said: "First tell me about what was going on this morning and then I'll go back with you."

He almost fainted from frustration and quickly stretched his neck several times in succession as he forced himself to swallow his own spleen: "But the reverie forest is being plundered!!" If he had had the nerve, he would certainly have knocked my brains out on the spot.

But I was fully as determined as he was. If he didn't tell me the truth, I wouldn't budge. In the end each of us settled for half a victory: I would return with him immediately; and on the way, he would explain everything to me.

Scorpion finally confessed the truth: the morning-bath spectators had been invited out from the city and

* Avenging a wrong suffered by a friend is a mark of *yich'i* (righteousness, nerve, guts, loyalty) and is sanctioned by Chinese folk mores; the government, however, has traditionally disdained *yich'i* since it is in fact a code outside the law.

were all upper class cat-people. Ordinarily the upper class would never have gotten up early, but the opportunity to watch an Earthman bathe was too rare to pass up; moreover, Scorpion had agreed to provide succulent reverie leaves for the occasion. Each person gave him ten National Souls (the standard monetary unit in Cat Country) for the privilege of watching me. And at no extra cost, each spectator got two succulent and juicy leaves of the very best quality.

"Why you bastard!" I thought to myself. "Putting me on display as though I were your personal property!" Before I had a chance to explode, Scorpion had a deceptive explanation all ready: "Look at it this way. A National Soul is a National Soul. Getting other people's National Souls into one's own hands is certainly an honorable undertaking. Now although I didn't talk it over with you beforehand," (he was walking fast, but the quick pace didn't seem to interfere in the least with his devious reasoning) "I knew that you certainly wouldn't oppose such an honorable undertaking. You'd still get to take your bath as usual, and I'd take the opportunity to obtain a few National Souls. The spectators would broaden their understanding, and it would be a profitable undertaking all round. Very profitable!"

"But who is going to take the responsibility for the people who died of fright during all your nonsense?"

"*You* scared them to death, so it doesn't matter! If *I* killed somebody," Scorpion continued pantingly, "then, although I'd get away with it, I'd still have to pay out a few leaves. After all, the law is nothing but a few words engraved on stone and you can always get around it if you have enough leaves; as a matter of fact, if you've got the leaves, you don't even have to worry about murder. With you, a foreigner, it's easier yet. You don't even need *leaves.* Kill anyone you please and no one will dare say anything; in any case, Cat Country law doesn't apply to foreigners. You wouldn't even have to spend a single, solitary leaf. How *I'd* love to be a foreigner like you! For instance, if you kill someone in the countryside, then as a foreigner, you can just leave him there as a snack for those white-tailed hawks and forget about it; or if you kill a man in the city, then all you have to do is go to the local courthouse and report it. Our judge will even apologize for inconveniencing you!" Scorpion seemed extremely envious of me and I even seemed to detect a few tears in his eyes. I was about to shed a few myself. Pitiful cat-people! What kind of life did they have? What guarantees were there for their rights and security?

"But those two who died were influential people. Won't their relatives make trouble for you?"

"Of course they will! Who do you think it is who's plundering the forest at this very moment? They sent scouts over quite a while back to see what you were doing. As soon as you were a good distance from the forest, they started pillaging. One of their people died, and now they're avenging him by stealing *my* reverie leaves! Hurry!"

"Are men and reverie leaves exactly equivalent in value?"

"The dead are dead, but the living still have to eat reverie leaves. Hurry!"

Suddenly it occurred to me—perhaps because I too had been contaminated by the cat-men, or perhaps because I had been struck by what he had just said about the living and dead—it occurred to me that I ought to get some National Souls out of him, myself. For if I ever left him—and after all the two of us really weren't good friends—what in the world would I use to buy things with? Since it was *my* morning bath that he had charged admission for, I certainly ought to be entitled to a share of the gate. Had I not found myself in that unusual situation, I don't think that such a low thought would ever have occurred to me. But since the situation was what it was, I'd have to look out for myself. The dead were dead, but the living still had to eat reverie leaves —he had a point there!

When we got close to the reverie forest, I stopped. "Scorpion, how much money have you taken in during the last two days?"

My question took him by surprise. He rolled the pupils of his eyes around: "Fifty National Souls and two counterfeit bills. Hurry!"

I turned around and walked away, taking great and decisive strides. He caught up with me. "A hundred! A hundred!" I kept right on going, and he kept adding to the amount until he reached a thousand. I estimated that in the last two days there had been at least several hundred spectators, and that he had certainly taken in much more than a thousand, but I was getting tired of the game. "All right, Scorpion, give me five hundred or we'll call it quits right here and now!"

Scorpion was well aware that for every minute he argued with me, he lost a few more leaves. With a pair of tear filled eyes, he answered, "It's a deal."

"If after this, you ever again try to make money off me

without telling me about it, I'll set fire to your reverie forest." I pulled out my box of matches and patted it. He promised it would never happen again.

By the time we got to the forest, there wasn't a soul there. No doubt, a scout had reported my imminent arrival and they had all fled in advance of our coming. Twenty or thirty of the trees on the edge of the forest were already completely bare. Scorpion let out a cry and collapsed on the ground.

9 *A Reluctant Servant of the Great Spirit* *

The reverie forest was truly beautiful. The leaves had already grown slightly larger than the palm of a man's hand. They were thick and of a rich green, bordered with a ring of burnished gold. The most succulent of the ripe leaves had become slightly mottled so that from a distance one would have taken the forest for a garden of mixed flowers. The sunlight from out the silver-grey sky fingered its way into the trees and made the colors of these flower-leaves still richer and even more serenely beautiful. They didn't have that kind of glossiness that sometimes glares into one's eyes, but were rather possessed of a gentle beauty that captivated the beholder and gave him a sense of tranquility. It was something

* The Chinese soldier's primary loyalty was often given to the warlord who commanded and paid him rather than to the country at large. Some of these "warlords" were actually quite good men, but there were many others who would allow their troops to plunder the countryside almost at will. Consequently, in much of China soldiers were feared as rapacious plunderers who lacked any real courage and were, at best, of questionable loyalty.

like looking at an old watercolor whose colors are still fresh, but whose paper has, in the course of years, lost its sheen.

And now every day, from dawn until dusk the forest was enclosed by a ring of spectators—and yet they weren't really spectators either. With eyes closed and noses thrust forward, they all inhaled the rich aroma of the leaves. Their mouths were open and watering so profusely that the shortest string of saliva was over two feet long. Whenever a breeze arose, without changing their stance in the slightest, they would crane their necks around and follow it so as to breathe in whatever perfume was contained in the air. They reminded one of snails slowly doing neck exercises after a rain. If by chance a dead-ripe leaf fell from a tree, they would immediately open their eyes, and their mouths would begin to twitch in anticipation; it was almost as though they had perceived the faint sound of the falling leaf with their noses! But before they could gather up enough nerve to go over and pluck up the precious leaf, Scorpion, in a flurry of fur, would beat them to it; and from all sides a cry would go up that sounded very much like the moan of a wronged ghost.

Scorpion transferred five hundred soldiers to guard the reverie forest, but he took care to station them over two miles from the forest itself. For had they been close to it, they would have been the first to steal the leaves. Actually he had no choice but to bring them there, for according to the customs of Cat Country, the harvest of the reverie leaves was a most important event, and troops had to be transferred for the sake of appearance if nothing else. Everyone knew that the soldiers wouldn't really protect anything, but it would be a public insult to the officers and men not to use them for this strange kind of guard duty in which they didn't feel responsible for guarding anything. Scorpion was something of a bigwig in the society and, of course, he didn't want people to criticize him; therefore, in order to avoid flouting Cat Country customs, he had to transfer the troops whether he wanted to or not. However, he did take the precaution of stationing them more than two miles away so that their rapaciousness would not lead to calamity. When the breeze grew a bit stronger and began to blow in the direction of the army camp, Scorpion immediately issued an order to the gallant five hundred to retreat a mile or so more in order to avoid the possibility that they might follow the scent and plunder every last leaf. The only reason that the soldiers followed his orders was that I was there; if it hadn't been for me, they would have long since mutinied. There was even a common saying among the cat-people that went: "If a foreigner so much as coughs, five-hundred cat-troops will fall prostrate from fear."

Apart from the five-hundred troops, Scorpion had twenty family retainers who served as his personal bodyguards; and it was upon these valiant men that he really depended for protecting the forest. All of them were blessed with a full and deep understanding of righteousness, and were fully loyal and reliable. But if by chance they took it into their heads to cut-up a bit, it wouldn't be beyond them to tie up Scorpion and take over the reverie forest themselves. However, because of my presence they didn't dare take it into their heads to cut-up; and thus they were able to preserve their deep understanding of righteousness and loyalty.

As harvest time drew near, Scorpion was really beside himself with activity: he had to watch his personal bodyguards to make sure that they didn't eat the leaves behind his back; he had to keep an eye on the wind direction in order to be prepared to order a more distant removal of the doughty five-hundred; he had to watch the spectators on the edge of the forest to make sure that he didn't lose so much as half-a-leaf of what dropped from the trees. In order to keep his own energy up, Scorpion was now eating up to thirty reverie leaves at a single sitting. It was said that if you could manage to eat more than forty at a time, you could go for three days without sleep; on the fourth day, however, you'd have the honor of joining your ancestors. Reverie leaves were funny things: if you took them in small doses, they would give you a lift, but you wouldn't feel like working; if you took them in large doses, you'd be able to work hard for a short time, but then you'd die. Scorpion was in a bind: he had to eat lots of the leaves in order to stay awake to watch over the forest, and yet he was well aware that if he ate too many of them, he would die. And yet he couldn't permit himself to cut down as though he were afraid of death—even though he was, in fact, terrified of death! Poor Scorpion!

He did cut down, however, on *my* evening meal of *regular* food. He felt that if I didn't have quite as much to eat in the evening, then I'd be more alert during the night. Scorpion was using the same methods to deal with me that he used on his own people. The security of the reverie forest was entirely dependent on me; therefore, I'd have to be alert at night; and therefore, I'd have to eat less at the evening meal. This was a good example of Cat Country logic: the ablest people ought to receive the lowest rewards. Once, I got so angry at the paltry amount that I was given that I threw the whole meal on the ground along with the eating implements. The very next day my food was again as abundant as it had always been. I had finally learned how to handle the cat-people, but I didn't feel too proud of myself.

Now a breeze began to blow the whole day long. This was the first time that this had happened in my experience on Mars. When I first arrived, there had been no wind at all. When the reverie leaves turned red, there was occasionally a slight breeze, but this was the first time that it had blown continuously. Tinged with every imaginable color, the reverie leaves swayed beautifully to-and-fro in the wind. After the sun had set Scorpion and his bodyguards worked straight through the night in the heart of the forest to build a large wooden frame; it must have been at least fifty or sixty feet tall. Though I didn't know it yet, they were preparing it for me. The light breeze that had blown all day and continued into the night was known in Cat Country as the "reverie breeze." The onset of the reverie breeze signalled a change in season. There were only two seasons in Cat Country: the first half of the year was the "passive season" (no wind); and the second half of the year was the "active season" (wind and rain).

In the midst of a morning dream, I heard a great racket outside my little room. When I crawled out to look, I saw Scorpion standing at the head of a column consisting of his twenty bodyguards. He had the tail-feather of a hawk stuck behind his ear and a large wooden stick in his hand. Each of the bodyguards seemed to be holding something too. I couldn't be sure, but it looked as though they were carrying various kinds of musical instruments in the ready position. Another wave of Scorpion's baton and the musical instruments began to make a racket. They blew their instruments in such a fashion that it was obvious that no one felt the slightest inclination to harmonize with anyone else. The high and low notes were equally unpleasant to the ear, and identically long and drawn out—so drawn out that the pupils of the bodyguards' eyes almost popped clear out of their heads before they took another breath. Having pulled in another lungful of air, they began blowing again, leaning first forward and then backwards in order to utilize every last bit of breath that they had, but still unwilling to take a fresh one. It seemed as though they wouldn't stop until they had collapsed inwards like a paper-bag when you suck the air out of it. As a matter of fact, two of them got so out of breath that they collapsed on the ground, but they still kept on blowing! The music of Cat Country lays great emphasis on the length and volume of a note. The percussion instruments were of wood and looked something like castanets. The musicians banged on them all they were worth, although there was no discernible rhythm.

Then the wind instruments grew shriller; the percussion instruments, more excited. It seemed as though the cat-musicians would have considered it an honor and pleasure to blow and beat themselves to death. After three rounds of this, Scorpion's stick went up in the air and, mercifully, the music stopped. All twenty bodyguards squatted down and panted for breath.

Scorpion took the feather from behind his ear, walked over to me very respectfully, and said: "The time has arrived. Please ascend the altar and oversee the harvest of the reverie leaves in the name of the God of Spiritual Brilliance." It must have been that I was hypnotized by the music, or perhaps it would be more accurate to say "stunned" by the racket, for although I felt like laughing more than anything else, without thinking, I obeyed. He placed the feather behind my ear and began leading the way. I followed, and the twenty musician-bodyguards fell in behind me. We arrived at the tall scaffold and Scorpion climbed up on it. He prayed for a while to heaven, and the musicians accompanied his prayer with a bit more racket. He climbed down and asked me to go up.

It was as though I had completely forgotten that I was a grown man; it was as though I were once again a playful child totally entranced by a new toy. Like a little monkey, I scampered up. When Scorpion saw that I had reached the highest point on the scaffold, he gave a wave of his stick and the twenty musicians scattered to all sides. Taking up their posts at a considerable distance from each other at the edge of the forest, they turned about and faced the trees. Scorpion scampered off only to return a while later leading a considerable number of soldiers, each of whom had a big club in his hand and a bird feather stuck behind his ear.

When they got to the edge of the forest, the whole formation halted and Scorpion pointed up to the scaffold. They all raised their clubs in my direction as if they were saluting me. You see, as the direct representative of the Great Spirit, I was supposed to have come to protect the reverie leaves for Scorpion, who was, of course, most beloved by the Great Spirit. If the soldiers, while harvesting the leaves, were to try to hide any of them away, or eat them on the sly, then I, as direct representative of the Great Spirit, would strike that erring soldier down with a bolt of lightning from my hand. The source of that "lightning" would be, of course, the *yishu* that I carried tucked inside my belt. The twenty musician-bodyguards were my aids and if they saw anyone trying any hanky-panky, they'd signal Scorpion with their instruments; he, in turn, would pray to me to loose a bolt of my lightning.

After the ceremony to the Great Spirit was over, Scorpion ordered the soldiers to divide into teams of two. One man would climb the tree to pick, and the other would stay on the ground to stack the leaves as they were handed down. No one was allowed to work on the trees closest to me. The reason for this, Scorpion told them, was that it would be dangerous to get too close to the direct representative of the Great Spirit; for if a breath came out of the nose of the Great Spirit's representative and touched one of them, then that man would immediately fall paralyzed to the ground like a wet rag and never be able to rise again. Therefore these trees would have to be left for Scorpion to pick personally. It seemed that Scorpion had been equally as successful in hypnotizing the soldiers as he had been with me, for they immediately broke up into teams of two and set to work!

Scorpion must have eaten an especially heavy meal of the best leaves, for he was running back and forth supervising things as fast as a shuttle on a loom. He had his club constantly poised against the possibility that he might have to bring it down on the head of an erring soldier. I heard later that every time they had a reverie leaf harvest, the landlord was expected to club to death a couple of the soldiers and bury them under the trees in order to insure a bountiful harvest the following year. Sometimes when the landlord hadn't had the foresight to provide himself with a foreigner like me to serve as the Great Spirit's representative, the soldiers would bury the landlord under the trees, instead, and make off with the entire harvest. Such mutinous troops would also steal the wood of the trees to make clubs, for an army of cat-men equipped with reverie-tree clubs was considered to be almost invincible.

And so it was that I came to be perched, like some giant and ungainly parrot, up there on the scaffold! Now what in hell was I doing that for? I was tempted to laugh, but refrained; after all, I didn't want to interfere with the customs of the cat-people. Since I had come here in the first place to observe everything that I could, I'd just have to play along with things, and join in their group activities no matter how ridiculous they might be. Fortunately there was a little breeze so that it wasn't too hot up there. I had Scorpion get someone to fetch me one of the grass covers that I had woven to cover my food with; for the time being, I used it as a sun-hat. I wasn't going to be a victim of sunstroke if I could help it.

Except for a feather behind the ear and a club in the

hand, there was no difference between a soldier and an ordinary cat-man. The club and feather gave them positions superior to those of ordinary cat-men, but then under the burden of Scorpion's hypnotic command, they probably suffered a bit more than ordinary cat-men too.

Soon I was able to see the trunks of the reverie trees that had been previously hidden by a dense growth of leaves. It was somewhat like watching silkworms strip a mulberry tree. Before long, the soldiers were all at the tops of the trees. I noticed that those who were closest to me were picking with one hand and shading their eyes with the other. They probably thought that looking at me directly would harm them in some way!

It isn't really that the cat-men can't work, I thought to myself. If only they had a good leader who would forbid them to eat the reverie leaves, they might really be quite productive. Supposing I were to drive Scorpion off and become landlord in his place; supposing I were to become their leader . . . but this was just idle thought and I didn't dare go too far with it, for I still didn't completely understand the cat-people to begin with.

Just as I was musing in this vein, I saw—the reverie leaves were few and far between now and I could see very well what was going on below—I saw Scorpion's club being zeroed in on the head of a soldier. I knew that even if I jumped down, I still wouldn't get there in time to stop him. But I felt that I had to make a try anyway, for in my eyes Scorpion was much more hateful than the soldiers and even if I didn't make it in time to save a man, I could still take advantage of the opportunity to show him a thing or two. Crawling to a spot that was only a few yards from the ground, I jumped down and ran over to them. But by the time I got there, the soldier was already lying on the ground and Scorpion was already issuing the order to bury him.

A man who doesn't fully understand the ways of thinking of those around him often hurts people out of the best of intentions, and so it was with me. When I jumped, the soldiers thought that I was about to begin unleashing bolts of lightning, and as I hit the ground I heard a number of thuds as they leapt down from the trees on all sides. The majority of them had probably suffered injury, for I heard them crying piteously. But I was too carried away by anger toward Scorpion to pay attention to them. Scorpion probably thought that I had seen him punishing a soldier and had come down to help. Since I had been so tractable in every other way that morning, it was natural perhaps for him to assume that I would serve as his flunky in everything. Hence, he was taken completely aback when I grabbed him. He himself probably didn't see anything at all wrong in killing a mere soldier.

"Why did you kill him?" I demanded.

"Because he was eating the stem of a leaf behind our backs."

"Do you mean to say that you think simply because a man eats the stem of leaf, you can. . . ." I didn't bother to go on. I had forgotten for a moment that I was in the midst of cat-people, and there's no point in reasoning with them. I beckoned to the soldiers standing around and said, "Tie him up!" They all looked at each other as though they didn't understand what I meant. "T-I-E H-I-M U-P!" I said it slowly and distinctly this time, but they still made no move. Their lack of initiative disheartened me. If ever I were to be given command of a body of troops like this, I'd probably never be able to get them to understand me. Their not daring to come forward was not at all out of affection for Scorpion, but was rather because they simply didn't understand me—that I might be doing all this to avenge the fallen soldier was totally beyond their comprehension. I'd gotten myself in another bind: if I let Scorpion off scot-free, he'd certainly lose all respect for me; but if I killed him, I wouldn't have him around to help during the many times in the future when I'd certainly need him. With regard to my future plans for taking in the sights on Mars—at least this part of the planet—he would certainly prove more useful than this motley crew of soldiers. Pretending to be calm, I asked: "Do you want to accept your punishment, or would you prefer to see me sit up there on the scaffold and let the soldiers steal the leaves without doing anything about it?"

When the soldiers heard me talk about permitting them to steal reverie leaves, they became so excited that a few of them misinterpreted my question as the go-ahead signal. While holding Scorpion in one hand, I had to kick two of them to the ground; the rest stopped dead in their tracks. Scorpion's eyes had already narrowed to a tiny slit; I knew how, in his heart of hearts, he must hate me. He had personally invited me in as the representative of the Great Spirit, and now here I was, turning on him and disciplining him before the very eyes of his own troops—that *must* have been hard to take. Of course, it would never have occurred to him that in killing a man for eating a piece of the stem of a reverie leaf he had done anything wrong.

In the end, he decided against calling my bluff and acknowledged my right to punish him. I asked him what compensation the soldiers got harvesting the reverie leaves. He said that each man would get two small leaves. At this point, all around us, the soldiers' ears pricked up. They probably thought that I was going to punish Scorpion by forcing him to give them extra leaves. Instead, however, I told him to give each of them a regular meal after the harvest just like the one that I had every evening. Upon hearing this, their ears all dropped flat against their heads and their vocal cords produced a sound something like that of a man choking on something while eating. To them, it was a most unsatisfactory way of resolving things. As for the dead soldier, I told Scorpion to indemnify his family to the tune of one hundred National Souls. He agreed. I asked the soldiers where this man's family lived, but not one of them said anything. The cat-people were not accustomed to helping out in anything that might be beneficial to someone else, even if that help only cost them a few words. That's something else that I didn't learn until I had lived in Cat Country for several months. Since we couldn't find out where the man's family was, Scorpion lucked out again and was saved a hundred National Souls.

10 *Being a Foreigner Does Have Its Advantages*[*]

The reverie leaves were all harvested. There was a breeze every day now and the temperature had gone down by ten degrees. From time to time black clouds floated across the grey sky, but there was no rain at all. It was at the beginning of the active season that the landlords took the reverie leaves into the city. Although deep down in his heart he was something less than happy with me, Scorpion had to feign an unfelt affection

[*] During the so-called "Century of Unequal Treaties"—from approximately the middle of the last century to the middle of this one—much of the internal administration of China was in the hands of foreign interests. While foreigners often competed in wringing concessions out of the Chinese, they usually stopped short of open conflict with each other, for that would endanger all of their positions in China. This was, understandably, very discouraging to the Chinese. For thousands of years "playing one barbarian off against another" had been a cornerstone of China's foreign policy. Now it no longer worked. For thousands of years, too, the Chinese classics—especially the *Poetry Classics*—were quoted, much as the *Bible*, to justify anything from love to murder; the author takes obvious delight in satirizing this tradition.

in order to get me to accompany him into the city. Without me, he knew that he wouldn't be safe and might well lose his life in protecting the leaves.

The reverie leaves were all sun-dried and baled. A team of two soldiers was responsible for transporting each bale and they took turns carrying it on the head. Scorpion led the way, carried by four soldiers. His spine was flattened out so as to rest on the four heads of the troops. Two tall soldiers held his feet in place, while another man brought up the rear, propping up his neck. In Cat Country this mode of travel was the most prestigious, if not the most comfortable. The twenty bodyguard-musicians marched on either side of the column with their musical instruments in their hands. If any of the soldiers did anything out of order, such as tearing a hole in one of the bales in order to enjoy the aroma of the leaves, then one of them would musically signal the fact to Scorpion. (In order for it to exist, everything in Cat Country must have a practical application and music is no exception, for musicians also double as spies.)

My position was right in the center of the column so that I could keep an eye on those to my fore and aft. Originally Scorpion had seven bearers set aside for me too, but I told him that I had much rather walk on the ground and had no desire for this kind of special treatment. But Scorpion wouldn't give in so easily. He quoted the Cat Country classics at me: * "And of bearers, our

* In traditional China the classics, especially the *Poetry Classic,* were often quoted to justify things for which no apparent basis could be found in logic.

emperor shall have two score and one; our feudal lords, three times five; and our nobles, seven . . ." He informed me that this was a custom that had been passed down from ancient times as a way of marking social distinctions. To destroy such a custom would be unthinkable and, furthermore, he just wouldn't permit it. However, I remained adamant. Then he quoted a folk saying to me:

> When a noble on his feet must go,
> In shame his ancestor's face hangs low.

I told him that my ancestors wouldn't feel the least bit ashamed. Then, on the verge of tears, he quoted two lines of their *Poetry Classic:*

> Raise high your face the blessed leaf to eat,
> And spend your life as one of our elite.

"To hell with you and your nobles!" I couldn't think of a suitable line of poetry to quote back at him and was reduced to this uncouth reply. Scorpion sighed; within the narrow confines of his heart, I am sure that he was swearing me into a bloody pulp, but he didn't dare express such critical sentiments openly.

We wasted almost two and a half hours just in lining up. Altogether Scorpion must have gotten up on, and down from, his bearers' heads at least seven times. It seemed that the cat-soldiers were determined not to get into an orderly formation. They must have been aware by now that I was not entirely on Scorpion's side, and for that reason, Scorpion no longer dared to break open their heads at will. And no matter how Scorpion swore at or castigated them, they just *wouldn't* form a straight line. At last Scorpion gave up and ordered them to forward-march no matter how uneven the formation was.

Just as we were finally about to depart, several white-tailed hawks flew toward us. Scorpion jumped down again and addressed his men: "It's very unlucky to meet hawks when setting out on a journey; we'll put it off until tomorrow." *

I pulled out my revolver. "If we don't go now, we're never going!" Scorpion's face turned green with anger. Flabbergasted, he opened and closed his mouth several times, but nothing came out. He knew that it wouldn't do any good to argue with me, but at the same time he also felt that setting out on a journey in violation of a taboo was a very dangerous business. He hemmed and hawed another ten minutes or so before he climbed back up on the heads of the bearers and prepared to set out. He was trembling all over when the column finally set into motion. I don't know whether it was because I had made him so angry that he couldn't lie steady, or whether it was because the bearers were intentionally playing tricks on him, but at any rate, before we had been on the road very long, Scorpion had already fallen off several times. But as soon as he fell off, he'd crawl right back up there again. You see, Scorpion had a heavy sense of responsibility for preserving the customs handed down by his ancestors.

All the places along the road where it was possible to

* In traditional China, before setting out on a journey—or undertaking anything important—people would often consult an almanac or fortune-teller to determine whether it would be a lucky or unlucky day.

write—on the bark of trees, on stone, on broken fragments of wall—were entirely filled up with large white characters. WELCOME SCORPION; SCORPION IS A GREAT MAN WHO EXHAUSTS HIS STRENGTH IN IMPROVING THE NATIONAL DIET; SCORPION'S SOLDIERS HOLD HIGH THE CLUBS OF RIGHTEOUSNESS; WITHOUT SCORPION WE WOULDN'T HAVE THIS YEAR'S BUMPER CROP. Scorpion had had the foresight to send emissaries on ahead to write out all of these things so that he might enjoy them as he went by.

We passed through several small villages where the inhabitants all sat leaning against broken walls. When the cat-soldiers passed in front of them, they all closed their eyes, not even daring to take so much as a peek. If they are afraid of the soldiers, I thought, why don't they hide? Or if they aren't afraid, why is it that they don't dare to open their eyes and take a peek? I just couldn't figure it out. But when I took a closer look, I began to understand. These were, it turned out, members of the village welcoming committee. I could tell because I saw that there were large characters written in the fine grey hair on their heads. One character on each man's head, so that several of them together formed such phrases as WELCOME SCORPION! Because the words had been written some time before by one of Scorpion's advance emissaries, the characters were already somewhat faded and indistinct. Although the villagers all sat with their eyes closed, Scorpion still nodded toward them in appreciation for the welcome, just as though the whole thing were for real after all. These villagers too were all under the "protection" of Scorpion. The run-down and filthy condition of the village, the emaciated, filthy, listless condition of the inhabitants—all testified to how well their protector had fulfilled his responsibilities. I began to hate Scorpion even more than I had before.

Had I been alone, I probably could have made the journey to Cat City in half a day; travelling with cat-soldiers, however, is the most rigorous exercise of one's patience that can possibly be imagined. I well knew that the cat-people could, in fact, travel with great speed, but not when they're serving as soldiers. For the faster a cat-soldier gets to the front, the sooner he dies. Therefore the cat-troops were all well known for being slow and deliberate. They would march calmly and slowly to the front as if half asleep, but when they closed with the enemy, their tempo would suddenly switch from largo to allegro—as they took off in the opposite direction.

It was somewhat past one in the afternoon. Although there were a few black clouds in the sky, the sun was as hot as ever and the mouths of the soldiers hung wide open; their fine hair was all matted against their bodies with sweat. I had never seen a less presentable body of troops. There was a reverie forest off in the distance and Scorpion issued an order taking us somewhat off our normal course so that we might pass through it. I thought that Scorpion was at last beginning to show some consideration for his men and planned to let them rest for a while once we got to the forest.

When we were almost there, Scorpion rolled down off his bearers and came over to confer with me. Would I be willing to help him plunder this forest? "It's really not all that important that we make off with a few reverie leaves, but it would be most beneficial to give the troops a little combat experience," he said. Before answering him, I looked around at the troops. I could tell from the leers on their faces that every last one of them knew what Scorpion had in mind. A few minutes ago they had looked totally exhausted, but now they didn't seem to be the least bit tired. It would seem that looting the countryside is exactly what the cat-soldiers are best cut out to do, I thought to myself. I realized that if I interfered with Scorpion's contemplated raid, the troops would hate *me* even more than they did Scorpion. Although I probably could control the whole lot of them for a time with my revolver, still if they really wanted to do me violence, there were just too many of them for me to guard against all by myself. Anyway, I thought to myself, the cat-people seem to consider mutual plunder as an entirely reasonable form of behaviour! Why should I interfere? Besides, even if I did stand up against them in the name of righteousness, who would be there to know about it and admire me for it? Apparently I too had been infected by the thinking of the cat-people, for of late my courage was often weakened by thoughts of preserving my own peace and security. I told Scorpion to do as he pleased.

I was well aware that this was a kind of backing-down, but I hadn't realized that by giving Scorpion an inch, I'd encourage him to take a mile: he immediately asked if I would be willing to take command of the raid. This I unhesitatingly refused. "Go ahead and plunder the place if you want to; I won't stop you, but I won't help you either!" As soon as we started moving toward the reverie forest, the troops seemed to smell plunder in the air; for without even waiting for Scorpion's order, they all set their bales on the ground and took a firm hold on their clubs. In fact, some of them had already run forward to join the attack. I had never before seen Scorpion display so much nerve; although he did not lead the foray in person, he did manage to look quite martial and even dashing. His eyes were popped out round and every fine hair on his head was standing on end. At a single wave of his club, the troops rushed in mass toward the forest. When they arrived, they began circling about the perimeter of the forest in a provocative manner as though they were trying to lure the guards out. They circled it three times, but there was no sound from within. Scorpion smiled, and with a loud cry, the troops hurled themselves into the forest.

Terrible cries issued from within. Scorpion's eyes were not popped out quite so round now, and he even blinked a few times. Suddenly, his troops were in full rout! Their clubs were gone and they were pounding their heads with both hands while screaming like banshees: "Foreigners! Foreigners!" Although Scorpion didn't seem to believe it, he didn't look quite as bold and full of derring-do as he had a few minutes previously. He just kept mumbling, "Foreigners? There can't be any foreigners." At this point someone rushed out of the forest in hot pursuit. Now Scorpion was really scared. "My God! There really are foreigners in there!" Quite a few soldiers came streaming out of the forest. The two who seemed to be leading were tall and had white hair all over. Each of them carried a shiny club in his hand. I assumed that they must be foreigners, for the clubs they carried were made of a steel-like synthetic that was far beyond the technology of Cat Country. I began to feel a bit uneasy, myself. For what if Scorpion should ask me to go and stop the two foreigners. How did I know what those shiny things in their hands were? And yet, even though plundering the reverie forest had not been my idea in the first place, I was, after all, Scorpion's bodyguard. If I stood by and watched him suffer defeat without making any attempt to save him, at the very least I should lose status. Besides, my entire future in Cat Country depended on my relationship to him.

"Hurry up and stop them!" Scorpion said. "Hurry!"

I knew that this was a question of duty that would admit no excuse; there was no point in hesitating. I pulled out my revolver and approached them. Much to my surprise, when the two white-furred soldiers saw me coming forward, they stopped advancing. Then Scorpion ran over to join us, and I knew that the danger was past. "Make peace! Make peace!" Scorpion whispered from behind. *Now* I was really thrown for a loss. Why didn't he tell me to fight them? Make peace? How? The "how" was much easier than I had anticipated, for in the midst of my confusion, the two white-furred soldiers spoke: "You are hereby fined six bales of reverie leaves to be disposed by the three of us as we see fit!" I looked all around: there were only two of them. What did he mean by three? Scorpion stood behind me and urged in low tones: "Make terms." Not knowing what else to do, like a simpleton I said right back to them: "*You* are fined six bales of reverie leaves to be disposed of by the three of *us* as *we* see fit!" When the two white men heard me say this, they smiled and nodded their heads as though they were very satisfied with my terms. I, on the other hand, was totally mystified by their reaction. Scorpion sighed and ordered his troops to bring up six bales of reverie leaves. When the six bales were on the ground before us, the two white-furred soldiers very politely invited me to pick out the first two. Only then did I realize that in saying "three" they were including me in. I was equally courteous in return and asked them to choose first. They picked out four at random and handed them over to the Cat Country soldiers under their command. Then they said to me: "Our leaves are almost harvested too. See you in Cat City!" And without further ado, they went back into the forest.

I was utterly confused and didn't know what to think. What kind of tricks were being played here? It wasn't until after I arrived in Cat City and questioned the foreigners that I understood the full ramifications of what had happened. The cat-people were no match for foreigners; thus, their only hope was that foreigners would fight among themselves. It would have required a tremendous amount of effort for the cat-people to make themselves strong and they were much too clever to be dumb enough to do *that* much work. It was much easier to pray to their Great Spirit to make the foreigners slaughter each other so that the cat-people might make a strength of Cat Country's weakness, or perhaps one ought to say, to make the foreigners as weak as themselves.

The foreigners well understood this and although they often had conflicts of interest in Cat Country, still they would never be willing to fight each other and thus enable the cat-people to take advantage of their quarrels. They saw very clearly that if they allowed disputes to arise amongst themselves, it would be a case of matching one sharp sword against another so that even the victorious one would suffer great loss. If, on the other hand, they united in order to bully the cat-people, then they could gain great profit without suffering the slightest loss. They not only honored this principle in the conduct of their international relations, but even as single individuals working in Cat Country they observed it rigorously.

Protecting the reverie forests was a good occupation for the foreigners. By agreement, they were responsible for protecting the Cat Country landlords from their own people. If it so happened that there were foreigners protecting the landlords, then neither side was permitted to infringe upon the rights of the other. If this condition were not honored, then the foreign guardians on both sides were to meet in solemn conclave and decide on the punishment to be meted out to the landlords. Thus, not only was it possible to avoid disputes arising between foreigners because of the cat-people's affairs, but it was also possible to preserve the superior status of the guardians. Thus they would never be used by the cat-people.

If you looked at it from the point of view of the foreign guardians, this was really a pretty good system. But if you looked at it from the cat-people's point of view . . . ? Almost despite myself, I began to feel sympathy for all the Scorpions of Mars as underdogs. But then it occurred to me that the Scorpions all seemed more than willing to accept this kind of treatment; they didn't seem to want to make themselves strong. They seemed to *prefer* inviting the foreigners in to bully their own people. Then whose fault was it, after all? Only people who have an equal share of guts can respect each other, and the people of Cat Country had simply lost theirs. No wonder other people toyed with them so much. For several days I couldn't get these disturbing thoughts out of my mind.

Going back a bit, after Scorpion had been punished, he continued on to Cat City as though nothing had happened; rather than having the slightest expression of shame on his face, he looked as though he had just returned from a great victory. The only thing he said to me was that if I didn't want those two bales of reverie leaves—he knew that I really didn't like reverie leaves all that much—he'd be willing to buy them back from me for thirty National Souls. I was certain that this quantity of reverie leaves was worth at least three hundred National Souls, but I didn't say whether I would sell them or not. I didn't want to lower myself by paying any attention at all to such a gutless coward. I didn't even so much as favor him with a growl of contempt. When the sun was on the western horizon, Cat City came into view.

11 *The Capital of Cat Country* *

As soon as I sat eyes on Cat City, for some reason or other, a sentence took form in my mind: *This civilization will soon perish!* It certainly wasn't because I knew all there was to know about the civilization of Cat Country that I thought this, for the bit of experience that I had gained in the reverie forest had only been enough to stimulate my curiosity and make me want to get to the bottom of everything. Nor was it because I viewed the civilization of Cat Country as a mere tragic interlude prepared for my entertainment and diversion. It was rather that I had hoped to utilize my sojourn in Cat Country to fully comprehend the inner workings of at least this one civilization and thus enrich my experience of life. I knew that it was possible that a whole civiliza-

* In the following pages, the author clearly has in mind crowded Chinese streets. Within the family or among friends, Chinese often carry the business of politely yielding precedence to each other to the point of absurdity; however, lined up for theater tickets or crowding aboard a bus, it is often a case of the devil take the hindmost.

tion or even a whole race might perish, for the history of mankind on my own planet, Earth, was not entirely wreathed in roses. And since the perusal of the past history of mankind on Earth had been at times enough to make me shed tears, imagine my feelings at the prospect of seeing a civilization breathe its last before my very eyes!

The life of a man, like a candle, seems to glow again with former brilliance just before going out; and an entire civilization on the point of extinction is not without a final, ephemeral splendor either. And yet there is a difference: a civilization on the edge of oblivion is not so conscious of its own imminent demise as is a lone man. It is almost as though the creative process itself had marked the civilization for extinction so that the good—and there are always a few good people left, even in a country that's about to expire—suffer the same fate as the evil. And perhaps in such a civilization, the few good people left will begin to experience a certain shortness of breath, will begin to draw up their wills, and will even moan over the impending fate of their civilization. But their sad cries, matched against the funeral dirge of their own death-bound culture, will be but as the chirps of lingering cicadas against a cruel autumn wind.

And yet Cat City was full of life, but behind this lively facade one was conscious of a skeletal hand, a hand that seemed ever ready to tear the skin and flesh away from the cat-people to leave nothing but a wasteland of bleached bones. And yet, despite all of this, Cat City was one of the liveliest places that I have ever seen.

The arrangement of the city itself was the simplest that I had ever encountered in all my experience. There was nothing that you could really call "a street," for other than an apparently endless line of dwellings, there was nothing but a kind of highway, or perhaps one ought to say "empty square." If one kept in mind what the layout of a Cat Country army camp was like, one could well imagine the layout of the city: an immense open square with a row of houses down the middle, totally devoid of color and utterly drowned in cat-people. That's all there was; this was what they called "Cat City." There were crowds of people, but one couldn't tell exactly what they were doing. None of them walked in a straight line, and all of them got in each other's way. Fortunately the streets were wide, and when it was no longer possible to go forward, they could switch to walking sideways as they crowded past one another.

It was as though the single row of houses formed a breakwater against which a tide of people pounded. I still don't know whether they had house numbers or not. But if we assume that they did, then a man who wanted to go from number five to number ten, would have to zig-zag his way for at least three miles. Once outside his own door, he'd be crowded into a sidewise progress and simply float along on the tide until he arrived at his destination; but if by chance, the direction of the tide should change before he got there, then he'd be crowded home again. However, if he hit things just right, he would probably make it to number ten. But, of course, one can't always be sure of hitting things just right, and occasionally he might be crowded back-and-forth so much that he would be taken even farther from his destination and might well fail to even make it home that day.

CHAPTER ELEVEN

There was a reason for there being only one row of buildings in the city. I worked that reason out in my imagination somewhat as follows. I assumed that in the beginning there must have been several rather narrow streets. Crowding about in the narrow lanes had doubtless resulted in wasting a good deal of time, and had probably cost a number of lives to boot. You see, in the eyes of the cat-people, "yielding the right-of-way" was considered to be most disgraceful; and keeping to one side of the street was seen as incompatible with their freedom-loving spirit. Thus, if they had built houses on both sides of the street, they would be forever bottled up between them, and it is likely that the bottleneck wouldn't break up before one row of the houses had collapsed under the pressure of the crowd. And thus it was, I concluded, that they had built their houses in one long line, making the streets on either side infinitely wide. However, they hadn't completely solved the problem of crowding even yet; but at least no more lives were lost. To be sure, crowding ten miles out and back in the course of a short trip would take you out of your way a bit, but it wouldn't place you in any mortal danger. Therefore we can cite this new and less dangerous arrangement as another piece of testimony to the humane spirit of the cat-people.

Furthermore, crowding along in this manner wasn't all that unpleasant; besides, when people crowded you off your feet and carried you along in the press, you were, in effect, getting free transportation. In all honesty, I must admit that this explanation is merely my own hypothesis and I dare not vouch for its correctness. To make a solid case for my theory, I'd have to go back and see whether or not I could, in fact, find traces of the old streets that I assume were there previously.

If it were simply a matter of crowding, it wouldn't have been all that unusual. But I discovered that the tide didn't merely roll to the left and right, but even had its risings and fallings! As I was watching the Cat City crowd, a pebble on the road caught someone's eye and an entire group of cat-people suddenly squatted down to examine it, thus occasioning an eddy on the surface of the tide. It was as though, come hell or high water they just had to see that pebble; soon they changed from a squatting position to a sitting one, and all around them more and more people began to squat, making the eddy grow larger and larger. Those in back, of course, could not see the stone, and, as they pushed forward, those who had been seated were crowded to their feet again. The more that people crowded, the higher up those who had been sitting in front were pushed until they were finally on top of their neighbors' heads. Suddenly everyone forgot the pebble, stood up and threw their heads back to watch those who now rested on their neighbors' heads, thus filling the eddy up again.

As though decreed by fate, two old friends happened to meet at the edge of the eddy that had just filled in. They immediately sat down for a chat and those around them also sat down to listen in on their conversation. This, of course, occasioned another eddy. Then the bystanders who were listening in on the chat began putting in their two cents' worth and before long, of course, a brawl ensued, causing the eddy to expand suddenly. As the fighting continued, the eddy kept getting larger and larger until it reached the edge of another eddy—one that had been formed when two old men had decided to play a game of chess on the street. Now the two eddies became one, and as more and more people began watching the chess games the brawl died out. And until the bystanders began kibitzing, the chess-game-eddy was possessed of a fleeting stability.

This human tide was interesting enough in itself, but the best was yet to come. A large crack suddenly appeared in the tide that reminded one of the parting of the waters of the Red Sea when the ancient Israelites crossed it. Had it not been for a similar miracle, I can't possibly imagine how Scorpion's reverie leaf formation could have gotten through the tide intact, since Scorpion's home—their destination—was smack dab in the center of Cat City.

Backtracking a bit, let me explain how it was that this miracle came about. One would have expected that as Scorpion's formation neared the city, they would have devised some way of skirting the edges of that human sea while they jockeyed for a position from which they might have worked their way over to his home. But no! With seven of them bearing Scorpion on their heads, they plunged headlong into the cat-surf! Then music was struck up. At first I thought it was a signal for the pedestrians to clear a right-of-way. But as soon as they heard the music, rather than shrinking back, the people all began crowding over in the direction of the reverie leaf formation until they were packed as tight as sardines in a can. I thought that it would be a miracle if Scorpion's men ever made it through.

But Scorpion was much more capable than I had imagined. *Bump-ba dump-dump-dump, bump-ba dump-*

dump-dump—lively as a roll of drums in a Chinese military opera, the clubs of the soldiers came down on the heads of the cat-people and a crack began to appear in the human tide. Thus the miracle of the Red Sea had been of Scorpion's own making. Strange to say, the people's eagerness to see what was going on was not abated one whit by the clubs, although they did fall back out of the way to open up a path. They kept on smiling at the formation. The clubs, however, didn't stop merely because of this friendly reception, but continued with a *bump-ba dump-dump-dump.* By dint of careful observation, I was able to make out a difference between the city cats and the country cats: the city cats had a bald spot where a part of the skull had been replaced by a steel plate that was placed at the center of the head and also doubled as a drum—clear evidence that they had had long experience with having their heads drummed by soldiers while watching exciting public spectacles, for experience is never the product of a single, fortuitous occurrence.

Originally, I had thought that the soldiers were beating their heads as they walked along merely in order to open up a path; but it turned out that this drum-playing served still another purpose. You see, the victims of all this drum-playing were not exactly angels themselves. None of those who were hindmost were willing to stay there but would push, kick, crowd, and even bite in order to make their way in the world and become foremost. Those who were already foremost, on the other hand, kicked back with their heels, poked back with their elbows, and leaned back hard in order to keep the hindmost in their proper places. Now the soldiers didn't beat those who were in the front rows exclusively; they also reached out with their clubs and played a *bump-ba dump-dump-dump* on the cat-heads in back. Thus all their heads hurt and this tended to make them forget somewhat the pain that they were causing each other. And so the soldiers' drumming served to reduce the hostility that they felt for each other. One may call this method "treating pain with pain."

I was completely wrapped up in watching them. To tell the truth, they exerted a compelling, though melancholy, attraction over me. It seemed that I just had to watch them. I was so taken up with observing them that I didn't even notice what that row of houses in the center of the square was like. I already knew that whatever the houses were like, they certainly couldn't be beautiful, for a foul stench continuously emanated from them. Now it may be possible for beauty to exist in the midst of filth, but I for one don't think so. I can't conceive, for instance, of a Taj Mahal resplendent beneath a coat of black mud and foul water. The people on the street didn't do much to improve things either. Whenever I approached them, they immediately cried out and shrank back as far as the press would allow; but then they would quickly rush back toward me again, a clear indication that the fear and respect that city dwellers felt for foreigners was not quite as intense as that of the country folk. Having dissipated their fear and surprise by crying out, the city dwellers then felt brave enough to come up to me and give me the once-over. If I had stood still on the road, I would certainly never have been able to move again, for they would have surrounded me so closely that you wouldn't have been able to get a drop of water between us.

Ten thousand fingers kept pointing at me. The cat-people are very straightforward: if they see anything fresh and new, they simply point it right out with their fingers. Still unable to completely rid myself of the vanity of a human being from Earth, I was most uncomfortable. I longed to take wings and fly away to some quiet, peaceful spot where I might sit down and rest for a while. My courage was gone and I simply didn't dare to raise my head. Although I am not a poet, I still possess a certain degree of the poet's sensitivity, and it seemed that these fingers and eyes were about to watch me away or point me away like a melting piece of ice. They made me feel like a "thing" with no personality left. But there are two sides to everything, and my not daring to raise my head had its advantages too, for the road was uneven, covered with potholes, and strewn with stinking lumps of mud. If I were to walk with my head up, at the very least I would make the lower half of my body as dirty as a pig. In spite of their very long history, it seemed that the cat-people had never once repaired their roads. (I must confess to being extremely disdainful of history, especially history that stretches into the distant past.)

Fortunately, I finally arrived at Scorpion's house. It was only at this point that I definitely ascertained that the houses in Cat City were about the same as that little hole that I had lived in in the reverie forest.

12 *We Foreigners Had Better Stick Together* *

Scorpion's residence was right in the middle of town—high walls on all four sides, with no windows and no doors. The sun was already about to set and the crowd on the street was gradually thinning out so that I could see clearly now that the houses both to my right and left were *all* four-sided affairs without windows or doors.

Several cat-heads appeared above the walls, but after a few shouts from Scorpion, they all disappeared again. Then after a bit, they came up again and lowered down several thick ropes with which they hoisted the reverie leaves over the wall, one bundle at a time. It turned dark and not a single person was left on the streets. After the greater half of the bales had been hauled in, the soldiers became impatient and were obviously nervous. I surmised that, despite their excellent vision in the dark, the cat-people didn't like working at night.

Treating me with the utmost courtesy once again,

* Most foreigners in China lived in little foreign enclaves where they were insulated from the Chinese populace and beyond the jurisdiction of Chinese law.

Scorpion asked me if I would be willing to stay outside all night and guard the bales of reverie leaves that hadn't yet been hauled inside. He explained that the soldiers would have to return since it was very late already.

It occurred to me that if I only had a flashlight, this would be an excellent opportunity to take a night tour of Cat City all by myself. Unfortunately, both flashlights were still in the plane; moreover, both had no doubt been smashed in the crash. Even though I had originally looked forward to staying with Scorpion so that I might see the inside of his house, I agreed. Judging from the experience that I had gained through living in the reverie forest, sleeping inside wouldn't necessarily be any more comfortable than sleeping in the open air anyway. Scorpion, pleased with my assent, dismissed the soldiers and pulled himself back over the wall on one of the big ropes.

I was left alone. A gentle breeze was blowing and the stars were twice as bright as usual. There was a strong hint of autumn in the air and I felt in good spirits. Unfortunately, there was a foul-smelling ditch outside the house that prevented me from tranquilly enjoying the hush of evening. I tore open one of the bales and ate a few of the leaves partially in order to dispel my hunger and partially in order to withstand the foul air.

I started rambling around and unconsciously began to think about a number of questions. Why was it that the cat-people were so raucously conspicuous during the day and so quietly hidden away at night? Was it a sign that the society was not secure? So many people all skulking into this single row of houses: no ventilation, no light, nothing but flies, foul air, and filth—was that living? Why were there no windows or doors? Why, of course! It must be that they were afraid of thieves! They had tossed hygiene to the winds for the sake of security; and yet such filth would breed diseases that would plunder their very lives from within. Once more I saw the giant finger of destruction pointed down at Cat City, and I trembled a bit.

A contagious disease like cholera, or scarlet fever, could sweep this entire city clean of all traces of life within a single week! The more I looked at the city, the uglier it was to me—a large ugly shadow under starlight that issued not the slightest sound, but only gave off a foul stench.

I took several bales of reverie leaves and spread them out on a spot far removed from the stinking ditch; I lay down on top of them and watched the stars. It wasn't an uncomfortable bed, but yet I felt a bit lonely and even began to envy the cat-people a bit. Filth, stench, and no ventilation—but at least, old and young, they lived together as a family. And me? Alone on Mars with only stars for company! Worse yet, I had to guard the reverie leaves for Scorpion! It was really quite amusing in a bitter-sweet way.

I was slowly dozing off, but two contradictory thoughts within my mind seemed to prevent me from crossing the threshold to dreamland. On one hand I felt that I ought to faithfully guard the reverie leaves for Scorpion; but on the other hand why should *I* care about his damned leaves? Just as I was at this half-awake half-asleep juncture, someone patted me on the shoulder. I immediately sat up, thinking that I was perhaps dreaming. Instinctively, I rubbed my eyes. There were two cat-people standing in front of me. (When you run into someone in a place where you definitely knew there was no one to begin with, you automatically think of ghosts. It seems that primitive superstitions can still catch us civilized people off guard and give us a good fright.)

Although I hadn't looked at them carefully, I was already certain that they were not ordinary cat-people, for they had had the nerve to slap me on the shoulder. I hadn't thought of going for my gun either; for the moment I seemed to forget that I was on Mars. "Please sit down." I don't know what prompted me to say this. Perhaps like other oft-used, polite phrases, it just came automatically.

The two cat-people sat down without the slightest reserve. Now that really made me feel good, for during my many days in the Cat Country no one had ever before freely and openly accepted my greeting.

"I am a foreigner too," said the thinner of the two. It was apparent that they had not rehearsed what they were going to say before coming, for they listened respectfully to what each other had to say. In conversation they were not at all like Scorpion, who monopolized things without anyone else getting a chance to get a word in.

"I've come from Earth," I said.

"Oh!" With one voice they expressed their astonishment. "We've wanted to get into contact with another planet for a long time, but have never been able to before. We are really quite honored to meet a man from

Earth." They stood up together as if to demonstrate their deference. I felt that I had entered "human" society once again, but I felt strangely uncomfortable for precisely that reason; I said nothing polite in return.

They sat down again and asked quite a few questions about Earth. I really liked these two; their speech was clear, simple and not overloaded with polite phrases, and yet in everything they said they still managed to express that kind of mutual respect that exists between friends. "Just right" is the best phrase that I can think of to describe it. If speech that is "just right" is the result of a clear thought process, then in intelligence these two were infinitely superior to Scorpion.

Their country—Light Country—was, they told me, a seven days' journey from here. Their occupation was the same as mine, safeguarding the reverie leaves for the landlords. After I had asked them quite a bit about Light Country, they got down to business.

"Mister Earth," (what a respectful form of address!) the fat one said, "we have two purposes in coming to you: in the first place, we'd like to invite you to live with us; and in the second place, we'd like to make off with these reverie leaves."

That second purpose really startled me!

"Explain our second purpose to Mr. Earth," said the fat one to the thin one, "he still doesn't seem to understand what we mean."

"Mr. Earth," the thin one said with a smile, "I'm afraid that we really gave you quite a start, didn't we? Put your mind at ease. We've certainly not come to use force; we've just come to talk things over. Now, to be sure, Scorpion's reverie leaves are in your safekeeping, but if you loyally guard them for him, he won't be especially grateful to you; and if you confiscate them, he won't especially hate you for it either. You have to realize that the cat-people have an entirely different way of looking at things than we do."

"But you're both cat-people too," I thought to myself.

He seemed to have guessed what I was thinking and smiled again: "That's right, our ancestors were all cats, just like—"

"My ancestors were apes." I smiled too.

"Why yes, then we are all animals; we are all capable of coming up with evil ideas because our ancestors were not very honorable to begin with." He looked me up and down and was probably acknowledging to himself that I really did resemble an ape. Then he said: "Let's get back to this business of Scorpion. If you faithfully guard his leaves for him, he won't be at all grateful to you. On the other hand, if you seize half of the reverie leaves, then he can spread it around that he has been robbed and that will give him a good excuse to jack up the price on what's left. A rich man will have been robbed and the poor will pay for it; no matter how you look at it, Scorpion won't take a beating."

"But that's Scorpion's business, not mine. As long as I have accepted his commission to guard the leaves, I ought not take advantage of him."

"You're perfectly right, of course, Mr. Earth. In our country we see things exactly the same way that you do. But it doesn't seem fair that we should be forced to be honest here in Cat Country while the cat-people themselves are free to engage in hanky-panky. To tell the truth, it's a disgrace to Mars that a country like this should still exist. We're so ashamed of it that we don't even bother to treat cat-men as men at all."

"For that very reason, we ought to be all the more honest and upright. Even if they aren't 'men,' *we* must still act as men ourselves." I said this very decisively.

The fat one picked up the conversation. "That's right, Mr. Earth. We certainly don't want to make you act against your conscience. Our intention in coming here was simply to warn you not to let the cat-people take advantage of you. We foreigners have to look out for each other."

"Excuse me," I asked, "But is Cat Country's present poverty and weakness due to the fact that a number of foreign countries have ganged up on her?"

"Well, that's part of it. But here on Mars, the mere lack of military power is, in itself, not enough to cause a nation to lose its position vis-à-vis other states. That only happens when the people lose their individual integrity and the country gradually loses its national integrity, for no one wants to cooperate with a country that has lost its integrity. One must admit that, on occasion, the other countries have dealt unreasonably with Cat Country. And yet who would want to damage the amity that exists between equal powers just for the sake of sticking up for a state that has no national integrity to begin with? There are a number of other poor and weak countries on Mars, but they haven't lost their international prestige merely because of poverty and weakness. Besides, there are many reasons for the weakness of a state.

To be sure, natural calamities and poor topography are enough to make a country weak and poor, and that kind of weakness and poverty can move others to sympathy. But lack of integrity is brought about by the people themselves, and this kind of self-inflicted debility is incapable of inspiring any kind of sympathy. Let's take Scorpion as an example. Now you came from Earth as a guest, not a slave. But did he ever invite you to go to his home to relax for a bit? Did he ever ask you if you were hungry? No. He only asks you to guard his reverie leaves. Don't get me wrong. I'm not trying to stir you up in order to get you to steal from him; I'm simply explaining to you why it is that we foreigners disdain the cat-people. Now let's get back to the first question." The fat one took a breath and let the thin one pick up where he had left off.

"If tomorrow, Mr. Earth, you demand to live in Scorpion's home, he'll certainly refuse you. Why? Well, you'll find that out for yourself later on. But at any rate, you have to have a place to live and that's partially our purpose in coming to you. Now, the foreigners here live in a separate place to the west of Cat City. Regardless of nationality, all of the foreigners live there in something like a big, happy family. The two of us are presently taking our turn of duty on the welcoming committee of the foreign enclave. It's our job to welcome people who already know of our enclave and to notify those who don't. We have people circulate around Cat City every day in order to report new arrivals to us. Why have we organized such a community? Because the filthy habits of the natives here are past all rectification: their food is little different from poison and their doctors—well, they really don't have any. There are other reasons too that I won't spell out for you right now. At any rate, our purpose in coming here proceeds entirely from concern over your welfare. I think that you can probably believe that, Mr. Earth."

I did have faith in their honesty. I also guessed a few reasons they hadn't explained. But since I had come to Cat City, I was determined that I should see it first hand. Perhaps it *would* be more beneficial to me if I saw another country first. (I could tell on the basis of these two men that the Light Country was undoubtedly much more civilized than Cat Country.) However, it is not often that one has the opportunity to observe the extinction of an entire civilization. It wasn't at all the case that I was observing Cat Country's history with the same attitude that I might watch a tragedy on the stage; it was rather that I really hoped that I might be of some help to the cat-people. I can't say that I felt any sympathy for Scorpion, but then Scorpion couldn't be taken as representative of all Cat Country. Nor did I suspect these two foreigners of lying; but I simply had to see for myself.

They guessed at what I was thinking and the fat one said: "You don't have to decide right away. We will welcome you whenever you decide to come. To get to the enclave, you go straight west from here—it is best to go at night when it is not so crowded—when you get outside the city, keep right on going and before long you'll come to it. Goodbye, Mr. Earth."

They didn't seem the slightest bit put out with me.

They were simply open and honest people who could well understand my position. I was really quite grateful to them.

"Thank you," I said. "I'll certainly visit your place in the future, but first I want to see the people here."

"Be careful what you eat! Goodbye." They spoke in unison.

No, I simply couldn't give up the cat-people as hopeless and go live in the foreign enclave. It certainly wasn't the case that the cat-people couldn't be trained for better things. Consider how tractable they were. They kept right on smiling even when the soldiers were using their heads as drums, and then when it turned dark, they went right to sleep without a peep out of them. Could one seriously think that such a people would be difficult to manage? I was sure that if they only had a good leader, they would be the most peaceful and law-abiding citizens of the universe.

I couldn't get to sleep. A number of lively and colorful scenes appeared before my eyes: the reconstruction of the Cat City into a place that would resemble a flower park . . . music . . . sculpture . . . learning . . . flowers . . . birds . . . order . . . cleanliness . . . beauty. . . .

13 *Three Generations* *

After Scorpion had moved all of the reverie leaves inside, he didn't even so much as thank me for my help. Where I lived, he told me was certainly none of his business, but I simply couldn't live in *his* home; for a thousand and one reasons, that was simply out of the question. Finally he said: "Besides, you'd lose status if you stayed with us! You're a foreigner. Why don't you live in the foreign settlement?" He had stated straight out what the two Light Country people had been too polite to say—what shameless candor!

Rather than taking offense, I explained to him in great detail my reasons for wanting to live in Cat City. I even went so far as to hint to him that even if it wasn't

* The rapid pace of social change in twentieth-century China was difficult to keep up with: radical youngsters often found themselves viewed with disdain as conservatives by the time they reached middle age and condemned outright as reactionaries in their declining years. The normal shift toward conservatism that occurs as one grows older was accelerated in modern China by disappointment after disappointment with a succession of weak governments and ineffective reforms.

convenient to have me live at his place, I'd still like to see what his home was like. Then afterwards, I would go and look for another place by myself. He wouldn't even let me have so much as a peek at his place. His refusal was, of course, anticipated. In the several months that I had spent in the reverie forest, I had never been able to find out where he lived. Perhaps he was afraid that I might make off with his leaves. I told him that if I really intended to abscond with his crop, I would have made my move last night. What would I have to gain by waiting until he had the leaves all stored away inside and then taking all the extra trouble to steal them back out again? He shook his head: there were women in his home who could not, of course, receive male guests. That was a very powerful reason. But I wouldn't do his women any harm by just looking at them—but "just looking," of course, wasn't what Scorpion had in mind.

An old cat-head appeared on top of the wall: a head of white hair and a pursed-up pig's mouth that looked like a quince dried in the wind. The old cat began shouting: "We don't want any foreigners! We don't want any foreigners! No, no, no!" This must be Scorpion's father.

I didn't lose my temper; on the contrary, I began to admire this old cat with the dried-quince mouth, for he was not only unafraid of foreigners but even dared to look down on them. Perhaps his disdain proceeded from ignorance, but no matter how you looked at it, there was something more to be said for his attitude than that of his son.

A young cat-man called me to one side, and Scorpion took advantage of the diversion to crawl back up the wall. A young cat-person! I had been hoping to meet one. When it turned out to be Scorpion's son, I was doubly delighted. I had gotten to see three generations. Although the quince-mouthed old man and Scorpion were still active and still enjoyed great power, still they were, after all, people who had seen their day. If I wanted to ascertain whether or not there was any hope of curing the cat-people's disease, then I'd have to take their pulse through their young people.

"You've come from a distant place?" Young Scorpion —actually, he had another name, but I called him this for the sake of convenience—asked me.

"Very, very far! Tell me is that old man your grandfather?"

"Yes. Grandfather thinks that all of our troubles were brought in by the foreigners and that's why he hates them so!"

"Does he eat reverie leaves too?"

"Yes. He thinks that since reverie leaves were brought in from abroad in the first place, he disgraces the foreigners by eating them so that the wrong is not on his part, but theirs."

A crowd started to gather around us. They all popped wide their eyes and let their mouths hang open as they watched me the way one would study a freak.

"Couldn't we find some quieter place where we might chat?"

"They'll follow us wherever we go, so we might as well talk right here. They're not interested in hearing what we say, anyway. They just want to see how you open your mouth and blink your eyes."

I found young Scorpion's candor delightful.

"Fine." I couldn't very well insist on the point, "And your father?"

"He's a 'new' man. At least he *was* a new man twenty years ago. Twenty years ago he was opposed to eating reverie leaves, but now he has inherited grandfather's reverie forest. Twenty years ago he came out for women's rights, but now he won't even let you inside the house because he doesn't want to expose his women to you. Grandfather often says that I'll be the same way later. He says that young people like new things and are curious about everything, but when they arrive at middle age, then they begin to look back fondly to the bequeathed patterns of their ancestors. You see, grandfather is totally ignorant of foreign things, and therefore he takes the rules handed down to us by our ancestors as the ultimate norms for getting along in the world. My father, on the other hand, knows something about foreign things. When he was young, he even wanted to copy everything from the foreigners. Now he merely uses what little he knows of foreign things as a tool for maintaining his own advantage. He uses foreign methods where he feels they are practically applicable and, in that regard, he is not so stiff-necked as grandfather. You see, father merely applies his knowledge of foreign things to practical ways of getting along in the world, but when it comes to the overall purpose of life, his views are no different from grandfather's."

I closed my eyes: in the light of his speech I could see the outlines of a painting of social change. Outside the edges of the painting there were perhaps a few rosy clouds, but inside the frame there was nothing but a sombre mist that was getting darker all the time.

Whether or not that sombre mist would be able to combine with those rosy clouds and thus brighten things up a bit, would depend entirely on whether or not Young Scorpion could throw a bit of strong light on the canvas. I expected much of Young Scorpion, although I really didn't know as yet what kind of person he was.

"Do you eat reverie leaves, too?" I suddenly asked. It was as though I had seized upon reverie leaves as the source of all evil, though I can't tell exactly why I felt that way.

"I eat them too," Young Scorpion answered.

The painting in my mind's eye now turned entirely black; there was not so much as a pinpoint of light in it anymore.

"But why?" I forgot about being polite. "Excuse my candor."

"If I didn't eat them, I wouldn't be able to take it!"

"You mean by eating them you can at least muddle through?"

Young Scorpion was silent for quite a while.

"Muddle through? Yes, that's it! I've been abroad and I have some notion of what the world's about, but living in the midst of a people that doesn't even think about solving its problems, I just muddle through. If I didn't muddle my way through, how would I live?" Young Scorpion smiled a smile that was not a smile.

"And individual initiative?"

"Useless! Against a mass of people who are so docile, stupid, pitiful, poor, easily satisfied, and even happy; against so many soldiers who only know how to wield clubs, steal reverie leaves, and rape women; against politicians who are intelligent, selfish, short-sighted, and shameless, who always have plans for themselves but are not interested in society—against all this you'd pose something as fragile as individual initiative? A brave gesture, indeed! But no matter how you look at it your own scalp is more worth looking after than someone else's."

"Do most young people think this way?" I asked.

"What's that? *Young* people? In Cat Country we don't have any young people! We only have different age groupings. If you want to count those who aren't too advanced in years as *young*, then we do have young people—young people who become old———." He was damning some group or other, but I didn't get the word that came after "old."

"Some of the 'young' people among us are even more antique in their thinking than my grandfather, and some of them are even narrower than my father, some. . . .

"You can't overlook the fact of an unfavorable environment," I interrupted. "We ought not be too hard on them."

"A poor environment *can* exert a bad influence, but from another point of view, it can also serve to awaken people. There always ought to be a little hell in all youth, but our young people are born half-dead. As long as they don't see an opportunity to get a little something for nothing, they're not so bad. But if they spot something that will afford them an advantage, then anything goes. Ordinarily they are critical of everything they see, but if it's a case of something that can bring them personal profit and gain, then they forget all of their criticisms and will approve anything."

"Excuse my saying so, but you are too pessimistic. You

have become a pessimist, possessed of a clear head, but lacking in courage. Because you yourself are lacking in initiative, you judge all other people from that point of view alone, and therefore you see everything as black and hopeless. But perhaps that's not actually the case. Perhaps if you looked at things from a fresh point of view, this society would not look so fearfully black after all."

"Perhaps. I leave the task of observation to you. Since you're from distant parts, perhaps you'll see things a bit more clearly than we do." Young Scorpion smiled faintly.

It seemed that the people around us had had their fill of seeing how I used my mouth and blinked my eyes, for now they began looking at my raggedy pants. There were still a number of questions that I wanted to ask Young Scorpion but we were so crowded in that I had to almost gasp for air. I asked Scorpion to help find me a place to live. He too exhorted me to go to the foreign enclave, carefully framing his words in a philosophic manner. "I really wouldn't like you to stay here and carry out that observation that you spoke of, for I'm afraid that your enthusiasm and hopes would be obliterated. But if you really insist on living here, then I can help you to find a place. It's a place that doesn't have anything to recommend it except that the people there don't eat reverie leaves."

"If I can just find a place to live, I won't worry about anything else. I'll be very grateful for your trouble!" I had made up my mind, once and for all, not to live in the foreign enclave.

14 A Rainstorm *

The original landlord, who had been an ambassador, had been dead for several years now. My landlady was the ambassador's widow. Besides the fact that she had, as the ambassador's wife, lived abroad for a while, there was something else quite distinctive about her: "We don't eat reverie leaves!" I think I heard her say that more than a hundred times a day. But it didn't matter who my landlady was; the important thing was that I had attained my goal of "climbing the walls" of a cat-home. I was as proud as any Cat Country kitten who had just learned how to crawl in and out of the house. Now at last I would see how the quadrangular cat-homes were arranged on the inside.

* Actively embroiled in the modern social revolution, Chinese women began demanding equality before the law, equal opportunities in education, and the right to freely choose their own mates. Educated men and women attacked the system of concubinage practiced by the upper classes, a system under which a man usually married a "main" or "proper" wife and then was free to buy as many concubines as he could afford.

When I had climbed half way up the wall, I began to feel a bit nervous. If I were to say that the wall was shaking, I'd not be telling the truth; however, it would certainly be no lie to say that earth kept falling off the wall at every spot that my hands or feet touched. I thought to myself that perhaps this cracker-crisp wall had some other use that I was as yet unaware of. By the time I got to the top of the wall, I couldn't tell whether it was my head that was reeling or the wall that was shaking.

Since the home had no roof to begin with, what did they do when it rained? I couldn't figure it out, and that made me all the more curious to live there for a while.

Five feet or so down from the top of the wall on the inside of the house there was a layer of boards; in the middle of this flooring a large hole appeared. I first saw the ambassador's wife when her head popped up through this hole to greet me.

My landlady's face was large and her eyes, ferocious. I could take that, but then her whole face was covered with heavy white powder and the fine grey hairs of her face poked through this layer of powder so that she looked like a thorny old frost-covered winter melon on which someone had hung a pair of glasses—and that did shake me up a bit.

"If you have any baggage, put it down on the boards. That area up there is all yours, but you're not to come down here. We eat once at the crack of dawn and once at sunset; don't be late to meals. We don't eat reverie leaves! Let me have your rent." It was apparent that the ambassador's wife was an old hand at conducting foreign affairs. I handed over the rent; I still had the five hundred National Souls that Scorpion had given me stuffed away in my pocket.

My situation was very simple. Since I, myself, was my only baggage, I had nothing to worry about so long as I had a place to live. My quarters? Just a layer of boards with walls on all four sides. There was no need to bother with tables and chairs; and as long as I didn't lose my head and fall through the hole in the floor, things would probably go along very smoothly.

There must have been more than two inches of mud on top of the boards, and the odor that it gave off was not something that one would expect in the home of an ambassador. All that sun and stinking mud was more than I could take; I'd simply have to go out. I began to understand why the cat-people lived on the streets during the day.

Before I had a chance to set out, the landlady came up through the hole, accompanied by eight other women, all of whom also had melon-like faces. All eight of them climbed straight over the wall without favoring me with so much as a glance. The ambassador's wife was the last one out; once outside, she rested her chain on top of the wall and said: "We're going out. See you again this evening. You see what a miserable predicament I'm in! Ever since the death of the ambassador, the responsibility for looking after these eight vixens has been entirely on my shoulders. I've no money, no man, and have to spend my days looking after these eight felinettes! And I don't even eat reverie leaves! My man was an ambassador, you know; and so I've been abroad, and that's why I don't eat reverie leaves. And yet, from morning till night, I have to look after these eight feline. . . ."

I hoped that she would hurry up and follow them down; otherwise who knew what those eight women might become on the tongue of the ambassador's wife. I guess she did have a sense of the appropriateness of things after all, for suddenly she was gone.

I was confused again. What was going on here? Were they eight daughters? Eight younger sisters of the late ambassador? Eight concubines? Yes, that must be it! Eight concubines! That was probably also the reason that old Scorpion hadn't wanted me to enter his home. There would be no fresh air at all down there under the boards. To think of a cat-man down there with eight "felinettes"—to borrow a word from the diplomatic vocabulary of the ambassador's wife—how stinking, dissolute, obscene, ugly! I began to regret having come here, for what was to be gained by observing this excuse for a house? However, since I had already paid my rent, I was determined to find some way of taking a look around down there no matter how repulsive it might be.

Since they were all out, why not go down right now and have a look? But the ambassador's wife had specifically enjoined me not to go down, and to do so behind her back wouldn't seem very honorable. Just as I was debating the morality of the question, my landlady's head appeared over the wall again.

"You hurry up and go out too. It would be very unseemly for you to stay here and peek about down below!"

I immediately climbed down to the street. Whom

would I go visit? I decided that Young Scorpion was the only one with whom I could get along, even though he was pessimistic. But where would I find him? He wouldn't be at home, of course; and trying to find him on the street would probably be as hopeless as looking for a needle in the ocean. Moving crosswise, I crowded my way out of the throng, and surveyed the street from a safe distance. I saw clearly now that the center of the city was taken up by government buildings and the residences of the nobility. These buildings were much taller than those on either side, and the farther you went to either side from the center, the lower and more dilapidated the buildings became. I concluded that the outer ones must be small shops and the dwellings of the poor. And that's all there was to Cat City.

At this juncture, ten or so women crowded out of the throng. I could tell they were women even at this distance because of their powdered white faces. They were coming toward me. I felt just a trifle uneasy, for from the impression that my landlady and Scorpion had given me, I had concluded that the local women were exceedingly submissive, upright, and moral. And if that were true, then ten or more women gadding about the street together couldn't possibly be entirely respectable. Since I was a newcomer here, I'd have to keep an eye on my reputation. As I reached this point in my thought, I began to run the other way.

"Are you beginning your research?" It was Young Scorpion's voice.

I turned around and took a second look; Young Scorpion was enfolded in the midst of the women. There was no point in running now. In less time than it takes to tell, I too was there in the middle of the group with Young Scorpion, fleshed in from all sides by cat-women!

"Why don't you try one?" asked Young Scorpion with a smile. He turned his gaze on the women. "This is Blossom; this is Revery (she's even more intoxicating than the reverie leaves); this is Star. . . ." He introduced all of them to me, but I can't recall all of their names anymore.

Revery came over and winked at me. A cold shiver ran down my spine: I simply didn't know what to do. What line was this bunch of women in? I didn't know. If they were all whores, then as a newcomer I'd have to watch my reputation; but if they were respectable ladies, then I'd have to watch what I said so that I didn't offend them.

To tell the truth, though I am not a misogynist, I have never felt too well-disposed toward women in the first place. Somehow or other I've always seen their penchant for making-up as an indication of dishonesty. I have, of course, encountered women who don't powder or rouge, but they haven't necessarily proved any more honest than those who do. This feeling has not at all diminished in me the respect that one ought to show to the opposite sex; in sum, with regard to women, my attitude is that of Confucius with regard to ghosts and spirits: respect them, but keep them at a distance. But what was the proper way of "respecting" this bevy of cat-women?

Young Scorpion seemed to be conscious of my predicament. He pushed them away in a teasing, playful manner and said: "Now that two philosophers have run into each other, there's no longer any need for you." In a flurry of giggles, they tactfully disappeared into the crowd again. I was still stunned.

"Most of the traditionalists take concubines; most of the modernists take wives. As a man who despises both the old and new, I neither marry nor take concubines, but simply play around with them. I muddle through. As with everything else, I just muddle through. What's the point in taking them too seriously?"

"The women who were here just now seemed to be. . . ." I really didn't know what to say.

"Oh, them. Seemed to be . . . ," Young Scorpion picked up the words that I had left dangling, "seemed to be *women*. Women are all the same. The way one treats them varies with a man's way of thinking: you can treat them rough, spoil them, respect them, worship them, or just fodder them down. But no matter how you treat them, they themselves will never change. My great-grandmother used make-up; my grandmother used make-up; my mother used make-up; and my younger sister uses it too. All of our present-day women use make-up, and their granddaughters will continue to use it. Whether you lock them in a room or turn them loose on the street, they'll powder their faces."

"You're being pessimistic again," I said.

"It's not pessimism. In saying this, I'm actually complimenting and exalting women. A man spends his whole day making a pompous fuss over nothing; he's a hopeless case. Sometimes he's a saint; sometimes, a sinner. But a woman, and a woman alone, remains constant from start to finish. From beginning to end, she's a woman, and from cradle to grave she never gives up trying. Somehow or other she always feels that there is something wrong with the face that she was born with and invariably tries to improve it with make-up of one kind or another. But even if a man did happen to feel that his face would be improved by a touch of powder, his scrupulous sense of honesty and purity would keep him from resorting to such camouflage. With his sparkling reputation still intact, he'd go off with his unimproved face and find something else to raise hell about."

His bantering tone put me into a reflective mood. Obviously pleased with himself, Young Scorpion continued: "The group that was here just now are all so-called 'new women.' They are the enemies of my father and the ambassador's wife. You see, my father hates them for being a new breed. For instance, if they were his daughters, they wouldn't sit about and allow him to sell them as though they were so many reverie leaves. No, they're a new breed, and he knows it. And if they were his concubines, they wouldn't passively allow him to lock them up in a room without putting up one hell of a fight. They're a new breed, and he knows it; and he hates them for it. However, this is not to say that they are stronger or abler than my mother or the wife of the ambassador; it's just that they are better at being women—feminine, helpless, thoughtless, and intractably stubborn. One must admit, however, that they have made improvements in the art of make-up; and they are very lovable. Even a person like myself who doesn't love anything is often moved to muddle through with them."

"Have they all received a modern education?"

My question so tickled Young Scorpion that it was a long time before he was able to recover himself.

"Education? Oh, education, education, education!" It seemed that Young Scorpion had slipped his trolley a bit. "In Cat Country, except for the schools, you'll find education everywhere. Grandfather's cursing people—education! Father's selling reverie leaves—education! The ambassador's wife superintending eight walking-dead felinettes—education! The stinking ditch downtown—education! Soldiers using the people's heads as drums—education! Powder being applied in thicker and thicker coats all the time—education for women! You'll find 'education' everyplace you look. Whenever I hear the word, I have to eat an extra ten reverie leaves just to keep from vomiting."

"Are there many schools here?"

"Yes. Haven't you been over to that side of the street to see them yet?"

"Not yet."

"You ought to go have a look. That side of the street is completely taken up with cultural agencies." He smiled again. "But please don't ask whether or not our cultural organizations have anything to do with 'culture.' At least, we have the buildings." He raised his head and looked at the sky: "Oh-oh, it's going to rain."

There were no heavy clouds in the sky at all, but there was a very cold gust of wind coming out of the east.

"Hurry home!" Young Scorpion seemed very much afraid of the rain. "We'll meet here again when it clears up."

It was as though the human tide had encountered an irresistible wind, for now it was rolling back toward the houses like a tidal wave. And even though I knew that

I'd still get wet back in the roofless house, I ran along with them. It was really something to see the cat-people madly climbing the walls of their homes. I'd seen a few obstacle-course races before, but I had never before seen an entire city climbing walls!

Another gust of wind blew out of the east and the sky suddenly turned black. A bolt of red lightning bracketed down to both ends of the row of houses and formed a triangle. To the tune of a clap of thunder, scattered rain drops as big as eggs started coming down in the distance, making gentle splashing sounds. In the midst of the grey clouds where the sky lowered over the land, it began to get bright, and another giant bolt of lightning came accompanied by a gust of cold wind. Now the rain deluged down from the sky and one could no longer distinguish the sound of individual drops. The sky grew black and everything around me disappeared into a darkness that was occasionally relieved by red splashes of lightning. Then high up in that waterfall that descended from the sky, an opening was rent and a tremendous bolt of lightning leapt out of nowhere to momentarily cleave the blackness. It shuddered once or twice against the black sky and then, like a startled snake, disappeared again into the forest of darkness as quickly as it had come and surrendered the field once again to blackness. By the time I arrived back at the house, I was thoroughly soaked.

Which home belonged to the ambassador's wife? I couldn't see clearly, and moved back several paces to await the temporary brilliance of a lightning flash. Then a huge one came, a blinding white flash; it was as though the largest devil in heaven had suddenly opened his eyes and quickly blinked several times. But it was a flash that was so bright that I couldn't see against its glare. I began to panic and decided to worry about whose house it was after I'd climbed in. By the time that I was half way up, I could tell by the feel of things that it was the right house; I recognized the way the walls swayed.

There was a great flash of lightning and then, after a pause that seemed centuries long, a peal of thunder that sounded as though the whole sky were caving in. I was conscious that the wall and I were no longer upright! We were leaning! I closed my eyes, and heard another peal of thunder. Where was I going? Who knew?

15 *Madam Ambassador's Story**

I was vaguely conscious of the sound of thunder moving off into the distance, but I was still in such a foggy state that I couldn't tell whether I was really hearing a roll of thunder or was merely dreaming. I tried to open my eyes, but couldn't; it seemed as though every last bit of mud from the walls of the landlady's house was plastered across my face. "Yes," I decided, "that really *is* thunder and I *am* awake." I started to feel about with my right hand, but discovered that I couldn't move it; it was pinned under some stones. I couldn't even see my feet or legs and felt for all in the world like a rice plant that some farmer had stuck in the mud.

I finally got my right hand free and began to wipe the

* Under the traditional marriage system, widows were not permitted to remarry. A somewhat indelicate proverb pointed out that a horse only has one saddle. As a reward for chastity after the death of her husband, a virtuous widow might hope for a posthumous memorial arch. Traditionally there was often intense rivalry between the usually elder head wife and the usually younger and prettier secondary wives or concubines.

mud away from my face. Madam Ambassador's house had become a large mound of earth. While struggling to free my legs, I screamed loudly for help. I wasn't thinking of myself, but of Madam Ambassador and the eight sexpots in her care, for I was sure that they were buried beneath all the rubble. But no matter how loudly I called, I couldn't seem to rouse anyone. There were still a few scattered raindrops in the sky. Remembering how deathly afraid of rain the cat-people were, I realized that no one would come out until the sky was perfectly clear.

I succeeded in extricating the half of me that was buried and began tearing away like a mad dog at the mudpile, with no time to even worry about whether or not I myself had suffered any injury. When the sky had fully cleared, all the cat-people came out. I kept on digging as I called to them for help. Quite a few came and stood off to one side watching me. I thought that perhaps they had misunderstood and explained to them that I didn't want them to save me, but nine women who were buried beneath the rubble. After they had understood my meaning, they all crowded forward for a better look, but not one lifted a hand to help. I realized that exclusive reliance on entreaty would be useless. I felt in my pocket. My National Souls were still there. "Anyone who comes and helps me dig, gets one National Soul!" They stood agape for a moment as though they didn't believe me. I hauled out two National Souls which I waved in their faces. They came up the mound like a swarm of bees. One would pick up a piece of stone and depart with it; then another would pick up a piece of brick and make off with that. I knew what they were up to, for taking advantage of every opportunity for personal profit was a prevalent custom in Cat Country. "All right! Go ahead and steal the bricks and stones! When you've stolen them *all* away, the people down underneath will be saved anyway!" And were they ever fast! It reminded one of a colony of ants making away with the separate grains of a little pile of rice. I hadn't imagined that the mound could possibly be moved away that fast! When I heard the sound of a voice from below, I was somewhat reassured. But then I became doubly nervous when I noticed that Madam Ambassador's voice was the only one to be heard. When the rubble had been entirely cleared, Madam Ambassador appeared through the hole in the flooring. She was in a sitting position; the eight vixen were strewn all around her. None of them were moving. I was going to help her up, but just as my hand touched her shoulder she began speaking.

"Aiyah! Don't touch me! I am Madam Ambassador! You've all stolen my house away and I shall report it to the Emperor unless you all act like honest folk and move the bricks and things back immediately!" Her eyes were still stuck together with mud so that she couldn't have possibly seen anything, but being familiar with the habits of the cat-people, she had apparently taken it for granted that they had already made away with the wreckage of her collapsed house.

All around me the cat-people were still gracefully scampering about in search of more booty. Since the bricks had already been moved away, now they had to content themselves with scooping up the dirt with both hands. I was struck by the way that economic oppression can cause people to feel that it's at least better to go home with a double-handful of mud than nothing.

Madame Ambassador clawed the mud away from her face. Her cheeks had been torn in two places and a mighty lump had risen on her forehead. Fire seemed to be shooting out of both eyes. She struggled to her feet and stumbled over toward one of the cat-people. I don't know how her aim could have been so accurate, but at any rate, she had the poor unfortunate's ear clamped between her teeth in less time than it takes to tell. She snarled fiercely out the sides of her mouth as she chewed on the ear, just like a cat that has caught a rat. The cat-man being bitten began to howl and belabor Madam Ambassador's belly for all he was worth. After they had been at it tooth and nail for a while, Madam Ambassador noticed the other women strewn about and relaxed her jaws in surprise just enough to allow the unfortunate cat-man to shoot away like an arrow. The people standing about gasped and moved back away from Madam Ambassador by ten feet or so as not to crowd her. She clasped one of the dead vixen and began to wail.

I melted. So she wasn't a heartless wretch, after all. I was tempted to go over to comfort her, but was afraid that in her present frenzied state she might well latch on to one of *my* ears. After she had cried for quite a time, she looked at me again.

"It's all your fault! You pulled my house down with all your climbing! You won't get away with it, nor will those rascals who made off with my house! I'm going to see the Emperor and have you all killed!"

"I have no intention of running away," I said slowly. "I shall simply stay here and do all that I can to help you."

"Since you're a foreigner, I guess I can trust you. But

as for that bunch of cat-rabble there, I'll see to it that the Emperor dispatches soldiers to search all their homes, house by house. Wherever a single piece of brick is found, that person will be executed. After all, I am the Ambassador's wife!" Angry spittle flew a long ways out of her mouth and finally with a wretching sound, she spat out a mouthful of blood.

I didn't know whether she really had all the prestige that she laid claim to, but at any rate, I began to calm her down for fear that she would go completely out of her head. I asked: "Now what do you want done with these eight ladies?"

"What have these eight dead sexpots got to do with you? I'm only worried about the living; I can't be bothered about the dead. Do *you* have some way of disposing of them?"

That stumped me. Since I'd never conducted a funeral in Cat Country, I didn't have the foggiest notion of what to do with the bodies. Madam Ambassador's eyes grew more and more menacing; a watery glow shone out from the pupils, but it wasn't wet enough to dampen in the least that wildfire of madness that emanated from the same source. It seemed as though all her tears had been dried in the foundry of those blazing eyes. Even the whites of her eyes seemed to throw out a magnetic sheen.

"Let me talk it over with you!" She cried out: "There's no one to whom I can turn. I've no money and no man. And I don't even eat reverie leaves! The wife of an Ambassador! Let me tell you about it!"

I could see that she was out of her head, for she seemed to have forgotten all about the burial business that she had just brought up, and simply wanted to cry on my shoulder.

"This," she grabbed one of the dead women by the scalp, "this dead sexpot was brought in by the Ambassador when she was only ten. Only ten! Even before her bones and tendons were fully matured, she was dedicated to the Ambassador's pleasure. For over a month she was all right as long as it didn't get dark. But once it got dark, she—this dead little bitch—she'd wail and wail; call for her father and mother; grab my hand and hold on for dear life; call me mother; call me kind benefactor; and beg me not to leave her. But I was a virtuous woman and couldn't say anything that would make it appear as though I were jealous of a mere ten-year-old. If the Ambassador wanted to take his pleasure with her, that was none of my business. After all I was the first wife and had to maintain a proper wifely attitude.

"But this poor little sexpot. . . . Whenever the Ambassador went to her, she'd scream to wake the dead and wail until she no longer even sounded human. When the Ambassador was about to enter her, how she'd plead! How she'd scream! 'Madam Ambassador! My savior! Save me!' But could I forbid the Ambassador his pleasure? It was none of my business. When it was all over she'd just lie there completely inert. I wouldn't know whether she was pretending to be dead or had actually passed out. Nor did I really try to find out. I'd just apply salves to her and get her something to eat. But do you think this dead bitch was at all grateful to me? And you should have seen what an imperious wench she became when she grew up. She became so possessive that I thought she'd swallow the Ambassador whole any minute. Then when he bought a new concubine, she went about whimpering and sobbing the livelong day, blaming *me* for not stopping him! But I had my position to think of. *I* was an Ambassador's wife. And if the Ambassador didn't buy a new sexpot every now and then who would respect him? What would become of our prestige? But this little bitch didn't have enough brains to understand that and actually blamed me for not stopping him! Bitch! Stinking Bitch! Goddamned sexpot!" Madam Ambassador pushed the corpse aside and grabbed hold of another.

"This little baggage was a whore. She ate reverie leaves all day and tempted the Ambassador to eat them too. I knew that if he became addicted, the government would never let him go abroad again. He'd be without a job! Without position! You should have seen the trouble she caused! But what was I to do? I couldn't prevent him from playing around with whores if he wanted to, but I couldn't sit idly by and watch him eat reverie leaves either, for then we'd never be able to go abroad again. The problems I've had! You can't possibly imagine how difficult being an Ambassador's wife really is! I had to watch that whore every minute of the day to see to it that she didn't take reverie leaves on the sly and at night I had to be on my guard lest she try to turn the Ambassador against me. And then the dead little bitch threatened to run away. She was constantly scheming up ways to escape. I had to have eyes in the back of my head to make sure that she didn't fly the coop! After all, if a concubine ran away, what face would we have left?" It seemed that the eyes of the Ambassador's wife were really shooting fire now, as she grabbed the head of yet another of the dead ladies.

"This . . . thing! She's the most despicable of them all! She's a *modern* sexpot. Before she had even come into the house, she tried to get the Ambassador to drive me and the concubines out so that *she* could be his *proper* wife. Hah! How did she think she'd get away with that! And anyway, it was *she* who had chased the Ambassador because of his rank. All the other sexpots were bought with money; this trollop *wanted* to be with him of her *own* accord. Just think, the Ambassador got into her pants without spending a single red cent! Think of how that cheapened the rest of us!

"But that wasn't the worst of it. Once she'd come into the house, the Ambassador didn't even dare *speak* to us! And if he went out, she'd go with him! She'd even insist on being with him when he received guests. She was so pompous that one would have thought that *she* was the Ambassador's first wife! Where did that leave me? It was perfectly proper, and even desirable, that the Ambassador should buy in a few more women, but there could only be *one* Madam Ambassador. I just *had* to punish her for her presumption. I began tying her up, and sticking her up on the platform whenever it rained. After she had been soaked three or four times, the little bitch couldn't take it any longer. She demanded that the Ambassador send her back home. She even had the nerve to say that the Ambassador had deceived her. But how could I let her go? Can you expect to get away with taking the position of 'Madam-Ambassador-In-Reserve,' having a battle with the Ambassador himself, and then just get up and leave when you feel like it? I, for one, have never heard of such a thing! Did she hope to marry someone else? Well, she wouldn't get off that easily if I had anything to do with it. It's difficult, I tell you! Being Madam Ambassador is far from easy! I had to watch her night and day. Then, fortunately, the Ambassador came by a new piece of baggage." She turned around and picked out another of the bodies on the ground.

"Now this one was fairly close to me. She wanted to form a united front with me in order to oppose that modern tramp. But women are all alike. They get nervous when they don't have a man around. If the Ambassador spent a night in the modern tramp's bed, then this one would cry the whole night. I set her straight. I said, 'And you think that someone like you, who can't stand to be away from him for a moment, could be the Ambassador's first wife? Why don't you take time to observe what I—his real first wife—am like! If you want to be an Ambassador's first wife, then you can't monopolize him. The Ambassador, after all, is not some peddler on the street who has to be content with sleeping with one woman all of his life.' "

The pupils of Madam Ambassador's eyes were all red now. She lifted the head of one of the dead women and bashed it on the ground several times. This was followed by a laughing spell and then she looked at me—instinctively I retreated a few steps.

"While the Ambassador was alive, they wouldn't let me relax for a single day. I'd have to keep my eyes on this one and be on guard against that one; I'd have to chew one out and beat up another. They didn't give me a moment's rest from morning until night. They spent all of the Ambassador's money and drained him of all of his male vigor; and after all that, when the Ambassador died, he hadn't left behind even one male child! It wasn't that he hadn't had any—all eight of them had given birth to male children, but not one had survived. How could they? When one of them gave birth to a child, the others would stay up the whole night working out ways to do it mischief. They were all competing to be the Ambassador's favorite and were scared to death that anyone who gave birth to a male child might be advanced to the position of first wife. On the other hand, I myself—the real first wife—was not nearly so jealous as they were. I didn't pay any attention to them. If one of them wanted to kill another's child, that was entirely her business; it had nothing to do with me. I wouldn't harm any of the children myself, of course, but then I wouldn't interfere in their intrigues either. After all, a first wife has to preserve a first wife's dignity.

"When the Ambassador died, he didn't leave me any money or male offspring—nothing but these eight playthings! What could I do? I certainly couldn't let them run away and remarry as they pleased; I just couldn't! Day in and day out I had to keep a close eye on them so that they didn't drag some man into their beds. I faithfully exhorted them from morning till night in order to make them understand the great principles of feminine morality. But do you think that they understood? It wasn't that easy. But I didn't give up either; I kept a tight watch on them day in and day out. What was I hoping for? There was really nothing that I could hope for, except that the Emperor might possibly understand my difficulty, appreciate my dedication and character, and reward me with money, perhaps even present me with an honorary tablet with STEADFASTLY CHASTE AFTER THE DEATH OF HER HUSBAND engraved on it. But . . . well, you heard me crying just now, didn't you?"

I nodded my head.

"What do you think I was crying about? This bunch of sexpots? Fat chance of that! I was weeping my own outcast fate. Wife of an Ambassador! I've never even eaten reverie leaves. And now the house has fallen in on me and utterly destroyed the evidence of all of my accomplishments. If I go to see the Emperor now what can I say to him? If he sits up there on the throne and asks: 'Madam Ambassador, upon the basis of what merit do you come to seek a reward?' What will I say? Supposing I report that I have been taking care of the late Ambassador's eight women in such a way as to preserve and uphold the highest precepts of feminine morality? Then His Majesty is bound to ask where they are. And what will I tell him? That they are all dead? Do you think he'll give me a reward when all proof of my merit has been buried? Not much chance of that. What will I say? Think of it! The wife of an Ambassador, a woman who has never eaten reverie leaves, a woman. . . ." Her head dropped down on her breast. I thought of going over to her again, but was afraid that she might give me another tongue-lashing.

She lifted her head once more, eyes fixed in a dead stare: "Wife of an Ambassador, a woman who has been abroad, who doesn't eat reverie leaves. And my reward from the Emperor! My honorary tablet! . . . Wife of an Ambassador. . . ." Madam Ambassador's head dropped down again. Her body sank slowly sideways to the ground, and came to rest between two of the others.

16 *Free Love and Other Things* *

I was extremely downcast, for the widow's lament had made me weep for all the women of who knows how many past centuries. I felt as though my hands were resting on the very darkest pages of Cat Country's history, a history that I was afraid to go on reading.

Not going to the foreign enclave had been a mistake, for now I was once again a homeless ghost. Where would I go? The cat-men who had helped with the house were still watching me. They were probably waiting around to see if they could get any more money. To

* In an effort to modernize, China sent large numbers of students abroad to study. When he got back home, a "returned-student" frequently had difficulty in readjusting to those aspects of his native culture that his foreign sojourn had caused him to view as backward or illogical. He was often dissatisfied with the customary practices of his stay-at-home countrymen and they, in turn, were just as often equally unhappy with what they saw as foreign ways. Young people tried desperately to break free of the restrictions of the traditional family system and to achieve true independence as individuals. The odds against success in this endeavor were very high and, even if attained, success would be accompanied by feelings of guilt.

be sure, they had already looted everything that Madam Ambassador had owned, but apparently that still wasn't enough to diminish their desire to come by a few more National Souls. My head ached terribly and in falling about on the rubble, I had loosened two of my teeth. Gradually, I was no longer able to think. Something in the back of my mind warned me that I was going to be ill. I took my whole pocketful of National Souls, in denominations of ten and five, and threw them all on the ground. Let the cat-men decide how it should be divided up or stolen, for I certainly didn't have the heart or energy to supervise.

There was no hope for the eight vixen, and now Madam Ambassador was finished too. A puddle of blood flowed out from under her body. Her eyes were still open as though, even in death, she still wanted to keep an eye on those eight little sexpots. I knew that if I didn't bury them, no one else would, and yet there was nothing I could do. I was afflicted by such intense grief and disappointment that I almost felt like ending my own existence.

I sat on the ground for a while. Then, looking at those bodies again, I felt that I'd just have to get out of there. I was totally drained and almost too exhausted to move, but I simply couldn't watch the women rot away before my very eyes, and so I left. Limping and hobbling alone in a most unsightly way, I probably lost a good deal of face for the entire foreign community. The street was crowded again.

I noticed a group of young people going from house to house with chalk, writing on the walls. The walls were still so damp that the words were not visible when they were first written but then a breeze would blow and dry the chalk to whiteness: SANITATION MOVEMENT. And then on every house appeared the words: EVERYTHING HAS BEEN WASHED CLEAN HERE. Although my head was throbbing, I couldn't help roaring with laughter. The cat-people really knew how to get things done! What better time to advocate cleaning up the whole city than right after a violent rainstorm? The intense rain had even cleared out the stinking ditch in the center of town. Sanitation movement, my ass! That was a laugh! I must have been slightly out of my head, myself, for I felt a strong urge to haul out my pistol and shoot a few of the chalk-toting bastards.

I seemed to remember Young Scorpion's having told me that the buildings over there were cultural agencies. I wound my way around to that side, not to visit the cultural agencies, but just to find a quiet place where I could rest and pull myself together. Somehow or other, I couldn't break myself out of the habit of thinking that buildings on a city street ought to be arranged facing each other, rather than laid out back to back in a single line as they were here. Pondering the novelty of this unique arrangement made me forget my headache a bit. Such a layout well suited the cat-people, for they didn't care about fresh air and light in the first place. The buildings were all back to back without even breathing space between them; rather than calling it a street, it would be more accurate to describe it as a giant brewery for diseases. My headache returned. Falling ill in a foreign country is apt to make one particularly despondent and I am no exception. I began to feel that I should never get back to China alive.

I didn't have time to be too fussy about where I sat down to rest, but simply collapsed at the first cool, shady spot that I found. I have no idea how long I slept, but when I awoke I found myself in an immaculately clean room. I thought that I was either dreaming, or else experiencing hallucinations brought on by my high fever. I felt my head. It didn't feel hot anymore! I was utterly at a loss. Still feeling somewhat weak, I closed my eyes again. Then, conscious of light footsteps in the room, I opened my lids briefly. It was the Revery who was "more intoxicating than reverie leaves!" She came over, felt my temples, and gently nodded her head. "He's better," she said to herself. I didn't dare open my eyes again; I decided to simply wait for the facts to explain themselves. Before long, Young Scorpion came and I began to feel a bit more secure.

"How is he?" I heard him ask Revery in a low voice. Before she had a chance to reply, I forced open my eyes.

"Are you better," he asked. I struggled to a sitting position.

"Is this your room?" My curiosity was returning.

"It's *our* room," he said, pointing to Revery. "I thought of asking you to come and live here in the first place, but I was afraid that father wouldn't approve; after all, you are father's man, or at least that's what *he* thinks. He doesn't want me to fraternize with you because he says that I've already picked up too many foreign ways."

"My thanks to both of you." I surveyed the room again.

"You're probably wondering why it's so clean. That's one of my foreign ways that father objects to." Both Young Scorpion and Revery laughed.

Come to think of it, Young Scorpion really *did* have a strong foreign flavor about him. Judging on the basis of his speech alone, he must have picked up a lot of additional vocabulary from foreign tongues, for in conversation he used about twice as many words as his father did.

"Is this your home?" I asked them.

"This is the office of one of the cultural agencies; we simply moved in and took it over. A man with enough prestige can occupy the buildings of any agency that he wants to. Since we have kept this place spotlessly clean, I think that we have nothing to be ashamed of with regard to the agency. No one else seems to bother himself about the question of whether or not private people ought to occupy public property, so we don't concern ourselves with it either. 'Muddling through'—that's the best way to describe our situation. Revery, why don't you give our friend some more reverie leaves."

"You mean I've already eaten some?"

"If we hadn't gotten some reverie broth into you, you wouldn't have come to yet. Reverie leaves make excellent medicine.* As a matter of fact, the reverie leaf is king of drugs here. No matter what you have, there's always the hope that the leaf can cure it. If you have a disease that can't be treated with reverie leaves, you might as well lie down and pull the sheet up over your head. Although the leaf can cure a number of serious diseases, it does have one peculiarity: it will cure an individual, but it will kill a whole society. That's one

* Similarly, opium was often used in China to treat diseases or even minor indispositions.

kink that we haven't worked out of it yet." Young Scorpion took on the air of a philosopher again.

After I had eaten some more of the reverie leaves, I was in much better spirits, but I no longer felt like doing anything. I began to appreciate the wisdom of the people from Light Country: there really was good reason for their living in their own enclave apart from the Cat Country, for once you got close to it, it would seem to reach out and grab you fast with a sticky hand so that you'd have no choice but to go the road that it dragged you. Cat Country was like an undertow in the ocean: get too close to it, and you'd be sucked in. If you wanted to sojourn in Cat Country, then you had to become a cat-man without any reservations; if you were unwilling to do that, then you'd better not go there in the first place. I had done all that I possibly could to avoid eating the leaf, and what was the result of all my resolve and effort? I, too, ended up eating the leaf. There seemed to be an absolute law at work: stay in Cat Country, eat the leaf; don't eat the leaf, don't stay in Cat Country.

If this civilization were ever to conquer all of Mars—and there were probably quite a few cat-people who cherished this pipe dream—then it wouldn't be long until the dissolution of the whole planet. Filth, disease, chaos, stupidity, darkness—these were the only distinguishing characteristics of this civilization. Although one could spot a pinpoint of light here and there, that tiny bit of light was certainly no match for so much darkness. Unless someone did something, the power of darkness would inevitably overwhelm the Cat Country. And yet the cat-people themselves didn't seem the least bit conscious of their impending doom. Perhaps Young Scorpion was conscious of approach of night, and seeing that the game was already lost, had begun to toy with his pieces while laughing at his own defeat. As for his father and the rest of the people—well, the kindest thing that one could say is that they were still dreaming. I had a million questions for Young Scorpion: education, the military, finance, produce, society, the family, politics. . . .

"I don't understand politics," he said. "Father specializes in politics, why don't you go ask him? As for the rest of the things you're interested in, there are some that I know about and some that I don't. The best thing is to go and see for yourself. Then when you've seen what you want to, come to me if you have any questions. Cultural enterprises is the only area that I'm up in. Father has a finger in every 'enterprise,' but since he can't oversee all of them himself, I take care of the 'cultural' ones. If you want to see schools, museums of natural history, libraries, just say the word and I'll arrange it so that you'll get your fill."

His words did even more for me than a big dose of reverie leaves. If I had political questions, I could go to Old Scorpion; if I had questions related to culture, I could go to Young Scorpion. With two such informants to rely on, I could be sure of gaining a fair knowledge of Cat Country.

I wondered if he intended to put me up indefinitely. I didn't dare ask, for to tell the truth, I didn't have the slightest intention of leaving this clean room if I could possibly help it. I really *wanted* to ask to stay but I simply couldn't bring myself to pant before them and wag my tail like a fawning puppy. I would wait. Young Scorpion asked me what I would like to see first. I'm ashamed to say that the leaves had made me so lethargic that I didn't feel like moving.

"Why don't you tell me a little about your own history?" I said. I hoped that I would be able to learn a bit more about his father as well as himself. Young Scorpion smiled. Every time he smiled, I somehow or other felt that he was lovable and despicable at the same time.

Young Scorpion was painfully aware that he was superior to other cat-people, and for that reason he didn't want to have anything to do with them for fear of soiling his hands. He acted as though he felt that being born in Cat Country was a personal misfortune and often spoke as though he were the only rose in a bunch of thorns. This was a part of him that I didn't like.

"My parents gave birth to me," Young Scorpion started speaking as Revery sat down to one side and gazed into his eyes, "but that has nothing to do with me. They loved me very much, but that has nothing to do with me either. My grandfather loved me very much too, but then all grandfathers love their grandsons, so there was nothing very remarkable in that either. It seems that there's really not much that's worth telling about my childhood." Musing back over the years, Young Scorpion raised his head slightly, and Revery raised her head slightly too in order to continue gazing into his eyes.

"Wait, there is one minor event that's probably worth your hearing about, even if it is not worth my telling about. My wet nurse was a prostitute. Although it is considered quite proper among us for a prostitute to be a wet nurse, I was not allowed to play with any other child. This was a part of the 'special education' given in our family. Why insist on a prostitute to look after the children? Well, we had money for one thing. We have a saying: 'Even devils are attracted by money.' Well, my wet nurse was one of those devils. Getting a whore for a wet nurse had been my grandfather's idea, for he felt that it was best to have soldiers look after girls and prostitutes look after boys, the reason being that they will soon communicate knowledge of sex to their wards. Their wards, in turn, having a thorough knowledge of the ways of man and maid, will marry early and produce offspring. And what better way is there to do justice to the ancestors than that? In addition to the prostitute, I had five teachers who taught me to read—five wooden excuses for men who taught me all the wisdom of Cat Country. Then one day one of my wooden mentors unbent a bit and ran away with my wet nurse, an indiscretion that resulted in the expulsion of his four wooden colleagues.

"Father sent me abroad when I grew up, for father thought that anyone who knew a few words of a foreign tongue must be omniscient, and he could well use an omniscient son. After four years I came back home, but much to father's dismay, I hadn't learned anything. I had only succeeded in picking up a few foreign mannerisms. This, however, in no way diminished his paternal affection for me, and he continued giving me money as usual. And what did I do? Well, I was happy to have the money to spend and passed my days making merry with Star, Blossom, Revery, and the other girls. Outwardly I was my father's Lieutenant-in-Charge-of-Cultural-Enterprises; in reality, I was nothing more than a parasite. I wouldn't lower myself by committing evil, but I was equally incapable of doing good. 'Muddling through'—the more I milk that precious expression, the more cream I get out of it." He laughed, and Revery laughed with him.

"Revery is a *friend,*" (Young Scorpion had again guessed what I was thinking.) "a *friend* with whom I live. This is another of my foreign mannerisms. I have a wife at home to whom I was married when I was twelve. My prostitute–wet nurse taught me all there was to know when I was six, so by the time I reached twelve, of course, I was anything but a stranger to the game. My wife is so talented that she can do almost anything, especially breed children—an excellent woman according to my father. And yet I *preferred* Revery.

"Father was quite amenable to my taking her into the house as a concubine, but I wasn't willing to do that. Since he has a dozen concubines himself, he sees taking concubines as perfectly normal behaviour, but he can't forgive her for simply *choosing* to live with me. Me, he can excuse, because my arrangement with Revery is one of the foreign mannerisms that I picked up abroad and he recognizes the existence of such alternative arrangements even though he may not approve of them. Grandfather, on the other hand, hates us both equally, for he simply doesn't recognize the existence of any foreign customs that might be brought forward to excuse my behaviour. Grandfather doesn't object to our relationship for any ill effect that it might have on either of us personally, but he does object to it because of the example that we set for the youth of Cat Country.

"You probably know that we cat-people look upon the relationship between man and maid as existing purely and simply for *that* kind of business. One takes a wife for *that;* and it's for *that* that one takes a concubine too; and why does one visit prostitutes if not for *that?* And this business of 'free love' that modern people make such a fuss over these days is, after all, still only for *that.* Once one has had enough reverie leaves to eat, then one's thoughts turn to *that.*

"Grandfather may have something in disliking me. You see I *am* a model to the youth of Cat Country, and it *was* I who set the precedent for marrying first, and then practicing 'free love' afterwards. It's for this reason, too, that the old people hate me down to the very marrow of my bones. You see, under the old custom of taking a first wife and then a series of concubines, it was clearly understood that the whole business was only for *that* to begin with, hence everybody—wives and concubines as well—could live together in perfect harmony. A little *that* here and a little *that* there resulted in the birth of many children, and that was all to the good.

"But this business of 'free love' is sticky. To begin with, if you have a wife at home, you can't very well throw her out to take your 'free lover' in; and your 'free lover,' on her part, is not likely to be willing to enter your household as a concubine. Thus, you have to establish her in a separate menage. (By now, if you don't set up a separate place, you aren't considered authentically foreign in your mode of life.) Well, at any rate, Revery and I started this fad. But because of the double menage arrangement, 'free' love has become quite expensive and some of the old folks feel that they can't afford it. But when they don't provide the young with sufficient money to carry on the new fad, then terrible family quarrels occur. Thus you see, Revery and I carry quite a heavy burden of guilt."

"Couldn't you just make a complete break with the old family system?" I asked.

"No, that wouldn't do at all! We wouldn't have any money! 'Free love' may be an admirable foreign custom, but there is an important native one that takes precedence over it: asking the old folks for money. Besides, if it weren't for the disharmony produced by the conflict of native and foreign customs, where would we get good material to practice our 'muddling through' on?"

"Can't the old people come up with any good way out of the impasse?"

"Now what in the world would you expect them to come up with? They begin with the premise that women were only made for *that* to begin with anyway. Since they take concubines themselves and approve of their children taking concubines, they are in no position to forbid 'free love.' There is nothing that they, we, or anyone else can do.

The chief result of taking wives, concubines and practicing 'free love' is an increasing number of children. The problem is: who is going to be responsible for the nurture of so many children? Neither we, the old people, nor anyone else has the answer to that one. We are always worried about the question of where to get some more of *that,* but we never concern ourselves with the question of our own children. The older men break their necks in taking concubines; the younger ones break their necks in making 'free love.' On the surface of it, there's a great deal of competition between the two systems, but in reality the whole thing is only for *that* anyway, and the result of all *that* is more little cat-men with nobody to look after them, nobody to feed them, and nobody to educate them. This is what we call *giant-size muddling through.* My grandfather muddles through. My father muddles through. I muddle through. And all of our youth muddle through. The single most hated expression in all of our Felinese language is *taking things seriously.*"

"And the women themselves? Do you mean to tell me that they accept *that* as their only function?" I asked.

"You tell him Revery, you're a woman," said Young Scorpion.

"Me? I love you, so there is nothing that I can say. If you want to go home to see that brood-mare wife of yours, go ahead; I don't care. But if you ever stop loving me, I'll eat forty reverie leaves at once and then Revery will be reveried to death."

I waited for her to go on, but she said nothing more.

17 *School Days* *

I didn't ask Young Scorpion about it directly, nor did he invite me, but somehow or other I ended up staying with them. I began my observation work the very next day. I had no definite plans as to what to examine first: it seemed to me that the best plan was simply to go out and investigate whatever I happened to bump into.

While I had been on the front side of the street, I had not seen many children. Now I discovered that the reason was they were all here on the back side of the single line of buildings. This made me feel very good, for it indicated to me that the cat-people did have one good point at least: they hadn't forgotten to educate their children. Since all the cultural organizations were on this

* Lao She sold manuscripts when he could. For a good part of his life, however, he earned his living by teaching. Having spent a good deal of time in the public school system before moving on to university teaching, he was quite familiar with the modern educational system. In both short stories and in novels, it provided him with one of his favorite subjects of satire.

side of the street, I knew that the children must have come over to go to school.

The children of the cat-people were the happiest that one could imagine. They were dirty; in fact, they were absolutely filthy, filthy past all possible description. They were thin, foul-smelling and ugly. Some had noses missing; others had eyes gone; and the heads of still others were covered with boils and scabs. And yet . . . they all seemed extremely happy! I saw one whose face was so bloated that it looked like a balloon; his mouth was so swollen that he couldn't open it, and there were bloodstains all over the lower part of his face. And despite all that, even *he* was smiling and merrily playing with the other children. The affectionate feeling that I had just entertained for the children of Cat Country suddenly vanished.

It seemed impossible to conceive of these children as coming from good homes or going to good schools. But they *were* "happy," weren't they? Only in a country where homes, schools, society, and the government are composed of muddle-headed idiots can such muddle-headed "happy" children be produced. Only in such a country can one find children who are filthy, thin, foul-smelling, ugly, deformed—and yet "happy"! These children were an index to the society and the state. They were a proper cross for their parents to bear. For it was most unlikely that when they became adults, they would make Cat Country not-dirty, not-thin, not-foul, or not-ugly; once more I saw the giant finger of oblivion pointed at the hopes of the cat-people. They had absolutely no future. Practicing polygamy, free love, and only caring about *that,* not one of them paid any attention to the future of their race. Love life! Facing imminent oblivion they still had time to worry about *love life!* Such devils hardly deserved to live!

And yet, what did I mean by judging them so hastily? I decided that it would only be fair to see what their schools were like before damning them out of hand. I followed a group of children to a school consisting of a large main gate and four walls that enclosed a patch of empty ground. As the children entered, I stood outside and peeked in. Some of them were rolled up into a wrestling mass of flesh in one corner of the yard; some were climbing the walls; others were making drawings on the walls; and still others were carefully examining each others private parts at a corner of the wall. They were all very gay, for the teachers hadn't come yet. After I had waited for I don't know how long, three adults came in. They were all skeletally thin as though none of them had had a single good meal since birth. They used the wall to support themselves as they came slowly shuffling along. Whenever there was a slight breeze, they would come to a dead stop and tremble a bit before going on. Still leaning against the wall for support, they slowly entered the school gate. The children continued rolling, climbing, making noises and examining each other's private parts. The three men sat on the ground, panting with wide-open mouths. When the students got even noisier than before, the trio simply closed their eyes and plugged up their ears. It almost seemed as though they were actually afraid of offending the students! I was beginning to lose track of time when the three men stood up and began exhorting the students to take their places, something that the children had apparently decided they would never do, for after at least an hour of exhortation, they still hadn't budged.

Fortunately, at this juncture the three teachers (for I had decided by now that they definitely must be teachers) caught sight of me. "There's a foreigner outside the gate." That's all that they said, but immediately all the students, faces toward the wall, sat down. It was apparent that not one of them dared to look a foreigner in the face.

I decided that the middle of the three men must be the head of the school. He announced: "First we shall sing the National Anthem." However, no one sang; they merely went blank for a while. Then he said: "Next let us offer up a silent prayer to the Great Spirit." At this point it seemed that the students had already forgotten that there was a foreigner outside, for, pushing and yelling, they began to yell and swear at each other again. "There's a foreigner outside!" he reminded them and they all quieted down again. "And now an address by our esteemed chancellor." One of the trio took a step forward and addressed the backs of the students' heads.

"Today you are all graduating from the university. What a grand and glorious thing!" I almost passed out from the shock. This bunch of . . . university graduates? But I decided that it wouldn't do to let my emotions run away with me and calmed myself in order to listen to the rest of the chancellor's speech. "What a grand and glorious thing it is that you have all graduated from this, the highest academic institution. Having graduated from this school, you understand everything and are in possession of all knowledge. In the future, the responsibility for all of our national affairs will be upon your shoulders. What a grand and glorious thing!" The chancellor then let out a long and musical yawn and concluded with: "That's all." The two teachers clapped for all they were worth and the students started raising hell again.

"There's a foreigner outside!" said the chancellor and they quieted down again. "And now an address by an honored colleague." The chancellor hadn't said which one, and hence the two teachers outdid each other in polite yielding of the honor. They went on like that for quite a while, and then finally one of them whose face was as thin as a dried-out squash took a step forward. I could tell that this gentleman was a pessimist because two large tears clung precariously to the corners of his eyes. In the most melancholy tones imaginable he began.

"Today you are all graduating from this, the highest of all academic institutions. What a grand and glorious thing! (One of the clinging tears let go.) All of the schools in our nation are the highest types of academic institutions. What a grand and glorious thing! (The other tear let go.) I hope that after graduation you will all remember what the head of our school and I have done for you. What an honor and privilege it has been for us to have the opportunity to serve as your faculty. However, before you set out into the great world, there's a bit of personal business that I must share with you. My wife died of starvation yesterday, and what a grand and. . . ." He couldn't go on, for now he was producing tears like rain. Only after a monumental struggle was he able to regain control of himself so that he could continue. "Please don't forget your faculty after you go out into the world. If you make money, then help with money; if you obtain a large stock of reverie leaves, then help with reverie leaves! You are aware no doubt that we have not been paid for twenty-five years. You. . . ." He lacked the strength to finish; his body went somewhat awry and he slipped down to a sitting position.

"Present the diplomas!"

The chancellor moved some thin stone slabs from the base of the wall and arranged them in front of his feet; I couldn't see too clearly, but they must have been engraved. "Everyone at this graduation is first in his class. What a grand and glorious accomplishment! The diplomas are all here and since everyone of you is first in his class, you can simply come up and get them in any old order you please. Assembly dismissed!"

The chancellor and the other teacher helped the pessimist, who was sitting on the ground, to his feet. With slow steps all three left. None of the students bothered to come forward for their diplomas. They simply resumed climbing the walls, rolling on the ground, and raising hell in general. "What kind of circus is this?" I thought to myself. I was totally baffled. I decided to go back and ask Young Scorpion about it.

Young Scorpion and Revery were both out. The only thing I could do was to go back out and continue my observation; then after I had made a general survey I'd go back and ask Young Scorpion to explain the details.

Set off a little to the side of the school that I had just visited was another school. The students all appeared to be about fifteen or sixteen. Seven or eight of them had someone pinned to the ground and seemed to be hacking away at him with knives. To one side of this group was another knot of students who were busily tying up two people. I thought that perhaps this was a laboratory class in physiology in which the students were practicing dissection. And yet, tying up living men did seem to be going a bit too far, even if it were in the interest of science! I hardened my heart and forced myself to watch; I was determined to see it through until the end so that I would find out what was going on here after all. When they had the two men tied up, they tossed them down by the foot of the wall; neither of them made a sound. They were probably already scared unconscious. The ones who were practicing dissection went on cutting and yelling.

"Let's see if you can still tell us what to do now? You dead beast. Let me tear off an arm here!"

"Make *me* study, will you? Forbid me from horsing around with the girls, will you? With our whole society as black as it is, you've still got the nerve to tell *me* to study, have you? You won't allow us to do *that* with the girls on school property, huh? I'll tear out your heart, you dead beast!" A chunk of bright red came flying through the air.

"Have you got those two rotten beasts tied up yet? Carry one of them over here!"

"Shall we bring the principal or the history teacher?"

"The principal!"

So it was their principal and a history teacher that they were dissecting! My heart was about to leap out of my mouth! Perhaps the principal and teacher did deserve death, but I just couldn't stand idly by and watch the students butcher two people alive. I no longer cared who was right and who was wrong in all of this. Just from the point of view of humanity alone I couldn't stand by and watch the students—or anyone else for that matter—commit murder on a whim. I pulled out my pistol. Actually, they would have all run away had I just yelled, but I was furious and felt that only a pistol could do justice to such a pack of little beasts. Of course, they really weren't worth wasting a bullet on, but I was beside myself.

I fired once and immediately occasioned a great crash. The concussion collapsed the walls. I had goofed again. I should have known that in Cat City walls cannot stand any sort of shock after a heavy rain. I had wanted to save the principal and had only succeeded in crushing him along with his students under the walls. I didn't know what to do. I couldn't simply throw up my hands and run away, for even the would-be assassins were still fellow creatures and therefore deserving of my help. But how could I save them?

I noticed that, fortunately, this wall was made entirely of dirt! It occurred to me that I had been too self-abasing in condemning myself for the principal's death, for this principal was probably a man who was looking to be killed. Judging from the way the school was put together, one would guess that he had misappropriated the building funds. Perhaps that's why the student had wanted to kill him. Although I went on conjecturing to myself like this, I didn't allow my hands or feet to rest for a minute; I went on pulling and tearing at the rubble and before long I had succeeded in hauling a few people out. As fast as I got one out, he'd run away like a madman without so much as even looking at me. They were like carrier pigeons released from their cages. Now I began to feel relieved. I even began to feel that this trick had been fun. Last of all, I pulled out the principal and teacher. They, at least, couldn't scamper away, for their hands and feet were still tied. I set them aside for the moment and started kicking every part of the rubble to see if there were anyone left. There probably wasn't, but I went over it again to make sure. Having satisfied myself that I had gotten everybody, I came back and loosened the ropes around the mud pies whom I had just rescued.

After what seemed like ages, the two men opened their eyes. I didn't have any drug for such an emergency, nor did I have anything alcoholic with which I might bring them around; I had to sit back and wait for them to recover themselves. Although I was dying to put a number of questions to them, I didn't have the heart to start interrogating them right away. The two men sat up slowly and I saw that there was still a look of terror in their eyes. I smiled reassuringly and asked: "Which one of you is the principal?"

A look of utter panic appeared on their faces and they began pointing at each other. I thought that perhaps they were still in a state of shock. Then slowly, stealthily, lightly, the two men stood up. I thought that they were going to stretch and loosen up a bit, but when they were all the way up, they nodded to each other and were off as fast as a pair of dragonflies chasing each other during their courtship dance. Zip! And they were out of sight. Pursuit would be useless. I was no match for a cat-man in a footrace. I sighed and sat down on the heap of rubble.

Now why had they done that? Of course! How silly of me to forget how suspicious, petty, and deceptive the cat-people could be. When I asked who the principal was, they had pointed at each other. Each, having just been snatched from the clutches of death itself, wanted to sacrifice the other in order to protect himself. They thought that I was going to do mischief to "the principal," hence they had yielded the honor to each other, and then had escaped at the earliest available opportunity. Hah, Hah! I began laughing like a madman!

I wasn't laughing at them alone, I was laughing at their whole society. Everywhere one looked in it, one found suspicion, pettiness, selfishness, and neglect. You couldn't find an ounce of honesty, magnanimity, integrity, or generosity in the entire society. In a society where principals are dissection material for their students, how could you expect a man to claim the honor of being principal?—darkness, darkness, total darkness. Was it possible that they were unaware that I had saved their lives? Very possibly, for in such a dark society, the very concept of saving another man's life was probably unknown. I thought of Madam Ambassador and the eight little sexpots. They were probably still rotting away back there. The principal, the teacher, the professor, the ambassador's wife, the eight little vixen—did any of them have anything worthy of being called "life"? Without realizing it, I had begun to shed tears.

18 *Young Scorpion as Historian*

The following is what Young Scorpion told me: "When the people of every other nation of Mars were still in a state of barbarism, we were already in possession of an educational system, for Cat Country's is an ancient culture. Our present system of education, however, was plagiarized from abroad. In saying 'plagiarized' I don't mean to imply that we ought not to copy from others. But I do think that imitating other people can prove an extremely tricky business. To be sure, copying and learning from one another is a fine thing. One might even say that it is an important impetus to the advancement of human civilization. But while *we* found that it was imperative for *us* to study the new educational institutions of *other* states, none of *them* has adopted *our* old system. This gives some indication of the relative value of the two systems.

"If we were really able to do a good job of copying so that our educational system might stand on a par with that of any other country, then even though we were merely copying, still no one could cast aspersions on our ability. However, although we have been practicing the new system of education for over two hundred years now, we are still in a state of utter chaos. This proves that we aren't even capable of imitating. The result is that while we can no longer practice our original system, we can't learn anyone else's either. You see, as a pessimist, I readily grant that our people are retarded. The renaissance of a retarded people is bound to be a joke, and hence our new educational system is a travesty.

"You asked why you saw small children being graduated from the university. You're much too honest, or perhaps one ought to say 'stupid.' Didn't you realize that that too was a joke? Graduate? That was the first day of school for all of those children. If you're going to play the fool, then go whole-hog with no reservations. That's one thing we *can* be proud of: when we play jokes, we let out all the stops. The history of our educational system for the past two hundred years has been a history of tomfoolery, and now we are rapidly approaching the end of the script. We've exhausted all the humor from the situation. No one today, no matter how witty he may be, can milk that script for any more laughs: it's gone dry.

"When the new educational system first went into effect, our schools were divided into a number of levels like any other country's, and the students had to start at the bottom and work their way up, one step at a time, through a system of examinations before they could be graduated. But in the course of two hundred years of improvement and advancement, we gradually did away with examinations! Any student who put in the required time could graduate when the time came regardless of whether or not he attended classes. However, there remained, of course, a status inequality between a primary school graduate and a university graduate. Now, since we didn't require either primary school students or university students to attend classes, why should anyone be satisfied with second best? Therefore we decided on a thoroughgoing innovation: anyone who went to school would be counted as a university graduate on the first day of classes. Let him graduate first, and then . . . come to think of it, since he has already graduated, there is no 'and then.'

"Actually, this was the best of all possible systems for Cat Country. You see, statistically we have the highest number of university graduates of any country on Mars. Of course, being first numerically makes us feel good, makes us downright proud. We Cat Country people are the most practical people on Mars. If you want to estimate the relative worth of things, the most practical way is to count. And when you start counting the number of university graduates—well, no one else can match us. It's a fact. Everybody knows it's a fact, and everybody smiles with satisfaction.

"The Emperor, himself, is very pleased with the system; if he weren't enthusiastic about education, how would we have so many university graduates? Thus, he has done well by his people and is pleased. The teachers also like the system, for under it, everybody is a university professor; every school is the highest academic institution in the land; and every student is first in his class. Think of the honor and glory! Heads of families are pleased with the system too. Every seven-year-old brat is a university graduate, and the intelligence of the children is, of course, a credit to the parents. And the students? Well, they love it. If a child is lucky enough to be born in Cat Country and survive until the age of six or seven, he is sure to attain the status of university graduate.

"From an economic point of view, the system is still more marvelous. You see, when schools were first established, the Emperor, himself, had to pay the cost out of his own pocket; and yet the students who went through the system often had the nerve to oppose the Emperor's wishes and made trouble for him. As far as the Emperor was concerned, this was nothing else but spending his own money to buy trouble. But under our new graduate-the-first-day system, the Emperor is able to produce a huge number of graduates every year without spending one red cent. Furthermore, the students produced by the new system are much more tractable and get along very well with His Majesty.

"Of course, quite a few of our teachers do starve to death, but the number of university graduates goes on increasing anyway. In the beginning, the principals and teachers were paid, with the result that they were at each other's throats from morning till night in such fierce competition for salaries that a few were killed every day. Sometimes they even incited the students to riot so that no one got any peace. Now that the Emperor doesn't give them any money, what is there for them to fight about? If they demand their pay, he simply ignores them; and if they press him too hard, he calls out the troops with clubs to play a tune on the tops of their heads. The students used to back them up in their demands, but now, since they all graduate the first day anyway, even the students won't help them. Since they can't look to any quarter for support, they have to content themselves with waiting around until they starve to death.

"Thus, for the heads of households, the question of tuition for their children is solved at one fell swoop. All they have to do is send their brats to school on the first day and their educational responsibility is ended. And since the parents have to feed the children, whether they go to school or stay at home, why not let them go to school and pick up a degree and a little status? There are no expenses for books and writing materials anyway, for people don't go to school in order to study in the first place. They go to pick up status, and they get it—on the very first day! What do you think of our system?"

"Why do you still need principals and teachers?" I asked.

"To explain that, I'll first have to say something about the evolution of the system over the past two centuries. You see, in the beginning, the schools offered a variety of curricula. Some of our students studied engineering; some studied commerce; and some studied agriculture—but what was there for them to do after they graduated? Those who had studied engineering picked up a bit of foreign technology, but since we have no industry, what use was it? Those who studied commerce learned something of foreign business methods, but here in Cat Country we only have street peddlers. Any large scale enterprise that opens up is immediately confiscated by the military. Those who studied agriculture learned foreign methods of farming, but since we don't plant anything here but reverie leaves, what use was it?

"Since under this kind of educational system, our schools were totally unrelated to the society around them, what could the students do after they graduated? There were only two alternatives: become an official or a teacher. Of course, to be an official you had to have connections. If you had an influential friend at court, then you could rocket to the top immediately, no matter what you had studied in college. But not everyone was lucky enough to have money and pull, and for those people the next best thing was to teach; after all, having received a modern education, they couldn't very well lower themselves to become manual laborers or peddlers.

"Thus the society was gradually divided into two kinds of people: university graduates and non-university graduates. The former were determined to go into teaching and officialdom; the latter became manual laborers and peddlers. For the time being I won't take up the question of the influence of this situation on politics, but merely confine myself to its effects on education. It turned our educational system into a cyclical one: I study; I graduate; and then I teach your children. Your children study, graduate, and then teach my children. They constantly imbibe the same old line of learning, and consequently their characters deteriorate bit by bit every day. How can I best explain it? There were more and more graduates every day and, except for those who become officials, they all wanted teaching assignments. There just weren't enough schools to go around and the results, of course, were ludicrous.

"The only purpose of this cyclical system of education was to pass on a reading knowledge of a few immortal textbooks; it had nothing to do with the cultivation of personal integrity. Sometimes in competing for a chair, one or two years of civil war would be stirred up with so much slaughter and bloodshed that one might really have thought that people were laying down their lives to elevate our cultural level when as a matter of fact the whole thing was only over salary.

"Gradually the Emperor, politicians, and militarists all began cutting into the operating expenses of our educational institutions. Then the educators began throwing all of their underlying energies into organizing movements to demand back salary. Teaching stopped altogether and the students, having discovered what their teachers were really like, got into the habit of skipping classes. It was at this point that there began that Graduate-the-First-Day Movement that I just told you about. And that movement, of course, slit the jugular vein of the entire system—operating expenses. The Emperor, the politicians, the militarists, and the heads of households all wholeheartedly approved of the Graduate-the-First-Day Movement because of the money that it saved.

"Everyone considered education to be useless anyway and nobody respected the hacks who were its purveyors; thus everyone was more than content to make the saving. And yet no one dared to close the schools down completely for fear of foreign ridicule. And so, the doors of the schools remained open as before and the number of university graduates even increased, but no money was spent! Since the doors were open to everyone, 'cyclical education' became 'universal education,' in other words, no education at all. But the schools *were* open for business as usual. Thus it was that our educational system became the biggest joke that Mars had ever cracked.

"When this movement had reached full maturity, it did not reduce in the slightest degree our principals' and teachers' enthusiasm for education. They still fought with each other over positions tooth and nail. You're wondering why.

"Well, you see, in the beginning the schools really did look like proper schools: they had desks, chairs, and equipment of every kind. When the system was still supported by a yearly budget, principals and instructors used to make money by selling school property. Then the principals began fighting for the principalships of the larger schools with the highest annual appropriations, and the result was widespread bloodshed. No matter how you look at it, you must admit that the Emperor handled this situation in a most humane fashion: he simply discontinued the annual appropriations for the schools. Having done this, he was far too embarrassed to be so strict as to go on and forbid the sale of school property. Well, the competition over principalships came to an end, and then, one by one, the schools turned themselves into wholesale bargainlands. Everything that could possibly be moved was sold. Thus it is that now every school is nothing more than an empty piece of ground surrounded by four walls.

"You're probably still wondering why it is that people continue to want to be principals and teachers. Well, in the first place they don't have anything else to do anyway. Furthermore, every other consideration aside, the rank of teacher or principal is still useful; the road to advancement under our cyclical system of education is from student to teacher, and from teacher to principal. To be sure, the principals and teachers have no hopes of obtaining any salary, but they *can* use the school system as a ladder to officialdom. And so it is that while there is no *education* in our schools, there *are* students, teachers, and a principal; and, moreover, every single school is the 'highest academic institution.' And when a student hears that his school is 'the highest academic institution,' he's so bowled over that he's not apt to worry about anything else. Since there's no education to be had in the schools, what do people who *really* want to study do? They revive the old system and hire family tutors. Of course, only the wealthier families can afford this. The vast majority of children still had to go to the public schools to come by their ignorance.

"The utter failure of this system of education has resulted in even the shadow of Cat Country's last hope being obliterated. The very first period during which the new educational system was tried was contemporaneous with the corruption of the 'new learning' which the new system was supposed to introduce. The new system had to be transported to us from abroad simultaneously with the new learning. If one calls learning 'new,' then that is a clear indication that learning is always advancing and developing, gathering new truths to itself every minute of every day. But as soon as the *new* system and the *new* learning arrived here, they both grew white hair as quickly as a vegetable moulds during rainy weather.

"You see, trying to adopt another country's institutions and learning wholesale is about as naïve as trying to graft another man's flesh onto your own without first preparing your own body to receive the transplant; you can slap a new piece of flesh on your own arm, but unless you've made some provision for nourishing it, it's idle to expect it to grow. Similarly, when you grab hold of a whole pile of new knowledge, yet lack the inquiring spirit needed to nurture it, the inevitable result is cyclical education. You learn A and teach A, but never add to it. And thus it was that we corrupted the new learning.

"During the initial period of borrowing, our people entertained an idle hope. Although they became aware of the folly of thinking that a piece of new flesh cut from another man's body would insure one of eternal life, they still clung to another superstition. For somehow or other, they always felt that as soon as new knowledge arrived—no matter how little—they would immediately become as vigorous and prosperous as the foreigners. In retrospect, I think that we can forgive them this arrogant pipe dream, for at least they still hoped to do something with the new learning. But today people are aware of schools only as places where people compete for principalships, where instructors are beaten, and where student movements occur. They take all of these things and lump them together with the new learning, and then stand around and curse the whole witches' brew. By now they think that the new learning is not only incapable of strengthening the state, but is enough to destroy the people. And so we have now advanced from corrupting the new learning to damning it outright. The heads of some families dismiss all the new learning and hire tutors to teach their children the traditional stone classics. Consequently the cost of our old stone books has gone up ten times, much to the satisfaction of my grandfather who sees this as the victory of our national heritage over foreign learning.

"My father was very pleased too. He immediately sent his sons abroad to study, for he felt that now they would be the only ones capable of understanding everything on the basis of foreign learning; he expected that when they came back home they'd really be able to fleece our native ignoramuses brought up on the stone classics. As a clever and active man, father has always considered the new learning as useful. He has never felt that the new learning should be widespread, but rather that it is enough for a few people to pick up enough of the foreigner's tricks to make us strong. However, most people are closer to grandfather's position than they are to father's. Like him, they see the new learning as a combination of magic and witchcraft capable only of confusing the mind and blurring the vision so that sons begin to beat their fathers, girls begin to curse their mothers, and students begin killing their teachers; in sum, they see it as utterly useless. But somehow or other, I have always felt that the more we vilify the new learning, the closer we are to the end of Cat Country.

"You will ask the reasons for the collapse of the new education. That's something that I don't know myself, but I have a *feeling* that it's due to a certain lack of integrity. Think about it for a minute. When the new educational system first arrived, why was it that people wanted it in the first place? It wasn't that they hoped that students would broaden their understanding, but rather that they thought they could use it to get rich. Nor was it out of any desire to let people understand new truths; it was rather out of the wish that we'd be able to make new and better consumer goods. In other words they wanted all that education could provide, except the most important part—that concerned with inculcating integrity and stimulating a love of learning. By the time the new schools were established, there were many bodies physically present in the schools, but few men of integrity. The principals were there to make money; the faculty was there to make money; and the students were there preparing themselves to make money.

"People looked upon the schools as they would a new-style restaurant, but no one paid any attention to the question of what the food was like. Of course, the schools themselves had two strikes against them because of the environment that they were in—a weak state built upon a decadent society composed of an emperor without integrity, and politicians without integrity, hoodwinking a populace that was even more lacking in integrity. Of course, it's true that in an impoverished state like ours there are quite a few people whose personal integrity has been worn away by hunger and poverty. I won't deny that, but I will deny that it provides adequate grounds on which to defend the individuals in charge of our educational system. Why did we promote education in the first place? To save the nation. And how were we to save it? Through the promotion of learning and the perfection of individual character. Our educators ought to be held responsible for not acting in such a way as to achieve those twin goals, and for not being willing to sacrifice a bit of personal advantage in fulfilling the functions of principals and teachers.

"Perhaps I expect too much from the teaching profession. People are people, and a teacher fears hunger just as much as a prostitute does. Hence, one might object that it's not fair to put so much of the blame on the shoulders of the teachers. I don't like laying it all on their shoulders either; but when you think of it, there are some women who will not lower themselves to become prostitutes even when they are dying of hunger. Shouldn't teachers also have enough backbone to grit their teeth and show an equal amount of integrity?

"One might argue that since the government delights in taking advantage of honest men, it would be foolish for teachers to be too upright, for the more upright they were, the more the government would take advantage of them. But no matter how bad the government may be, one would think that the educators might at least have considered using the weight of public opinion as a counterbalance against the government. For if our educators had integrity themselves, then they could turn out students with a sense of personal integrity; and it is unlikely that the society at large would be so insensitive as to be unaware of the high quality of students produced. And if the people at large saw our educators as wise and loving fathers, and if the students that those educators produced were able to achieve things in society, then it would be doubtful that the government could afford to treat education lightly or could go on refusing to provide funds for it. I think that ten years of an educational system that turned out students of integrity would change the entire face of Cat Country. However, our new system of education has already been in operation for two centuries and you have seen the results.

"If even our old system of education was able to foster honesty, a love of parents, and an obedience to rules, how is it that the new and improved system has failed to make a comparable showing? Everybody says —especially the educators themselves—that it is because of the dark evils of society. But whose responsibility is it to get rid of those evils? The educators only know how to blame social conditions, but have entirely forgotten that their responsibility lies precisely in making society a better place to live in. To be sure, society is black, but they have forgotten that their own personal integrity should serve as a bright star in the night sky. And since they have forgotten even that, what hope is there? I know that I am too extreme and perhaps somewhat idealistic, but shouldn't our educators also have at least some modicum of idealism? I also realize that neither the government nor the society gives our educators sufficient support. But who can expect anyone to *want* to help a group that is itself as evil as the society or the government?

"You saw teachers being butchered, but it ought not to surprise you, for it is only the inevitable consequence of an educational system that has no notion of the importance of character and decency. Since the teachers are totally devoid of integrity, can one expect the students who follow in their footsteps to be any different? This general lack of character, both inside and outside of the educational institutions, has a still worse consequence: it prods our people into taking a backward leap into history of tens of thousands of years, back to the cannibalism of antiquity. The progress of our species is exceedingly slow, but our retrogression is lightning fast;

for as soon as people lose their self-respect, they will revert to barbarism with amazing rapidity. Moreover, we've been at this regressive kind of education for over two hundred years now!

"During every day of the last two centuries, the heads of our schools have been fighting each other. The teachers have been constantly at each other's throats. And the students have either been fighting among themselves or against their teachers and principals. Fighting has brutalized them; and every fight that they have engaged in has added just that much more to the barbarity that they have been cultivating within themselves. And thus, now it is a very common occurrence to see students butchering teachers, professors, chancellors, and principals. However, it would be foolish of you to entertain feelings of compassion for our principals and teachers. You see, our education moves in cycles; the students whom you saw will one day themselves become teachers and principals and then it will be their turn to be victims. Luckily the addition to the educational system of a few more potential victims doesn't make any difference to society anyway, for no one pays any attention to who's killing who inside the schools in the first place.

"In a society as dark as ours it seems that people, like little animals, instinctively start sniffing to the right and clawing to the left as soon as they are born in the hopes of finding something to eat. Even as children, they'll put forth every last ounce of energy to grab the tiniest advantage or profit. And then comes the day when they're old enough to attend school where, as luck would have it, they come into contact with teachers and principals like the ones that you've seen; it's very much like a pack of cubs encountering another pack of old and hungry wolves. They're bound to try out their claws and teeth. The possibility of obtaining the most minute personal advantage is enough to fire up that residue of barbarous nature in them inherited from their most primitive ancestors. Thus a single book or reverie leaf is enough to result in corpses being strewn all over the countryside.

"Engaging in student movements is a natural manifestation of the ardor of youth and can certainly be forgiven; but our student movements cannot be explained as simply as all that. Our young hopefuls usually find some pretext for starting a riot, and then they pull down houses and destroy everything in sight. When it's all over they take the bricks and the choicest of the debris back to their own homes, brimming over with satisfaction at having gotten a little something for nothing. And their parents are usually as pleased as they are; since the family property has been augmented by a few bricks and sticks, they consider that their children's participation in the student movement was not in vain. Thus the students go looking for opportunities to destroy things so that they can cart the more worthwhile debris back home. Nor are their principals and teachers any better: they'll steal anything they have a chance to.

"Chancellors of universities, principals, faculty members, and students—from top to bottom, they all deserve to die. The fact that the students murder their principals and teachers is a kind of divine retribution; and the fact that the students will someday be murdered once they have become principals and teachers themselves is another manifestation of poetic justice. This then is our system of education. You must admit that an educational system that is capable of turning people into animals certainly cannot be counted as totally devoid of all accomplishment!"

Young Scorpion laughed.

19 *Of Scholars Old and New* *

Since Young Scorpion was a pessimist anyway, I had to take much of what he said with a grain of salt. And yet, with my own eyes I had seen teachers and principals being butchered, and students being graduated on their first day at school. Therefore, no matter how much I might suspect the validity of what he said, I had no real basis upon which to challenge his statements. The only thing I could do was gather more evidence from still another direction.

"Aren't there any scholars in Cat Country, then?" I asked.

"You bet your sweet life, there are! Carloads!" I could

* During the first part of this century, many conservative Chinese scholars still pursued antiquarian interests and spent much of their time stridently proclaiming the superiority of the spiritual civilization of the East over the crass materialistic one of the West. On the other hand, the younger and more modernized scholars had—at least according to their critics—often picked up no more of Western learning during their sojourns abroad than an expensive taste for foreign things.

tell that Young Scorpion was getting ready to have some more fun. As I had expected, he continued his speech without allowing me time to ask my next question.

"From one point of view, an abundance of scholars is a mark of cultural distinction; and yet, if you look at it another way, it's also a symptom of cultural decline. It all depends upon how you define 'scholar.' But rather than having *me* define 'scholar' *for* you, perhaps it will be better if I call some of them in so that you can get a good look at them."

"You mean 'invite' a few of them in, don't you?" I corrected the verb.

"I mean just what I said. I'll *call* some of them in; if I *invited* them, they wouldn't come. You're not familiar with the personality traits of Cat Country scholars yet, but stick around a while and you'll see what I mean. Revery, go and call a few of them in. You can tell them that I'll pass out reverie leaves when they get here. Why don't you have Star, Blossom, and some of the other girls go with you. Then you can split up and each of you can go fetch a few."

Revery went out tittering.

There didn't seem to be anything worth asking about in the interim, and I settled back to wait for the arrival of the scholars. Young Scorpion brought out some reverie leaves and we had a leisurely chew. Out of the corner of my eye, I detected just the trace of a devilish smile of anticipation on Scorpion's face.

Having delivered the invitations to the scholars, Revery, Star, Blossom, and the other girls came back to announce that the scholars would soon be along. They sat down making a circle of which I was the center.

They stared at me as if they wanted to speak, but didn't quite dare.

"Be careful," Young Scorpion said with a smile, "You are about to be cross-examined."

"We would like to ask about a few things, if you wouldn't mind."

"Fine. But I ought to warn you that I don't know a great deal about female things," I said, imitating the smile and tone of voice that Young Scorpion used in addressing them.

"Tell us what Earth women are like," they all asked as if with a single voice.

I felt relieved, for I knew that I could give them a fairly entertaining answer. "Well, let's see . . . our women all rub powder on their faces (they all 'Oh-ed!' at that) and arrange their hair to make it look as beautiful as possible. Some wear it long; some, short; some comb it into a part; and still others comb it straight back. And every blessed one of them uses perfume and aromatic oils." As they looked at each other's very, very short hair, their mouths all dropped wide open; then they closed them again in unison, seeming utterly disappointed.

"They dangle pearls and other precious stones from their ears so that when they walk these little baubles swing to and fro in a most pleasing manner." They all began to feel the tiny cat-ears set toward the backs of their skulls, and one of them—I think it was Blossom—seemed so disappointed that she would have liked to wrench her ears right off her pretty little head. "Earth women wear very pretty clothes. It's rather curious, for although they have beautiful clothes, they're always devising ways to expose a little more of their flesh. The charming result of all this is that they're partially hidden and partially exposed at the same time; they're really much more interesting looking than women like you who go completely nude all the time." I had decided to tease them a bit.

"By going stark naked, you reveal only the beauty of the flesh; and when you come to think of it, one color—even flesh color—gets a bit monotonous after while. By wearing clothes of different hues, our Earth women are able to look colorful and varied at the same time. That's the reason that, although they are not really opposed to going nude, they continue to wear some scrap of clothing even in the hottest month of summer.

"What's more, our Earth women all wear shoes made of leather and brocaded satin that have raised heels. They stud the toes with pearls and embroider flowers on the heels. Does that sound pretty to you?" I waited for a reply, but there was no reaction; they just sat there, their mouths all forming large zeros. "In antiquity our women sometimes bound their feet until they'd get them as tiny as this." I brought my thumb and forefinger together to give them an idea of the size. "But nobody binds a girl's feet anymore. Now we've changed to. . . ."

Before I had finished my sentence, they all asked with a single voice: "Why have you stopped binding them? Why? That's a stupid thing to do. Such tiny feet must have been very cute, and then to set off such cute little feet with pearls set in the toe of the shoe—that must have been exquisite!" It seemed that they were all genuinely worked-up over the painful custom's falling into disuse—and I felt that I'd better calm them down:

"Don't rush things! I haven't finished yet. All right, they quit binding their feet, right? But *then* they all started wearing high heels! The toe of the shoe was here," I pointed to the tip of my nose, "But the bottom of the woman's heel was way up here." I pointed at the top of my head, "Just think, they could add five inches to their height and twist the bones of their feet out of shape to boot! Better yet, sometimes they even had to lean against walls just to walk; and if a heel broke off, they'd have to limp along like hobbled horses!" They all seemed to feel much better now. And as they sat around me there on the floor, the more they came to admire the women of Earth, the more disappointed they were with themselves. As I finished my disquisition on shoes, I noticed that they had all slipped their feet out of sight under their buttocks.

I waited for them to ask me some more questions, but it seemed that my description of high-heeled shoes had cast them under a spell. Then suddenly they all burst forth in another flurry of questions.

"How high are the heels?"

"You said they have flowers on them, right?"

"Don't the heels make a click-clack noise when the women walk?"

"How do the bones get twisted out of shape? Does it happen naturally because the women wear such shoes, or must the bones first be bent awry before such shoes can be worn?"

"Can you make shoes of human skin as well as animal hide?"

"What kinds of flowers do you embroider on them? What colors do you use?"

I could see that had I been a shoemaker, my fortune would have been assured. I was just about to tell them how, in addition to learning to wear high heels, our Earth women have also learned how to take jobs, but just at that point the scholars came in.

"Revery," said Young Scorpion, "Go and prepare some reverie leaf juice." Then he addressed Blossom and the other girls. "Why don't you go somewhere else to continue with your discussion of high heels."

One after another, eight scholars came through the door, bowed toward Young Scorpion and then sat on the floor. With upturned faces, they all sat staring at the ceiling. Not one of them deigned to acknowledge my presence with so much as a glance.

Revery brought in the juice, and after they had all had a good leisurely drink, they seemed even less inclined to notice me. Actually, it was all to the good that they ignored me, for that gave me an opportunity to observe *them* closely. They were all extremely thin and exceedingly dirty. There was a satchelful of dirt in each of the little ears perched on the backs of their heads, and suds of saliva had collected at the corners of their mouths. Their movements were very slow, even slower and stealthier than Old Scorpion's by several times.

The power of the juice had begun to reach down to the roots of their being. They opened wide their eyes and stared at the ceiling again. Suddenly, one of them began speaking.

"Am I not the foremost scholar in all of Cat Country?" His eyes quickly swept all around and even seemed to pause on me a bit.

The other seven had all been aroused to movement by

his question: some scratched their heads; some gritted their teeth; and others stuck their fingers in their noses. Then they said in unison: "You? The foremost? Even if you threw in your father—and your grandfather for that matter—the three generations of you would still all be bastards!"

I was sure that they were about to come to blows, but much to my surprise the scholar who had arrogated first place unto himself began to laugh. Perhaps he has grown accustomed to being abused, I thought to myself.

"My grandfather, my father, and myself have been studying astronomy now for three generations. Who do the rest of you think you are anyway that you feel qualified to criticize such an eminent family of astronomers?

"The foreigners have to use all sorts of gadgets and mirrors when they do research in astronomy, but it's been our tradition for generations to use the unaided eye! The unaided eye, gentlemen, the unaided eye! How can the foreigners compare to us? Moreover, we pay attention to discovering the relationship between the stars in the sky above and good and bad fortune in the world of men below! Are the foreign astronomers capable of that? And as for being foremost scholar, let me tell you that while I was observing astronomical phenomena last night, the Star of Scholarship appeared over my head! Now if I'm not the foremost scholar in all the land, I'd like to know who is!"

Young Scorpion laughed and said, "If I'd been standing outside with you last night, couldn't I say that the Star of Scholarship had appeared over my head too?"

"The words of His Highness, Young Scorpion, are absolutely correct!" said the Astronomer bowing to the superior wisdom of his young ruler.

"The words of His Highness are absolutely correct!" the other seven chimed in.

For what seemed like ages nobody said anything.

"Speak!" Young Scorpion ordered.

One of them stood up. "Am I not the foremost scholar in all of Cat Country?" His eyes, too, made a quick sweep in all directions. "Can *astronomy* even be counted as scholarship in the first place? Everyone *knows* that it can't. In order to take up any kind of study, you must first be able to recognize our written characters. Therefore, philology is the only branch of learning worthy of the name. I've been studying philology for thirty years. Thirty years! Who among you can possibly have the gall to dispute my position as first scholar? Who?"

"Ah, go blow it out your ass!" they all suggested in unison.

However, the philologist was not, it seemed, as easygoing as the astronomer. He grabbed hold of a historian and yelled: "Who do you think you're talking to anyway! First of all, pay me back what you owe me! Did you or did you not once borrow a reverie leaf from me? If you don't pay me back immediately, then I'll twist your head clean off your shoulders or else I'm not the foremost scholar!"

"*I* borrowed a reverie leaf from *you*? I, a world-renowned historian, borrowed a reverie leaf from the likes of *you*? Let go of me! Don't get my arm dirty!"

"So you think you can eat a man's reverie leaves and

then just forget about it, do you? Well, we'll see about that. Just wait until I finish my *Comprehensive Discussions of Philology* and see if your surname is to be found in it. As the foremost philologist of all Cat Country, I shall proclaim to the rest of the planet that the character used to write your surname is not to be found in the written characters of archaic Felinese. Wait and see if I don't!"

At this point the historian seemed genuinely concerned, and began to plead with Young Scorpion. "Your Highness, Your Highness, hurry up and give me a reverie leaf so that I can pay him back. Although I am the foremost scholar and historian in Cat Country, as Your Highness well knows, scholars don't have any money. Since I am indigent, then perhaps at sometime I actually did borrow a reverie leaf from the bastard. I don't really remember. Speaking of reverie leaves, Your Highness, there's something else that I just have to bring up. Please put in a word for us with His Old Highness, your father, and ask him to distribute some more reverie leaves to the scholars. It doesn't matter so much when ordinary people are without reverie leaves, but when we who are scholars are without them—especially me, the *foremost* scholar—then how are we to pursue our scholarly activities?

"You see, Your Highness, only recently I have been engaged in further research on the methods of punishments employed in antiquity and I have established beyond all doubt that the ancients used to skin people alive. I shall present you with an article on this in the near future with the humble request that you pass it on to your father. Ask him to pass it on to the Emperor when he's through with it so that his Imperial Highness may revive this fascinating, and culturally rooted, mode of punishment. Should I not be counted as foremost scholar of the realm on the basis of this discovery alone? What do you think you are anyway, you mere philologist. History is the only genuine discipline."

"And is history written with characters or isn't it? Give me back that reverie leaf that you owe me!"

Young Scorpion had Revery give a reverie leaf to the historian. The latter tore it in two and handed half of it over to the philologist. "All right I'll pay you back, although I really shouldn't."

The philologist accepted the half and then said through gritted teeth: "You've short-changed me by half. All right, it'll be a wonder if I don't make off with your old woman after such treatment. You just wait and see!"

The words "old woman" seemed to make the rest of the scholars unusually excited. They all addressed Scorpion in chorus: "Your Highness! Your Highness! Why should it be that we scholars are only allowed one wife apiece so that we have to get excited and talk about stealing other people's old women? We are scholars, Your Highness. We bring honor upon the whole nation. We preserve and pass on the learning of our ancestors unto our children, grandchildren, and the posterity of the nation for ten thousand generations to come. Why shouldn't each of us have three wives at least?"

Young Scorpion didn't say anything.

"All you have to do is go to the heavenly bodies for an

example. A large star is bound to have several small stars around it. Since this is the way of heaven, should the way of man be any different? I believe that the position of foremost scholar is, in and of itself, clear evidence that a man is entitled to several wives. What's more my own wife's 'that' is not too much fun to use anymore!"

The philologist followed the astronomer with proofs of his own. "Just on the basis of the word alone, we can tell that it should be 'old women' in the plural, not the singular. In olden times our ancestors used the woman radical with amazing frequency in creating new words. Isn't the plural form of the original word patent evidence in itself that our ancient ancestors intended the plural use of women too? On the basis of my position as foremost scholar, I can demonstrate that 'wives' never had a singular form. What's more. . . ." The rest of what he had to say is not fit to record.

Each of the scholars, one after another, by virtue of his position as "foremost scholar of the realm," offered proofs of his own for the plurality of "wives." And each of them brought forth some evidence that is not fit to print. Listening to their speeches, I gained the general impression that in the eyes of these eminent scholars, women were nothing more than "that."

Young Scorpion remained silent.

"Perhaps His Highness is a bit fatigued," they said. "We. . . ."

"Revery, give them a few more reverie leaves and tell them to beat it," said Scorpion, closing his eyes.

"Thank you, Your Highness. Thank you for your understanding!" They intoned the same formula in unison.

Revery brought in a bundle of leaves and each of the

scholars grabbed as many as he could. They cursed and reviled each other while snatching the leaves, and between curses they bowed in the direction of Young Scorpion to express their thanks. Still cursing each other, they walked out.

No sooner had this group of scholars left than a group of young scholars came in. Apparently they had already been waiting outside for a good long time, but because they wanted to avoid contact with their seniors, they had forced themselves to be patient all this time. (You see, in Cat Country experience had shown that whenever junior and senior scholars came into contact, at least two of them were sure to die.)

In appearance the junior scholars had it all over their seniors. They were neither filthy nor emaciated and, what's more, they were full of life. They bowed to Revery, greeted me, and then sat down. To me this was all very gratifying and I began to feel that there was still some hope for Cat Country after all.

Young Scorpion whispered to me: "These are the young scholars I told you about who have spent several years abroad and know everything there is to know."

Revery brought out the reverie leaves and they all started wolfing down opium-laden leaves with real gusto. I felt a chill pass over my heart.

After eating their fill of leaves, they started chatting. But what was it they were talking about? I couldn't make out a single word! In my association with Young Scorpion I had already picked up quite a few of the new words that had been taken into Felinese, but I still couldn't understand the conversation of these young scholars. I could only hear sounds: *Gulu-baji, didung-*

didung, hwala-fuszji—it sounded something like that.

Since I was anxious to understand what they said, I began to get a bit flustered. Furthermore, they were continually talking at me and I couldn't say anything in return, but was reduced to nodding my head like an idiot. (Then a few words began to get through.)

"Mr. Foreigner, what is that you're wearing on your legs?"

"Trousers," I answered. I was a bit mixed-up myself at this point.

"What are they made of?" asked a young scholar.

"How are they made?" asked another.

"What academic rank does the wearing of trousers betoken?" asked yet another.

One asked: "Does your honorable country have two classes, the trousered and the trouserless?"

What was I to answer? The only thing I could do was play the fool and put on a forced smile. Obviously disappointed at not having obtained a reply from me, they came over and began to feel my raggedy trousers with their hands. Having finished their examination, they all started in again with that *gulu-baji, didung-didung, hwala-fuszji* until I thought I'd smother under their blanket of unintelligible sounds. After an interminably long time, they all left and I had a chance to ask Young Scorpion what they had been talking about. "You're asking me," he said with a smile. "But who am I supposed to ask?" As far as I know, they weren't talking about anything."

"But what did *hwala-fuszji* mean? That's one sentence that stuck with me," I said.

"*Hwala-fuszji?* They also said *tung-tung-fuszji* a lot;

do you remember? They say lots of things like that. For the most part, when they talk, they just string a lot of foreign nouns together so that nobody understands them. They don't understand what they're saying themselves, but they enjoy the lively atmosphere that all those foreign sounds create. You have to be able to speak like that in order to be considered a modern scholar. *Hwala-fuszji* seems to be the most popular expression these days. It doesn't matter whether parents beat a child, or the Emperor eats reverie leaves, or a scholar commits suicide—you can use *hwala-fuszji* to cover every case. Actually the expression means 'chemical action.' The next time you run into them, all you have to do is babble out '*hwala-fuszji, tung-tung, fuszji*,' and '*fuszji* everybody,' and they'll all think that you are a scholar too. Just use these sounds in places where you can throw in nouns. Don't worry about verbs, and if you want to turn one of them into an adjective just add an *-ous* and say something like '*hwala-fuszji-ous*.'"

"What did they mean by examining my trousers?" I asked.

"The girls ask about high heels and the modern scholars ask about trousers; it's all the same thing. The young scholars are all a bit effeminate. They're vitally interested in cleanliness, esthetic appeal, and new fashions; the old scholars are only vitally interested in a frontal assault on a woman's 'that.' The modern scholars are terribly concerned with making a good impression on people, and I'll be quite surprised if they aren't all wearing trousers within the next few days. You mark my words!"

The atmosphere in the room felt suddenly stifling,

and, without paying any further attention to my host, I went out for air. Just outside the door I ran into Young Scorpion's blossoms; they were using the wall to support themselves while they practiced walking on their toes with a piece of brick tied under each heel.

20 *Books and Relics by the Pound**

There are things to be said for the pessimist; for one thing, it takes *some* thought before one arrives at it. Granted the pessimist's thought may be unsound and his will, weak; but at least he does use his brain. Thinking in this vein, I came to like Young Scorpion a bit more. As far as the two groups of scholars were concerned, I pinned all my hopes on the younger ones. Perhaps they were just as mixed-up as their seniors, but on the outside at least they were lively and optimistic; and I thought that a touch of this lively optimism was just what Scorpion lacked. If Scorpion could only rouse his own courage and be as lively and happy as the young scholars, who knows what great enterprises he'd be able to undertake in order to benefit his fellow cat-men. If he could

* Many Chinese were incensed by the fact that ancient relics, documents, and works of art were often spirited out of the country by foreign armies or sold out of the country by corrupt native merchants and officials. Even today a great number of China's most ancient relics and most beautiful works of art are to be seen only in foreign museums.

only secure the aid of a few optimists! I was anxious to meet with the young scholars again to see if they'd be willing to help. I found out where they lived from Revery and the girls.

On the way I passed several schools, but I didn't have the heart to go in and see what they were like on the inside. It wasn't that I was going to take Young Scorpion's word for everything, but rather that the schools were all of the same uninviting style: four earthen walls surrounding a stretch of open ground. Even if they weren't as bad as Young Scorpion had painted them, I had to admit that there didn't seem to be much about them that was worth seeing. I did glance about at the male and female students who were walking past on the street though, and that was enough to depress anybody.

Their attitude, especially those who were a bit older, was exactly like that of the seven cat-men who served as Old Scorpion's bearers—inordinately proud and self-satisfied, as though each of them thought himself a living god and was at the same time totally oblivious to the fact that Cat Country was a disgrace throughout the planet. I thought that perhaps I ought to make some allowances for them, for their teachers must certainly have been utter ignoramuses in order for the students to get that way in the first place. And yet how was it possible for young people of twenty or so to be callous and insensitive enough to actually remain unaware of what was going on around them? How could they manage to live in this kind of hell and still saunter about with such a self-satisfied and arrogant air? What did they have to be so self-satisfied about? Didn't they have any feelings? I was almost on the point of grabbing one of them and demanding an answer, but I decided not to waste my time.

One of the modern scholars that I was looking for was one of the curators at the Museum of Antiquities. I decided to pay him a visit and at the same time take advantage of the opportunity to make a tour of the museum. The structure in which the collection was housed was rather large; it was at least two or three hundred feet long. A doorman sat outside the main entrance; his cat-head was tilted back against the wall and he was lost in a sweet and mellow nap. I poked my head inside and looked about, but no one else was around. Was it possible that the museum could open all of its doors to the public without anyone around to look after things? That was strange, especially when you consider how fond of stealing things the cat-people were. Not daring to disturb the doorman, I went right on in. After passing through two empty rooms, I came upon my new friend. He proved to be extremely clean, lively, and well-mannered; without thinking about it one way or another, I began to like him. I learned that his name was Cat Lafuszji. I knew for a fact that Lafuszji was not a common name in Cat Country and concluded that he must have taken it during his studies abroad. I was terribly afraid that if we got into a conversation, he would deluge me with a flood of words with *fuszji* tacked on the end of them, and, therefore, I told him straight out that I'd like to see the museum and hoped that he would be good enough to give me the guided tour. I was sure to be all right as long as I could keep him from *fulaszji*-ing.

"After you, after you! Please go in!" Cat Lafuszji was in high spirits and acted most graciously. As we entered an empty room, he said, "This is where we store the stone implements that were used ten thousand years ago; they are displayed according to the most modern methods. Look around at your leisure."

I looked all about, but there was nothing there! "Well, here we go again," I thought to myself. Before I had a chance to ask him what the joke was, he pointed to the wall and said, "This is a stone jar, ten thousand years old. It has foreign characters inscribed on it and is worth at least three million National Souls."

So that was it! Now I began to understand. There was a row of small characters inscribed on the wall; what he probably meant was that a stone jar worth three million National Souls at one time *had* been displayed in that location.

"This is a stone axe from ten thousand and one years back; it's worth two hundred thousand National Souls. This is a set of stone bowls from ten thousand and two years back; they are worth one and a half million. This is . . . three hundred thousand; this is . . . four hundred thousand!"

Everything else aside, I really admired him for being able to remember the price of every ancient relic with such fluency. We entered another empty room and with the same attentive courtesy as before, he said: "This is the room where we store books and documents from fifteen thousand years back. They are the most ancient on the entire planet and are all arranged in strict accordance with the most modern methods of classification." He began reciting prices and titles from memory, but there was nothing to be seen save a few black bugs on the wall.

After having seen ten such rooms in a row, Cat Lafuszji had all but exhausted my patience. But just as I was on the point of thanking him and saying goodbye in order that I might escape to the outside and get a breath of fresh air, he led me toward a room outside of which more than twenty cat-men stood on guard, clubs in hand. Now this room certainly *couldn't* be empty! Thank heaven! I was glad that I hadn't left earlier, for as long as there was one room filled with things, my trip would not have been in vain, even though I had to travel through ten empty rooms to get there.

"You've come at precisely the right time. Had you come a few days later, you wouldn't have gotten to see any of these things," said Cat Lafuszji in the most sincere and courteous of tones. "In this room we have some pottery from twelve thousand years back, all of it displayed in accordance with the most modern methods of classification. Twelve thousand years ago our pottery was the most exquisite on the entire planet. Later on—about eight thousand years ago—the pottery industry died out so that today nobody knows how to make it anymore."

"Why?" I asked.

"*Yaya fuszji!*"

Now what was *yaya fuszji* supposed to mean? Before I had a chance to ask, he continued: "These pieces of pottery are the most valuable things on the whole planet. Up to date we've already sold a total of three hundred billion National Souls worth of them abroad! Our asking price really wasn't very high either; if the government hadn't been so anxious to sell, we probably could have gotten at least *five* hundred billion. We once sold some stone implements that were not even ten thousand years old and got two hundred billion for them, but this time the government was just too anxious, and consequently the sale was a flop.

"The government's failure in agreeing to sell for such a low price is not really all that important, but the fact that we who work in this line had to take a cut in kickbacks *was* something worth worrying about. What are we supposed to live on? Our salaries haven't been paid for several years now. If we hadn't hit upon the device of taking kickbacks on the sale of antiquities, we'd have been reduced to a daily diet of air a long time ago. Of course, the amount made through the sale of ancient relics is nothing to be sneezed at, but you have to bear in mind that those of us who are responsible for looking after the national antiquities are all modern scholars; living expenses are much higher for us than for the old-fashioned scholars. Everything that we use has to be brought in from abroad, and the money we spend for a single item would cover the living expenses of the old-fashioned scholars for a good long time. It's really quite a problem!" A hint of melancholy actually crept across Cat Lafuszji's otherwise perpetually happy face.

Why had they allowed the pottery industry to die out? *Yaya fuszji,* whatever that meant. And why had they sold their ancient relics? So that the scholars could get their kickbacks! Of the hopes that I had pinned on the modern scholars, not one shred remained. I no longer had the heart to continue with my questioning; I could no longer even bring myself to stoop to talking with the man. I simply felt like clasping one of those ancient relics to my breast and having a good cry. There was no point in asking anything more. The government treated the sale of ancient relics as one of its sources of finance, and the modern scholars were only interested in getting kickbacks or reporting the prices of the ancient relics . . . what more was there to ask? However, I just had to ask one more thing.

"When you've sold everything and there are no more kickbacks to be had, what are you going to do then?"

"*Yaya fuszji!*"

At this point it finally dawned on me that by *yaya fuszji* they meant what young scorpion did by "muddling through," magnified ten thousand times! I began to hate Cat Lafuszji, and to hate his *yaya fuszji* even more.

Once you've grown accustomed to eating reverie leaves, it's not too easy to work up a rage anymore, and so I didn't give Cat Lafuszji a few belts as I should have. It seemed that I was not taking things so much to heart any more. After all, what was the point of a Chinese going into a rage over the domestic affairs of Cat Country. I saw clearly now that the modern scholars were simply people who had been abroad and had seen or had heard a little about new methods of classification and display. They were really totally incapable of making judgments and entirely incapable of distinguishing good from bad. They simply went through the motions of doing their jobs on the basis of what little knowledge of new methods they had. What a terrible shame that their pottery industry had died out. But the only reaction that they thought it was worth was *yaya fuszji*. And how painful it was to think of their own antiquities being sold abroad. But again, their only reaction had been *yaya fuszji*. They had no backbone, no judgment, and no character. They had simply taken a trip abroad in order to arrogate unto themselves the title of "scholar" in order to be able to *yaya fuszji* in comfort.

I ran out without even bothering to take my leave of Cat Lafuszji. As I ran back through the empty rooms, I seemed to be conscious of the sound of sobbing, and here and there I seemed to see ghostly shadows cover their faces and weep. If the ghosts of these ancient relics had consciousness and I were one of them, then I should have inflicted a hideous death on those betrayers who had sold me, and that whole lot of modern scholars should have died spouting blood from all seven bodily openings!

Having reached the street, I calmed down a bit. On second thought it occurred to me that living in a society as black as this one, being sold abroad might actually be counted a stroke of good fortune. Since theft and destruction were the two most ingrained habits of the cat-people, it was certainly much better that the precious relics of their past be sold to foreign countries where people would preserve them, rather than being destroyed by the cat-people themselves. But however fortunate the betrayal might have been from the point of view of the relics, it was certainly no justification for the scurrilous behavior of Cat Lafuszji. Of course, one had to admit that the sale of ancient relics had not been his fault alone, but that brazen attitude of his was past all forgiveness. Shame? It seemed that he didn't know the meaning of the word.

As I see it, pride in one's history is perhaps the most difficult of all natural feeling to eradicate, and yet it seemed that the youth of Cat Country were actually able to sell off the treasures of their own heritage without the slightest trace of feeling. What's more, Cat Lafuszji was a *scholar;* if that's what the scholars were, one could well imagine what the rest of the populace must be like! I no longer retained a single iota of hope for a renaissance of the cat-people. The expenditure of too much energy is sometimes enough to bring about the demise of an individual or even a nation, but one still admires those who, having tried too hard, cough up their blood and die of exhaustion. That would never happen to the cat-people! Cat Lafuszji and those like him only knew how to *yaya fuszji*—utterly hopeless the whole lot of them!

I didn't have the heart to go looking for any of the other new scholars, nor did I feel like seeing any of the other cultural agencies. For I knew that every new man I met would reduce that much more of my hopes for finding the ideal leader for the cat-people, and each new cultural agency that I visited would only cause me to shed a few more tears. What was the point in it?

Young Scorpion had had the right idea: he had not taken me to see these things, nor had he explained beforehand what I should encounter. He had simply suggested that I go and see for myself; his acting in this way carried with it a significance that went far beyond any words that he might have used.

I passed a library and felt like going in to see it, but was afraid of being the victim of an empty-bookshelf hoax. But then I saw a group of students come out. They must have gone there to read, I thought, and my interest was aroused again. Although the library didn't seem to have been very well kept up, it was still intact and really quite presentable.

As soon as I went through the front door, I saw that there were several large white characters brushed on the wall that looked as though they had just been written: LIBRARY REVOLT. Now who was it, I wondered, that the library was supposed to revolt against? Since I'm not really all that bright, I couldn't figure it out right away. Entirely wrapped up in pondering the meaning of the characters on the wall, I took a few more steps when out of a clear blue sky, someone on the floor grabbed me around the legs and shouted, "Help!"

There were ten or so people lying on the floor. I recognized the one who had me by the leg as one of the modern scholars. Their hands and feet were bound. As soon as I untied them, they took off into the distance like fish that had been thrown back into the water. Finally, only the modern scholar was left.

"What happened?" I asked.

"Another revolution. It's the Library Revolution this time!" He said tremblingly.

"And whom is the library revolting against!"

"No, that's not it. *They're* revolting against the library! Look here." He pointed to his legs.

He was wearing a pair of short pants. But what did that have to do with the library revolt?

"Well, it was this way. You wear trousers, right? Well, we modern scholars specialize in the introduction of foreign scholarship, mores, and customs; hence, we too began wearing trousers as a kind of revolutionary enterprise."

"Is revolutionary enterprise as easy to engage in as all that?" I wondered to myself.

"Well, at any rate, I started wearing trousers and that's where the trouble began. The university students next door noticed this new revolutionary enterprise and came over demanding trousers of me. You see, I am the head librarian and whenever I sell library books, I always have to give the students a cut of the profits because they too are ardent followers of Everybody Shareskyism. I have to sell books or I wouldn't be able to live, but when I make a sale I had better be sure that they get their cut. You see adherents of Everybody Shareskyism will kill a man without thinking twice about it. They're so used to Shareskyism that when they saw me start to wear trousers, it was natural that they wanted their 'sharesky.' But where in the world was I to get enough money to make trousers for everyone? And so they started a counter-revolution. My wearing trousers was originally a revolutionary enterprise, but since *they* couldn't afford to wear trousers, they decided to turn the revolution on *me*. They tied us all up and confiscated all of my savings!"

"But didn't they steal any books?" I wasn't too worried about the losses of an individual.

"There are no books to steal. We finished selling them fifteen years back. We don't do anything now except put things in order."

"But if you have no books, what's left to put in order?"

"The rooms. We're preparing another bit of revolutionary enterprise: we're going to turn this library into a hotel. We'll still call it a library, but we'll be able to rent out rooms and take in a little money. Actually in the past soldiers have often commandeered the place for quarters anyway; at least civilians will be a bit more tidy." I really admired cat-people's business sense, but I didn't dare listen to any more lest my silent admiration turn into open vituperation!

21 *Anyone for a Brawl?**

There was another heavy rain during the night, but like all rains in Cat Country it was totally incapable of inspiring one with poetic feeling; and no matter how I tried to settle my spirits, I couldn't rid myself of a certain tense anxiety. Sounds of collapsing buildings followed hard one upon the other, and the whole city was as a ship battered hard by a storm, a ship on which there was not a single cabin that was not constantly assailed by quaking terror. It occurred to me that a few more days of such heavy rains would be enough to totally destroy Cat

* From hedonism to communism, twentieth-century China was introduced to a whole panorama of programs each of which claimed to be *the* way of saving the nation. For thousands of years, monolithic unity and conformity had been the rule in Chinese politics. The concept of pluralism was basically unknown; hence, when political parties were organized along Western lines, the results were often disastrous. One of the most valued concepts in traditional Chinese thought was that of "harmony"; stripped of its deceptively pleasant overtones, "harmony" often meant total and unquestioning conformity to one truth or orthodoxy. Thus a competition of truths—political parties—was squarely against the grain of the traditional Chinese political system.

City, an extinction that would perhaps be a merciful end. It was not that I hoped for such an inhumane thing, but rather that I was depressed and anxious about the cat-people. Why were they living? And, after all, what kind of life was it that they were living? I still didn't understand Cat Country. I was only aware that history is capable of perpetrating wild and absurd errors, and I had a vague feeling that I was watching the cat-people suffer punishment for the sins of history. I readily grant that this may have been an overly abstract and somewhat mystical way of thinking, but that is how I felt at the time.

Everybody Shareskyism—I thought of that expression again. Since I couldn't get to sleep anyway, I passed the time in idle dreaming. Regardless of whether this expression, like so many of the other foreignisms used by cat-people, had any meaning or not, the cat-people had, I thought, suffered greatly from its harmful effects. I thought of what I'd been told about there being a number of students who believed in Everybody Shareskyism. If I were to stick to my plan of finding out everything there was to know about Cat City, then it would be necessary for me to gain some understanding of their political conditions. From the history of the various nations on the Earth, I had learned that students often serve as yeast to the bread of political thought, for the minds of students are the most sensitive, even though their enthusiasms are also the most shallow. If it turned out to be the case that the intellectual sensitivity of Cat Country's students was limited to the acceptance of a few new and quaint expressions, then I had better close my eyes to the future of their civilization! I realized that it was not fair to blame only the students, but because I had originally entertained so many hopes for them, I could not but express a double measure of censure. I would simply have to look into their political system. I was so anxious to see Young Scorpion again that I couldn't get to sleep all night. Although he had told me that he didn't understand politics, I felt that at least he'd be able to fill me in on some of the historical background of Cat Country. Without such historical depth, I would not be able to understand the contemporary scene, for I had, after all, lived here for only a very short time. I got up very early in order to buttonhole Young Scorpion before he went out.

"Tell me about Everybody Shareskyism," I said as though I too had become an enthusiast.

"It's a kind of political theory that holds that everyone lives for the sake of everyone else," replied Young Scorpion, chewing on a reverie leaf. "Under this kind of political system everybody works, everybody's happy, and everybody's secure. Society is a great machine and each individual is a part of the works. Each man is a happy, secure and useful little bolt or cog. It's really not bad."

"Has any country on Mars ever before practiced this kind of theory?"

"Many have. It's been practiced for over two centuries now."

"And Cat Country?"

Young Scorpion's eyes filled with such despair that I was quite alarmed, and it was a long time before he was able to speak. "Yes, we made quite a commotion about it too. I use the phrase, 'made a commotion' out of design, for we have never really 'practiced' any theory."

"What do you mean by 'made a commotion'?"

"If you spank your child because he is naughty and, having found out about it, I give mine a good hiding too, not because he is naughty, but because you have spanked yours and I feel that I must do likewise—then with regard to family affairs that would be 'making a commotion.' The same applies to politics."

"You seem to be saying that you never work out your own ways of dealing with your own affairs, but always 'make a commotion' on the basis of other people's ideas as fast as they come up with them. To make an analogy, it's as though you never build your own houses but always live in rented ones."

"Or perhaps it would be an even closer analogy to say it's as though, while there's no reason for us to do so, we insist on wearing trousers simply because we've seen other people with them on. And then, rather than having them cut to the measure of our own legs, we simply go and buy any old pair of ready-made ones."

"Tell me something of your past history," I said. "Even if you did only 'make a commotion', still even a commotion should have made some change in the status quo, shouldn't it?"

"And all change is necessarily improvement and progress, is that it?"

Young Scorpion was really quite a guy! I smiled and waited for him to go on. He reflected for a long time before saying: "Where should I begin? Altogether there are twenty-some countries on Mars and each one has its distinctive political system and typical reforms. When by chance one of us hears about the distinctive system of another country, then the rest of us 'make a commotion.' Or if perchance we hear that such and such a country has made a certain political reform, then we rush in to make a similar 'commotion.' As a result other people's distinctive systems still remain their own, and their reforms engender genuine changes, but we remain forever what we are. If you're interested in what it is that's distinctive about us, it's this: the more 'commotions' we make, the worse shape we're in."

"But, theory aside, let me have a few facts, no matter how disconnected they may be," I entreated him.

"Well let's begin with 'brawls.' "

"What does 'brawl' mean?"

"Well it's the same as with trousers: we didn't have any originally. I don't know whether or not you have a thing like brawls on the earth or not. No, they're not really 'things,' but rather a kind of organized political group. Everybody bands together to support a certain political position or program."

"We have that too. We call them 'political parties.' "

"All right, call them 'political parties' or whatever you like. At any rate when they get to us, 'political parties' are translated into 'brawls.' You see, from ancient times the Emperor kept tight reign on everyone and the common people were never allowed to express their opinions. Then suddenly the news arrived from abroad that the people ought also have the right to take a hand in government affairs. Well, to us—no matter how we thought about it—that could only mean one thing: the people ought to have the right to stir up a good brawl.

Moreover, ever since ancient times we have always taken 'minding one's own business' as a standard of morality. And then one day, out of a clear blue sky, we heard that everybody ought to band together into parties or associations in order to mind other people's business. We started leafing through our ancient books, but try as we might, we couldn't find an appropriate word to translate the concept of 'party.' 'Brawl' seemed *closest* to it, and we settled on 'brawl.' Why else would people group together, if not to stir up a 'brawl'? Didn't I tell you that I didn't understand politics? Ever since we started having brawls, there have been a good many political changes. I can't enumerate all of them in detail, but I can give you some facts, rough though they may be."

"Go ahead, a rough outline will do very nicely." I was only afraid that he wouldn't go on.

"The first political reform probably came just after the demand was made that the Emperor let the people have a hand in the government. Of course, he refused, and at that point the People's Suffrage Brawl drew some military men into its ranks. The Emperor, seeing things take this inauspicious turn, made officials of the leaders of the brawl, and then they began to devote themselves so exclusively to their official duties that they completely forgot about the People's Suffrage Brawl.

"As luck would have it, at just that point some other people heard that we really didn't need to have an Emperor to begin with and they organized still another brawl: the Government by the People Brawl. The Emperor saw clearly that the only way to handle this brawl would be to organize a counter-brawl of his own. Anyone who joined the Emperor's brawl was paid a thousand National Souls per month. When the members of the Government by the People Brawl found out about it, visions of wealth began to dance before their eyes. They immediately panicked and fell over each other in reaffirming their allegiance to the Emperor. But the Emperor was still somewhat put out with the members of the Government by the People Brawl and only allowed them a salary of one hundred National Souls a month. They were satisfied at first, but not long afterwards he had to raise them to a hundred and three in order to hold their allegiance. The fact that these people were given a monthly salary for no work attracted everybody's attention and before you knew it, there were brawls of ten members, two members, and even some of only one. There was no end to the names that the brawls went by."

"Excuse me for asking, but did the real, down-to-earth common people take part in any of these brawls?"

"I was just getting to that. How could one expect the common people to take part? They were ignorant, uninformed, and uneducated. The only thing that they could do was stand around and wait until someone decided to exploit them; they were absolutely helpless. And yet every single brawl that was organized proclaimed that it was 'for the country and for the common people.' But when the leaders of the brawls obtained official posts, then they'd take the Emperor's money just like anyone else; and the Emperor's money was all milked out of the common people whom the brawl leaders claimed to want to help in the first place. And if they couldn't get official positions, then they'd ally themselves with the military and put the people in shackles that way. The more brawls that were organized, the worse off the common people became and the poorer the country got."

I butted in again. "Do you mean to say that there were no good people in the brawls? Wasn't there a single one who was genuinely devoted to the interests of the country and people?"

"Of course there were! But you have to remember that even 'good people' have to eat, and even 'revolutionaries' have to make love. Food and love both take money. And thus people began to shift their interests from revolution to devising ways of making money. Once they had enough money for food and a wife, they became slaves to their salaries. They lost all hope of getting out from under, and all thoughts of revolution, politics, country, and the common people were consigned, once and for all, to oblivion."

"Do you mean that nobody who has food and a job will engage in political activity?" I asked.

"The common people are too ignorant to be interested in revolutions. The rich people are well-informed enough to revolt but, of course, they don't dare do anything. For if a rich man so much as moves, the Emperor, or the military, or brawl members will immediately confiscate his property. But if he just braves things through patiently without making a move, then he can purchase a minor post and preserve at least some of his property, although he may not be able to hold on to all of it. But if he made any move at all, he would lose everything he had. So that rules out the common people and the rich folk as potential revolutionaries.

"The only people who can safely engage in politics are people who have been abroad, or students in the schools, or gangsters, or local bandits, or military men who can read a few characters. You see when these people move into politics, they are bound to gain, and when they retire from politics they can be certain of suffering no loss. If they 'make a brawl,' they'll have enough to eat; and if they don't 'make a brawl,' they'll still have enough to eat. Thus, in our country revolution has become a kind of profession.

"Consequently after all these years of 'making brawls,' only two striking features have emerged: first, in politics we have had change but no reform, so that the more that democratic ways of thinking have been developed, the poorer our people have become; and secondly, the more political brawls that have been organized, the shallower our youth have become. The students spend their time in politics instead of study; consequently, even when they do achieve positions of power—even though they may genuinely want to save the country—they are so poorly educated that all they can do is stand back and stare at the things to be done like blank-eyed idiots. For during their school years when they should have been acquiring the ability and knowledge necessary for handling national affairs, they wasted their time in engaging in politics. This really pleased the old folks no end; for although they were just as ignorant as the young people, still they had many more wicked ideas about how to get along in the world than did the young. Since the young people didn't have time to learn anything in school, when they finally did achieve positions of power, they had to go to the old people to find out how to do things, and that's just what the wily old foxes were waiting for. Thus our revolutions looked after themselves, but the real directing power behind them has always remained in the hands of those wily old foxes.

"Since the ideas of the young people are muddle-headed and the schemes of the old people are sly, everybody has come to believe that politics is a kind of muddling through carried out on the social plane. If one is good at this kind of muddling through, then one obtains everything his heart desires; and if one isn't good at it, then he falls flat on his face. As a result of all this, the students in our schools don't bother to study anymore. All they do is memorize a little of the new jargon, learn a few of the old people's crafty schemes, and then present themselves to the world as political geniuses."

I let him rest for a while and then said: "You haven't gotten to Everybody Shareskyism yet."

"Well, the more brawls that came into being, the more impoverished our people became because everybody's efforts were devoted to the brawls and nobody paid any attention to economics. At that point Everybody Shareskyism arrived in Cat Country. Shareskyism emphasized the people and was strongly grounded in economics. Until the arrival of Shareskyism, despite the large number of revolutions we had gone through, the Emperor had never fallen. For whenever a new brawl became popular, the Emperor would simply announce that he believed in the same program and would even like to become leader of the brawl. Then he would secretly contribute funds in large amounts and the brawl members would make him head. Therefore, a poet once praised our Emperor as 'Ruler of the Ten Thousand Brawls' *

"However, when Everybody Shareskyism arrived, everything changed. One of our Emperors was actually murdered, and at long last a brawl actually came into power, the Everybody Shareskyism Brawl. Since this brawl advocated getting rid of everyone except honest-to-goodness peasants and workers, quite a few people were killed; but there was nothing unusual about this, for in Cat Country we have always killed people without so much as a second thought. Actually it might not have been a bad idea if they had really slaughtered all of the superfluous people, sparing only peasants and workers. But cat-people after all, are still cat-people and even when killing people they are bound to introduce some variations on the theme: for instance, if a man gave enough money, he was spared; and those who had someone influential to put in a word for them were also spared. Consequently those who ought to have been killed, were not; and those who ought to have been spared, on the contrary, lost their lives. The ones who ought to have been killed but weren't wormed their way into the Everybody Shareskyism Brawl and started corrupting it with wily schemes from within. The result was that more and more people died every day, but the orthodox principles of the brawl were never put into practice.

"But the best was yet to come. Everybody Shareskyism advocated allocating jobs on the basis of ability

* In ancient times, the Chinese emperor was known as "Ruler of the Ten Thousand Chariots."

while at the same time equalizing compensation for all jobs. To realize such a program, it would have been necessary to reconstruct our economy and revamp our education. However, the members of our Everybody Shareskyism Brawl didn't understand economics to begin with and had even less conception of the problems involved in creating a new system of education. Consequently when all the killing was over, everybody just stood around and stared blankly at each other. They had hoped to build the new society on a base of peasants and workers, but they didn't have the foggiest notion of what agriculture was or what work was.

"For openers, they equalized the distribution of land. After everybody had acquired his fair share, reverie trees were planted and everyone bore up as best he could until the trees reached maturity. The workers were eager to work, but there was nothing for them to do. And so they killed off some more people, in the belief that the minority left after the slaughter would be easier to provide for. It's as though one were to say that when your skin itches, you'll be much better off if you tear off that part of it. That's about all I have to say about our experience with Everybody Shareskyism.

"It was exactly the same as with all the other political theories that came from abroad. In other countries they were really good programs that prescribed the right medicine for the right disease. But when they got to us, they so changed that rather than being cures, they turned into the carriers of fresh diseases. We ourselves never carefully examined either the new programs or our old problems; consequently, we suffered all the pain associated with revolution, but derived none of the benefits. Other people revolt in order to put new plans and policies into practice. We revolt only in order to 'stir up a brawl.' Because we are fundamentally lacking in knowledge, we are forced to turn our attention away from attacking problems to attacking people. Because we concentrate on attacking people, everybody utterly forgets about the lofty character that is demanded of people engaged in revolutionary enterprise and can do nothing but attack each other in the basest ways imaginable. And so the result of several years of Everybody Shareskyism, other than slaughtering people, is for everybody to stand around and stare blankly at each other.

"In the end the leader of the Everybody Shareskyism Brawl became our next Emperor! From Everybody Shareskyism to the throne—what a non sequitur! What a nightmare! But when you come to think of it, there's nothing very odd about it, for cat-people have never understood what government is in the first place. Having royally bungled Everybody Shareskyism, we had no choice but to set up an Emperor again. And with the Emperor back, at least we were able to put an end to all of our indecision.

"To this very day, we still have an Emperor and he is still known as the 'Ruler of the Ten Thousand Brawls'! And down to this very day we still have people who believe in Everybody Shareskyism too."

Young Scorpion was weeping.

22 *Some Generals Prefer Boudoirs to Battlefields*

Even if everything that Young Scorpion said were true, it still didn't constitute a constructive critique. What good was there in being so pessimistic? Of course, having come from a peaceful and happy China, I was inclined toward optimism and somehow or other felt that there was still some hope for Cat Country. (A healthy man usually finds it difficult to understand why a sick one takes such a dim view of things. People should always keep up their hopes—as a matter of fact, hope is really one of mankind's responsibilities; for despair is a sign of self-abandonment, while hope is the mother of all endeavor.) I didn't believe for a moment that if the cat-people united their strength, they could still fail to achieve any positive accomplishments. There were many, many factors that inhibited the development of Cat Country and prevented their politics from getting on the right track. On the basis of what I had seen and heard, I was not fully aware of all the difficulties that they faced, but the cat-people were, after all, still *peo-*

ple; and people are creatures who are capable of surmounting any difficulty that may face them.

I decided to go and find Old Scorpion and see if I could get him to introduce me to a few of the leading political figures of Cat City. If I were able to meet a few clear-headed people, perhaps I could obtain some critical opinion that was more substantial and constructive than that which Young Scorpion had given me. Actually I ought to have interviewed the common people first, but they were so frightened of foreigners that I couldn't really think of any way of getting close to them.

Of course, given the lack of an informed populace, one couldn't reasonably expect to find a well-ordered political system. But on the other hand, precisely because the populace *was* uncritical, it should be somewhat easier to get a political movement going if one could only find a genuine statesman who was willing to exert himself on behalf of the people and nation. Even though I had never relished the prospect of being the minion of an intrepid leader, I decided to continue my search for the ideal hero; perhaps I'd find just such a leader among the leading political figures of Cat Country. I happened to arrive just at a time when Old Scorpion was holding a party. I assumed that since he was one of the most important personages in Cat City, I'd be sure to find some statesmen among the invited guests. This should be an excellent opportunity.

I had not been to this side of the street for several days now. The street was as bustling as ever; it brought to mind the swarming of ants, though it didn't remind one of their industry. I didn't understand what attraction this broken-down old city possessed that it could arouse in people such a longing to be in it. Perhaps it was because the rural economy had totally collapsed, making city life appear at least preferable to life on the farms. There was one improvement: because of the frequent rains recently, this section wasn't nearly as foul-smelling as it had been. It seemed that the Old Man in the Sky * had sparked a "Sanitation Movement" for them!

Old Scorpion was not at home even though I arrived at precisely the time we had agreed upon. In the meantime, I was entertained by the man who had brought food to me while I was in the reverie forest. Since we were acquaintances of sorts, he told me straight out: "If you make an appointment for noon, then you ought to come in the evening; and if you make an appointment for the evening, then you ought to come at dawn. And sometimes, you simply ought to come a few days later. It's our custom you know." I was very grateful for his advice and went on to ask him who the guests were. I had decided that if there weren't any people among the guests whom I wanted to meet, I would simply leave now and not come back.

"The guests are all important personages," he said, "otherwise we wouldn't be able to get foreigners to come." Fine then, I'd be sure to come back, but where would I go to pass the time meanwhile? I suddenly came up with an idea. I'd interview him! I still had a few National Souls left in my pocket. I gave them to him. The rest of it, of course, was easy going. You see, Na-

* A Chinese, not Felinese, term.

tional Souls are the keys to the cat-people's mouths. We went up on the roof and I conducted my interview there. I asked him what the people milling about below did for a living.

"You mean these people?" He pointed down to the human sea on the street. "They don't do anything."

Here we go again, I thought to myself. "Then how do they get their food?"

"They don't eat food; they eat reverie leaves."

"And where do the reverie leaves come from?"

"If one man becomes a major official, then a mass of people get enough reverie leaves to eat. In other words those people down there are all relatives and friends of officials. When a man becomes a great official, he *plants and sells* reverie leaves; but he sets some aside to distribute to his relatives and friends. If a man becomes a minor official, then he *buys* reverie leaves and is still able to distribute some to his relatives and friends. And if a man doesn't become an official at all, then he just waits around for a few reverie leaves to come his way."

"There must be a large number of officials then."

"Except for the unemployed, everybody is an official. I'm an official myself." He smiled ever so slightly. Perhaps he intended this smile as revenge for my contemptuous treatment of him in the past (I had pulled off a piece of his scalp in the reverie forest).

"Do all officials have money?"

"Yes. The Emperor gives it to them."

"But if nobody plants crops or works, how does the Emperor get his money?"

"He sells national treasures and land. You foreigners

love to buy our land and national treasures; otherwise we'd have no income." He was right. The Museum of Antiquities, the Library—all of it fit together in a single piece.

"And how about you, yourself? Do you see anything wrong in selling off land and treasures?"

"As long as we get the money, it's all right."

"Then all in all, I take it that you have no economic problems?"

This question seemed a bit too deep for him and it was quite a while before he replied. "In years past economic problems did give us a lot of trouble, but nobody talks about that anymore."

"You mean that in years past people did till the soil and work?"

"That's right. But now the countryside is almost empty. Of course people in the city still have to buy things, but the foreigners sell them to them now. And since there's no longer any need for us to plant crops or work, everyone is idle."

"Then why do people still want to become officials? An official certainly can't be idle. And since a man gets reverie leaves to eat whether he's an official or not, why does anyone want to burden himself down with official responsibilities?"

"But when you're an official, you get more money, can buy more foreign imports, and can even take on a few more wives. If you don't take a post, then all you get is a small allowance of reverie leaves. Furthermore, being an official is certainly no burden, for there are more officials than there are things to do. Sometimes our officials can't find anything to do even when they want to."

"I have another question. If reverie leaves are all you have to eat, how is it that the Ambassador's wife didn't eat them?"

"Well, it's *possible* to eat ordinary food if you want to, but it's terribly expensive. If you want meat and vegetables, you have to buy foreign imports. And let me tell you that when *you* insisted on ordinary food back there in the reverie forest, you cost the boss a pretty penny. Madam Ambassador was an oddball. If she had been willing to eat reverie leaves, people would have supplied her free of charge, but nobody had enough money to keep her in meats and vegetables. She used to take her eight sexpots out to the countryside to gather weeds and wild vegetables."

"And meat?"

"There's no place to get any meat, unless you buy it from abroad. When people were still getting by on a diet of half reverie leaves and half ordinary food—this was a long time back—the people ate up all the fresh meat so that there was not a single animal or bird left. Have you ever seen an animal or bird here in Cat Country?"

I thought about it for a while and concluded that he was right. "But wait a minute, how about those white-tailed hawks?"

"You're right. They're the only ones left. If it weren't for the fact that their meat is poisonous, they would have been extinct a long time ago too."

You cat-people, yourselves, are on the verge of extinction, I thought to myself. Ants and bees have needs, but no economic problems. But even though they're free of economic problems, they still have the instinct to go on working; in that respect, they are much superior to cat-people. The cat-people no longer had any economy or government worth talking about, but even so they still couldn't resist competing against each other until they had created chaos. I don't know who had been guilty of creating such inferior products—creatures who had neither the instinct of ants nor the wisdom of human beings. Perhaps the god who had made the cat-people intended them as a joke. They had schools, but no education; politicians, but no government; people, but no personal integrity; faces, but no concept of face. One had to admit that their god had gone a little too far with his little joke.

But, no matter what, I was still determined to have a look at those important personages. I had already been forced into admitting my own inability to come up with a solution to the cat-people's problems; now I'd see if their own bigwigs had any ideas. On the surface of things, the solution to their main problem seemed ridiculously simple: carry out an equal redistribution of reverie leaves and thus bring into being a Reverie Leaf Everybody Shareskyism. But this would lead them right on down the leafstrewn path to oblivion! No, one couldn't do that. One would have to turn them back, prohibit the consumption of reverie leaves, revive agriculture and industry! That was the only way to really prevent them from accomplishing their own destruction. But who could possibly shoulder a responsibility of such magnitude? For such a task was certainly nothing else than trying to transform gnats and flies into human beings! But what monumental strength, what unflagging effort, and what iron decision would be necessary if the cat-people were ever to make that transformation! Were they capable of it? I seemed to be getting as pessimistic as Young Scorpion.

Old Scorpion returned. He was somewhat thinner than I had remembered him in the reverie forest, but he seemed as wily and full of schemes as ever, if not more so. There was no need for me to stand on ceremony with him, and so I asked straight out: "Why have you invited all these guests?"

"No reason in particular. Just getting together for a chat."

I could tell from this that there was certainly something important afoot. There were many questions that I wanted to ask him, and yet I had somehow or other conceived such a loathing for him that I felt that the less I said to him, the better I would feel.

The guests continued to arrive. I had never seen any of them before, and they weren't the least bit like ordinary cat-people. As soon as they saw me, they all called me "old friend." I rudely announced that I was from Earth. My somewhat impolite intention, of course, was to show that "old friend" was inappropriate. However, they seemed to interpret this sour note in my speech as the sweetest of harmonies, for they went right on calling me "old friend" with redoubled pleasantry. A dozen or so additional guests arrived. I was in luck: they were all politicians. I soon observed that this new group could be divided into three factions.

The first was Old Scorpion's faction. They used "old friend" with great fluency, although there was something a bit strained in the way they said it. The members of this faction were all a bit older than the others and I was reminded of the "wily old foxes" that Young Scorpion had told me about.

The members of the second faction were a bit younger and especially courteous to foreigners. They were constantly smiling, but their smiles were such vacant ones that you could tell at a glance that their pride was based entirely on the fact that they had just begun to learn some of the old foxes' wicked tricks, though they had not yet mastered their entire line of depravity.

The third faction was the youngest. Their use of "old friend" was so unnatural that one would have thought that they were ashamed of saying it. Old Scorpion made a point of introducing me to this third faction. "These 'old friends' have just come from *over there,*" he said. What he meant wasn't very clear to me, but given the situation, it wasn't convenient to press him. A bit later it dawned on me that by "over there" he meant the schools. The members of this faction then were brand new hands at politics. I was very curious to find out how people who had just come from "over there" had gotten hooked up with these old foxes.

The feast began; this was my first one in Cat City. We began with reverie leaves, just as I had expected. When we had finished, I anticipated that I might well see some new mischief. I wasn't disappointed. Old Scorpion announced: "In order to welcome our newly arrived friends from 'over there,' we'll let them select the prostitutes for the evening."

The ones who had just arrived from "over there" smiled, winked, and were bashful and proud at the same time. They all began mumbling to themselves: "Everybody sharesky. Everybody sharesky." I felt as pained as one does when a loved one is on the verge of death. This then was what their Everybody Shareskyism amounted to! When they were still "over there" they had continuously advocated new programs and *-isms.* But as soon as they arrived "over here" they began "Everybody Sharesky-ing" the local whores. That was the limit! Since there was no point in saying anything, I sat back to see what would happen next.

The prostitutes arrived and everyone had another round of reverie leaves. From beneath the grey hair on the faces of the young politicians a rosy glow began to show through, and they started glancing furtively at Old Scorpion. The latter smiled and said: "Please make yourselves perfectly at home. There's no need to stand on ceremony." Upon this invitation, the young politicians took the prostitutes by the hands and led them down below. Old Scorpion, of course, had already prepared pleasure rooms for them.

After they had gone down, he smiled at the two remaining groups of politicians and said: "All right, now that they've gone, let's get down to business." My guess had been right; he had invited them here because something important was afoot.

"Have you all heard about it already?" Old Scorpion asked.

The old ones showed no reaction at all; it seemed that their eyes were all turned inward on their own worlds. One of the middle-aged ones started to nod his head, but sensing that no one else was nodding, simply continued the upward motion of his face to make it look as though watching the sky had been his intention in the first place.

I laughed out loud.

Everyone became even more solemn, a solemnity that they expressed with a serious laugh. You see, they *had* to join me, for I was a foreigner.

A long time passed and, then finally one of the middle-aged ones summoned the nerve to speak. "I've heard a little bit, but I'm not sure—I've absolutely no idea as to whether the news is reliable."

"It's reliable enough. My troops have already been defeated!" Old Scorpion was perceptibly shaken. It must have been his personal bodyguard that had been defeated for him to get that worked-up about it.

Everyone was quiet again. As time passed their breathing slowed down so much that one would have thought that they were afraid they'd damage the hair in their nostrils if they breathed too hard.

"Gentlemen, shall we pick a few prostitutes to keep us company?" suggested Old Scorpion.

That brought them back to life. "Fine, fine! How can one come up with any good plans without women? Bring on the girls!"

Another group of prostitutes arrived and everyone was quite jovial. By now the sun was about to set, but from start to finish, no one had discussed anything that had anything to do with politics.

"Thank you! Thank you! See you tomorrow!" They all led their prostitutes away.

The young politicians crawled back up again, the faint flush in their cheeks now replaced by a touch of greyish-green. They didn't even say thank you, but just kept muttering "Everybody sharesky."

I concluded that a civil war had started and that Old Scorpion's troops were losing. He had, no doubt, invited all these people over in order to seek their help; but apparently they weren't willing to come to his aid. If my guess was right, then their refusal to help Old Scorpion might prove a good thing for Cat Country.

Scorpion seemed genuinely worried. As I was leaving, I asked: "How were your soldiers defeated?"

"The foreigners have invaded!"

23 *Hawk*

Although the sun had not yet completely set, there was not so much as a ghost to be seen on the street. Slogans, however, had already appeared on the walls in huge white characters: ABSOLUTE RESISTANCE; TO SAVE THE COUNTRY IS TO SAVE ONESELF; DOWN WITH AGGRESSION-ISM. . . . My brain was a murky ox rolling in the mud. Although I was the only one on the street, I felt as though there weren't enough air to go round in this living city of death. Old Scorpion's "The foreigners have invaded!" still sounded in my ears like a mournful tocsin. But why had they invaded? It was obvious that Old Scorpion was scared out of his wits or he would have explained the situation to me in greater detail. But scared as he was, he had not forgotten his social obligations and had not neglected to provide his guests with prostitutes—that was past all comprehension! And that bunch of politicians! The enemy was invading and they still had the heart to call in whores and take their pleasure without so much as mentioning a word about the affairs of state! More than ever, I felt that I would never understand how the minds of the cat-people worked.

The only thing left to do was go and look for Young Scorpion. Although I didn't approve of his overly pessimistic attitude, I had to admit that he was the only clear-headed person around. Besides, after seeing the politicians, how could I blame him for his pessimism any more?

The sun was below the horizon. A beautiful layer of clouds tinged half the sky red with the reflected rays of the dying sun. And below the clouds, a tenuous mist reflected the cruel melancholy of the land, setting off in even brighter hues the glory of the sky. A gentle breeze blew against my chest and back. Not so much as a dog's bark was to be heard. Even in primitive times, I thought, things must have been somewhat livelier than this. And this was a great city! My tears fell like strung beads.

I arrived at Young Scorpion's place and went to my room. There was someone sitting in the shadows and although I couldn't see clearly enough to tell who it was, I could make out that it wasn't Young Scorpion, for this man was taller.

"Who is it?" He asked in a loud voice. I could tell from his tone that he was no ordinary representative of the cat-people, for none of them would have dared to ask a question so boldly and aggressively.

"I'm the man who came from Earth," I answered.

"Have a seat, Mr. Earth!" There was a slightly imperious tone to his voice, but it was so open and frank that one didn't mind.

"Who are you?" My tone of voice was a bit gruff too, as I sat down beside him. Now that I was closer, I saw that he was not only tall, but very broad as well. The hairs on his face were so long that they seemed to cover over the openings to his ears, mouth and nose. The only thing exposed in the heavy tangle of hair that was his face, was a pair of very bright eyes which reminded one of two bright little eggs in a bird's nest.

"I'm Hawk," he said. "People call me 'Hawk,' but that's not my real name. Why 'Hawk'?—Because they're afraid of me. In our country good men are seen as fright'nin' and hateful—that's why they call me Hawk."

I looked up at the darkening sky and saw that now there was only a single puff of cloud left; it was tinged with red and hung like a lonely flower over Hawk's head. I went blank for a moment and couldn't think of anything to ask him. My mind was still preoccupied with the glorious image of a Martian sunset.

"I don't dare go out in the day and so I waited until this ev'nin' to come lookin' for Young Scorpion," he volunteered.

"Why not in the daytime?" It seemed that only the first half of his statement had gotten through to me and thus I emphasized that part of it.

"There's nobody, 'cept Young Scorpion, who's not my enemy. Why should I go out in the daytime and make things tough on myself? I don't live in the city. I live in the mountains. I walked all night yesterday and hid all day today. Just got into the city a little while ago. Have you got anything to eat? I haven't had a bite all day."

"I've only got reverie leaves."

"No thanks. Wouldn't touch 'em if I were starvin'! A man can't move out after eatin' reverie leaves."

In my experience, this was the first cat-man with any guts. I called Revery in hopes that she could cook up something. I was sure that she was there, but apparently she didn't want to come to us.

"Forget it. The women are all afraid of me too. What's so bad about goin' hungry for a few days more or less anyhow? Seein' as I'm about to turn in my chips anyway, why should I be afraid of goin' hungry?"

"But the foreigners have invaded, haven't they?" I managed to ask.

"Right. That's why I'm here lookin' for Young Scorpion."

"But how can he help? He's too pessimistic, too much the romantic." I really shouldn't have criticized my friend like that, but at times candor can be a virtue.

"He's that way because he's smart. As for bein'—what was the second thing you said he was *too* of? I didn't catch what you meant. But no matter what it was, if I had to find a guy who would die with me, he's the only one who would be up to it. Pessimists are afraid of livin', but they aren't afraid of dyin'. Most of our people go on livin' happy as you please; they'd still live happy as ever even if you starved 'em down till there was nothin' left 'cept a sack of skin. You see, they're born that way—they just don't know enough to be pessimistic. Maybe I oughta say they're born without brains. Young Scorpion's the only one around who knows enough to take a dim view of things. That makes him the second good person in Cat City—that is, if you count me as the first."

"You're a pessimist?" Although I thought him a bit gruff and arrogant, I didn't doubt his intelligence.

"Me? Hell no! It's exactly because I'm not a pessimist that everybody's afraid of me and hates me. If I'd only picked up a bit of Young Scorpion's pessimism, they wouldn't have driven me into the mountains in the first place. The difference between me and Young Scorpion lies right there. He *despises* those witless people who have lost all sense of personal integrity, but he doesn't dare offend 'em. I don't hate 'em, but I do feel like knockin' some sense into their heads and lettin' 'em know that they still don't look up to scratch as people. So, I *do* offend 'em. But if push comes to shove, Young Scorpion's as ready to die as I am."

"Were you in politics before, too?"

"Yup. Now take my own way of livin'. I'm against eatin' reverie leaves, against whorin' around, and against takin' a lotta wives. So I try to talk people out of reverie leaves, whores, and concubines. This way I manage to offend the old guard, the new school, and everybody in general. There's somethin' you oughta know, Mr. Earth. Here with us, anyone who wants to suffer hardship or gain a little learnin' is thought to be a hypocrite. For instance I walk on my own two feet and never have to call in seven bearers to carry me around. But when other leaders see me refusin' to be carried around like a bale of leaves, when they see me walkin' on my own two legs—what do you think their reaction is? Do you think that they take me as a model? Hell no! They say I'm puttin' up a front, call me a hypocrite!

"Whenever the politicians open their mouths it's always 'the economic' this or 'the political' that. The students are forever jawin' about this or that '-ism.' But try askin' 'em what they mean, and they just stare at you blank as a wall. And if you get a notion to study it out for yourself, they'll call you a hypocrite. And the common people? Give 'em a National Soul and they'll smile at you; tell 'em to cut down on reverie leaves and they'll give you a dirty look and call you a hypocrite. From the Emperor on down to the ordinary folk, they all take doin' bad things as the right road of life, all take doin' good things or standin' up under hardship as playin' the hypocrite. And that's why everybody wanted to kill me—to get rid of a hypocrite. Politically, I think that any political program, no matter what kind it is, oughta be grounded in economics; and any kind of political reform oughta be motivated by sincerity. But none of our politicians has any notion of economics and there isn't a sincere one in the whole lot.

"From beginnin' to end, the politicians have always taken politics as a kinda game. You give me a push; I give you a shove. Before long everybody is talkin' economics, and yet our agriculture and industry are already completely bankrupt. Under this kind of condition, if anyone like me tries to set up politics on a basis of integrity and good sense—Hypocrite! You see, if they didn't accuse me of bein' a hypocrite, they'd have to admit that *they* were wrong. Now when you admit you're wrong, that's a kind of constructive criticism in itself, but they don't understand that. A few years back, you could blame our political decadence on a bad economic system; but now we don't have any more economic problems that we can use for scapegoats.

"It would seem to me that if we want to get back to the past glories of Cat Country, we oughta start with the problem of personal integrity. But it's really too late.

Once integrity is gone, there's as little hope of gettin' it back again as there is of bringin' a man back from the dead. In the last few decades we've just had too many political changes, and with every change, the value of personal integrity has gone down just that much more. The evil always win and so now we're settin' up for the final victory, that's to say we're waitin' to see who's the evilest of all. If I start talkin' about integrity here in Cat Country, the word no sooner leaves my lips than people spit right in my face. In foreign countries *-isms* are all good, but once we get our hands on 'em, they all turn bad. It was through ignorance and lack of integrity that we transformed the crops that nature gave us into reverie leaves. But I'm still not pessimistic. My conscience is bigger than I am, bigger than the sun, bigger than all creation! I don't commit suicide, nor am I afraid of standin' against 'em. Wherever I can exert myself to improve things, I do. I know damn well that it does no good, but my conscience, as I've said, is much bigger than my life."

Hawk stopped talking and I heard only his heavy breathing. Although I'm not a hero-worshipper, I had to admire the man. Since he was vilified by tens of thousands of people, he wasn't the kind of man one would normally pick as the object of hero-worship. He was more like a sacrificial victim who cleanses away all the shame of his people; he was more like the founder of a religion.

Young Scorpion came back. He had never before returned so late and I was sure there was some special reason for his delay.

"I've come!" Hawk stood up and rushed to the side of his old friend.

"You couldn't have picked a better time." Young Scorpion embraced Hawk and the two men wept. I knew that things must be in a critical state, although I was still ignorant of the details.

"But," Young Scorpion's tone showed that he seemed to know that Hawk was fully aware of what was going on, "your arrival won't make a great deal of difference."

"I know. As a matter of fact, it's more likely that I'll get in your way, but I had to come. Our opportunity to die has finally arrived," said Hawk as the two men sat down.

"And how will you die?" asked Young Scorpion.

"I yield the empty glory of death on the battlefield to you. I have in mind a somewhat inglorious, but not entirely useless, end. How many men do you have now?"

"Not too many. Father's troops retreated before the battle started, and the soldiers of the other leaders are preparing to fall back at this very moment. I'm afraid that Big Horsefly's men are the only ones left who might be willing to take orders from me. But when they hear that you're here, I don't know what they'll do."

"I know," said Hawk calmly. "Can you bring your father's troops under your command?"

"There's not much hope of that."

"How about killin' one or two of their officers as a show of strength?"

"But my father didn't turn over his military command to me, and they know it."

"Why don't you spread a rumor to the effect that I have a big body of troops under me, but we all refuse to accept your orders, and. . . ."

"That part of it might work. Even though you don't have a single solitary soldier, if I spread a rumor, there will be some who will believe it. But then what do we do?"

". . . And then kill me and display my head in the street as a warnin' to any troops who refuse to accept your orders. What do you think of the plan?"

"The plan has its merits, but I'd first have to spread the rumor that my father has relinquished his command to me."

"Well then, you'd better get started. The enemy is almost here and we'll need every soldier we can lay our hands on. It's settled then. I'll put an end to *myself,* old friend, in order to spare you the pain." Hawk clasped Young Scorpion in his arms, but neither of them shed any tears.

"Wait a minute!" My voice interrupted them. "Wait a minute! What possible good are the two of you going to accomplish by doing this?"

"None at all," said Hawk with the utmost calm. "It won't do a bit of good. The enemy outnumber us and are better equipped; even if we were able to concentrate the entire strength of our country against 'em, we still might not come out on top. But on the long shot that our example may have some influence, perhaps we can bring about a great turning point in the history of Catdom. The enemy expects that we won't dare, or even be willin', to put up any resistance. But the two of us, if we accomplish nothin' else, will have at least taught our enemies not to despise us so. And if not a single person heeds our call to arms? Well, the answer to that is simple enough: Cat Country will have deserved its death and the two of us will have deserved to die too. There's no consideration of sacrifice or glory involved in this. It's just that while alive we'll have done nothin' to bring about the extinction of the country, and in death we'll have avoided becomin' conquered slaves. Conscience is bigger than life; it's as simple as that. Goodbye, Mr. Earth."

"Hawk!" Young Scorpion called him back. "If you take forty reverie leaves, your death will be a little less painful."

"All right." Hawk smiled. "When I was alive, I was called a hypocrite for not eatin' reverie leaves. By eatin' 'em now at the hour of my death, I'll make it easy for 'em to prove that I was a hypocrite after all. What funny twists and turns life takes. All right, bring on the blessed leaf. As long as I'm gonna do it that way, there's no point in goin' outside 'cause I won't mess things up anyway. You two can watch me breathe my last. A death with friends gathered 'round is not, after all, completely meanin'less."

Having brought in the reverie leaves, Revery immediately turned away and left. Hawk chewed them up one at a time, but apparently felt no need to say anything more.

"And your son?" asked Young Scorpion. The words were no more than out of his mouth but he seemed to regret them. "I really shouldn't have asked that."

"It's all right," Hawk said and then asked in a low voice, "When the whole country's on its last legs, who can afford to worry about a son?" He continued eating, but his chewing gradually slowed down. His mouth was probably already numb.

"I'm goin' to sleep now," he said very slowly, and having said it, lay on the floor.

After a long time had passed, I felt his hand; it was still quite warm and elastic. In an almost inaudible voice he said, "Thank you both!" And that was the last thing that he said. By midnight, however, he still hadn't breathed his last.

24 *A Walk with Revery*

Hawk was dead—I don't want to use the word "sacrificed," for he didn't consider himself a hero. For the time being I had no way of knowing whether his death would have the effect he had hoped for. All I knew was that his head was displayed in a basket out there in the street. "Let's go get a look at the head!" became a popular catchword in Cat City overnight. I, of course, had no desire to see Hawk's head, but I was curious to see what kind of spectators had come. Since Young Scorpion was now so busy that he didn't even have time for Revery, much less for me, I decided that I might as well venture out onto the crowded street.

The city was as bustling as ever—no, I really ought to say it was even more lively than usual, for there was a head to see now! That was even more fun for the catfolk than standing around to gawk at where a pebble had been! Before I got to the place where the head was displayed, I heard people say that three old folks and two young women had already been killed in the press of the crowd gathered there. The cat-people were apparently willing to sacrifice their very lives for the pleasure of the eye. What sensitive esthetes!

The spectators didn't criticize or discuss the event that they were witnessing at all. It seemed that they were only interested in crowding and cursing each other. Nobody asked, "Who is it?" or "Why did he die?" Not a single one. All I heard was: "The hair on his face is pretty long, isn't it?" and "His eyes are closed," and "Too bad they didn't display the body too!" If this were the only effect that Hawk's death had on these people, then maybe he was better off dead; for what point would there have been in going on living with a group of people like this?

After I left the crowd, I started walking toward the palace for I thought that there was bound to be something worth seeing there. The street was crowded and noisy. There was a continuous din from wind and percussion instruments as one band after another passed by in the streets. It seemed that there was just too much for the people to take in at one time. They wanted to get a good look at the head, but at the same time they couldn't tear themselves away from the bands. Now they'd go harum-scarum toward the band and then they'd fall over each other running back to the place where the head was displayed; they all seemed very unhappy that they had grown only one pair of eyes. From their shouts I learned that the bands were all wedding processions on their various ways to pick up new brides. There were so many people that I couldn't get a close enough look to see whether they carried the brides in palanquins as we do back home, or whether, like Old Scorpion, they used groups of seven bearers; and so I had to content myself with listening to the music. I didn't really have the heart to go gawking at wedding processions anyway, but I certainly *did* feel like asking someone why, in a time of national peril, everybody was in such a hurry to get married. But there was no one whom I could ask, for generally speaking, the cat-people don't like to talk to foreigners. I went back to look for Revery and found her weeping alone in her room. My arrival only seemed to make matters worse and she wept so bitterly that she could no longer speak. I had to comfort her for quite a long time before she regained enough calm to say anything.

"He's gone! He's gone off to the war! What's left for me?"

"He'll be back," I said somewhat untruthfully. For, although I hoped he would, I had no idea as to whether he'd come back or not. "He promised that we'd go off to the front together," I lied, "and so I'm sure he'll be back."

"Honestly?" She was smiling through her tears.

"Honestly. Why don't you go out for a walk with me? There's no point in staying here by yourself crying."

"I'm not crying." After wiping her eyes and putting on a little powder, Revery went out with me.

"Why are there so many marriages taking place right now?" I asked.

If being able to comfort a woman and stop her crying for a while can be counted as any kind of accomplishment, then perhaps I can offer that as an excuse for my own selfishness. And selfish I was, for I must confess that I wasn't thinking of her interests at all—Young Scorpion's eventual death in battle seemed a foregone conclusion—but was only interested in satisfying my own curiosity. Even today I still feel somewhat guilty about using her that way.

"Everytime there's a disorder, everybody gets married immediately to prevent the women from being despoiled by the soldiers."

"But what's the point in getting married with such fanfare?" The concepts of death and destruction had monopolized my heart.

"Well if you're going to get married, you might as well do it up in style. After all, the fanfare only lasts for a few days, but marriage is for a lifetime." Perhaps the cat-people had a closer grasp of life than I did after all! She suggested going to the opera. After falling for my lie about Young Scorpion, she had forgotten all of her troubles. "The Minister of Foreign Affairs is taking a daughter-in-law into his home and there will be opera sung in celebration. Have you ever seen an opera?"

Come to think of it, I really hadn't yet seen an opera performed by the cat-people. The idea flashed across my mind that it would be much more to the point to go and kill the Minister of Foreign Affairs who still had the heart to see an opera while Cat Country teetered on the edge of oblivion. But after all, I'm not the killer type, and so I decided that I might as well escort Revery to the opera. In coming to that decision, I had the vague and uncomfortable feeling that my own thought was already a bit Cat-Countrified.

There were soldiers stationed outside the walls of the Minister's home. The opera had already begun. A crowd of common people had gathered around to hear what they could. Whenever, excited by curiosity or the music itself, they'd surge forward for a better look or listen, the soldiers would grab tight their clubs and play a different tune on their heads. Cat-soldiers were really quite good at using clubs on their own people. As Young Scorpion's girl, Revery, of course, could have gotten us inside, skulls intact, but I didn't really want to see it anyway. If it sounded that god-awful at a distance, think of what it would be like when you got up close! After listening to it for a bit, the only impression I had was one of racket. To tell the truth, I wasn't able to appreciate the cat-people's opera.

"Do you have any music that's a bit more restful and elegant?" I asked Revery.

"I remember once when I was small I went to a foreign opera that was much more refined than this, but since no one understood it, it was never performed again. For a time the Minister of Foreign Affairs, himself, promoted foreign opera, but then he heard someone —a foreigner—say that there was tremendous value in our native music and then he began to promote the traditional opera again."

"And if in the future someone else—a foreigner, let's say—tells him that there's more value in foreign opera after all?"

"He wouldn't necessarily promote it again. You see, foreign opera really *is* very good, but it's a bit too deep. I don't think he understood it even when he was promoting it. Consequently as soon as he heard someone say that our own opera was good, he was only too glad to change back. He doesn't really understand music anyway, but at the time he was interested in making a reputation as a patron of the opera. Promoting the traditional opera had a double-barreled advantage built in: it would be very easy to do and it would be well-received by most of the people to boot. It often happens with us that when a new art or science arrives from abroad, our native product begins to develop again as a result of the outside stimulus. You see, it's not easy to understand new things, so we simply don't bother to try."

I guessed that Revery had been infected by Young Scorpion's pessimism for I thought that such an opinion certainly couldn't be her own. And although she said all of these things against the opera, she was still crowding forward as she spoke. Since she seemed to like the opera, all the while denying it, I thought that it would be indiscreet to go on asking critical questions. I suffered through the atrocious racket as long as I could before suggesting: "Let's get away from here." Revery didn't seem to want to go, but she didn't insist on staying either; however, in light of the little anti-opera speech that she had just made, she was probably too embarrassed to stay.

I wanted to see what was going on over in the direction of the palace and she had no objections. The palace was the largest structure in Cat City, but it was by no means beautiful. Today it was particularly ugly. There were soldiers in front of the wall and on top of the wall; in fact there were soldiers everywhere. But that wasn't the worst of it. The top of the wall was piled high with soft mud and the ditch at the base of the wall was filled with a stinking kind of water. I didn't understand the idea behind all this, and I asked Revery.

"Foreigners like cleanliness," she answered, "so every time we hear that they are about to invade, we pile filth up outside the palace and fill the ditch with foul water. Thus when the foreigners arrive, they don't dare barge right in because of their fear of dirt."

I didn't even have the heart to laugh.

Several heads appeared above the top of the wall; after a long while the cat-people to whom they belonged all climbed up and straddled the top of the wall. Revery seemed very excited. "It's an imperial edict! An imperial proclamation!"

"Where?" I asked.

"Wait a bit!"

I waited until my legs were numb, and then I waited some more. Finally a piece of stone with white characters on it was lowered from the top of the wall. Revery's vision was really sharp, for she reacted with an "Oh!" almost as soon as they started to lower it down.

"Well, what in the devil's going on?" I was a bit impatient.

"They're moving the capital! It's moving day for the Emperor! This is the end of everything! The end! What will I do if the Emperor leaves?"

She was genuinely worried. I thought to myself: "If that prospect so alarms you, what are you going to do when you discover that Young Scorpion is not here anymore either?" I was preparing to comfort her as best I could when another slab of stone was lowered down. "Quick, Revery, what does it say?"

"The army and civilian population will not be permitted to evacuate without explicit permission; only the Emperor and his officials are to leave." She read it for me. I really admired that Emperor; with luck, I thought, perhaps he'd trip and break his neck while running away. But Revery, on the contrary, seemed quite pleased.

"Well I guess things will be right after all. If everyone else stays, I won't be afraid."

I wondered how in the world everyone else could possibly stay. When the officials were all gone, where would they get their reverie leaves? Just as I was pondering this, another proclamation was lowered down and Revery read it for me: "From this day forward, no one will any longer be permitted to address His Majesty as 'Ruler of the Ten Thousand Brawls.' With imminent disaster facing us, all our people should be united as a single man; therefore, we ought to refer to His Majesty as 'Ruler of the United Brawl.' "

Revery commented: "At this point it would be much better if they would simply forget about brawls altogether!"

She continued reading: "The military and civilian population are, without exception, to unite in resistance. No one is to injure the state because of private interests!" I had a comment of my own: "In that case, why is the Emperor first to run away?"

After another long wait, the people on the top of the wall climbed back down again. It seemed that the issuing of proclamations had ended. Revery wanted to go back to see if Young Scorpion had come back, but I was more interested in going to see what was taking place at the government agencies. Even if I couldn't get in, I figured that I'd at least be able to see what orders had been posted outside. We went our separate ways: she to the east, I to the west. In her direction things were still as lively as ever; the sounds of the wedding procession bands and operatic orchestras dinned unpleasantly against my ears from the distance. The west side of town, on the other hand, was very peaceful; in spite of the portentious proclamations that had been set out for people to read, it seemed that the inhabitants of Cat City were much more interested in seeing weddings than they were in reading royal proclamations. In fact, seeing weddings seemed to be the most important thing in the world to them.

I was especially interested to see what was going on at the Ministry of Foreign Affairs, but when I got there, there wasn't a soul to be seen outside the building. I waited a long time, but no one came out or went in. Stupid! I should have remembered. The Minister of Foreign Affairs was holding a wedding; and of course, that was much more important than mere foreign affairs, even if it was wartime!

I began to wonder whether the cat-people had any foreign affairs to conduct in the first place; I knew enough of the illogic of Cat Country not to fall into the naïve trap of concluding that they must have foreign affairs simply because they had set up a Ministry of Foreign Affairs. Since there was no one around I decided to simply ignore protocol and go in to have a look around. The doors were open and no one was inside. Good! I could look around to my heart's content. The rooms were empty except for piles of stone slabs all of which were engraved with the word PROTEST. Now I began to understand. What they meant by "foreign affairs" was sending a PROTEST slab whenever anything happened. The foreign affairs officers were, in fact, "protest specialists." I started to look for documents sent to the cat-people from abroad, but I couldn't find any. The probable explanation was that few people paid any attention to protests from the cat-people to begin with, not to mention the fact that conducting this kind of foreign relations was probably very simple and didn't require many records. There was no point in making the rounds of the other government buildings. If their foreign relations were conducted as crudely as this, it was likely that within the various other buildings, one would not even find so much as a stone slab.

I continued on until I came out on the west side of the city where I found a number of government buildings clustered together: MINISTRY OF PROSTITUTION; DEPARTMENT OF REVERIE LEAVES; MINISTRY OF OVERSEAS CAT-PEOPLE; OFFICE IN CHARGE OF BOYCOTTING FOREIGN GOODS; SUBDEPARTMENT OF MEATS AND VEGETABLES; and OFFICE FOR PUBLIC AUCTIONING OF ORPHANS. (The list is not complete; these are just a few of the agency titles that struck me as particularly interesting at the time.) There were a number of other agency titles that my Felinese was not good enough to understand. Since anyone who wasn't unemployed was an official one would naturally expect a large number of government agencies.

I continued my way westward. This was the first time I had gone out toward the western suburbs. It occurred to me that I could go out and take in the foreign enclave while I was at it. But how could I be so heartless? I really ought to go back and see whether there was any news of Young Scorpion. I changed my direction and came back across the reverse side of the street.

I didn't run into any young people at first; they were probably all off to see the head or listen to the opera. But after I had been walking a while I finally did come upon a student group. They were all kneeling on the ground. There was a stone laid out in front of them with a few white characters written on it: SPIRIT DWELLING OF THE GREAT IMMORTAL UNCLE KARL. I knew that if I ventured over to ask them about it, they would disappear like a morning fog chased by the wind. I slipped up quietly behind them, and kneeled down to overhear whatever I could.

One of those in the front row got up, stood upon the inscribed stone, and addressed the group: "Long live Uncle Karlskyism! Long live Everybody Shareskyism! Long live *Pinsky-pansky Pospos!*" They all echoed his cries. After they had stopped shouting, the one who had stood up addressed them as they sat on the ground. "We must overthrow the Great Spirit and concentrate all of our faith in Uncle Karl, the Great! We must overthrow our fathers and teachers; and to hasten the recovery of our freedom, we must overthrow the Emperor and put Everybody Shareskyism into practice. We welcome the foreigners who invade us today, for they *pinsky-pansky pospos!* Let's go and take the Emperor into custody so that we can present him to our foreign comrades; that's our only hope. We must capture the Emperor immediately, and then we'll take all fathers and teachers and kill off every last one of them. When they're all dead the reverie leaves will all be ours; the women will all be ours; the people will all be our slaves; and even Everybody Shareskyism will be ours! Uncle Karl the Great has said: '*Pinsky-pansky pospos* is the *dinsky-dansky dosdos* of both upper and lower levels of *hingy-hongy hopo!*' And now, on to the palace!"

No one made the slightest move. "Let's go *right now!*" But still no one moved.

One suggested, "Why don't we all go home and kill off our fathers first?" And still another said, "There are too many palace troops; there's no point in taking a beating because of haste!"

They were all starting to get up.

"Sit down! All right, is it decided then that we go home and get rid of our fathers first?"

They all began turning to their neighbors, asking this and answering that.

"If we kill our fathers, where will we get our reverie leaves from?" asked one of them.

"But that's just the reason we ought to kill them. The reverie leaves are all in their hands," opined another.

"Since we are not agreed on a united course of action, let's split up and go our own ways. Let the kill-the-Emperor faction go and kill the Emperor and the kill-our-fathers faction go home and kill their fathers," said still another.

"But Uncle Karl the Great only took up the kill-the-Emperor *pogsomosky, He* didn't say anything about killing our fathers."

"Counter-revolutionary!"

"Let's kill that misinterpreter of the sacred words of Uncle Karl the Great!"

I thought that this would lead to immediate bloodshed, but for a long time, no one made a move. Things were hopelessly disorganized. Gradually the main body of students split up into several small groups. They all stood facing Uncle Karl the Great's spirit tablet. After quite a while each splinter group consisted of only one person, still facing the stone and making as much fuss as ever. After working up a lather about this, and flying into a rage about that, they were all exhausted. Summoning up every bit of strength they had left, they all faced the stone and cried: "Long live Uncle Karl!" And then they all departed, each going his own separate way.

What kind of circus was this?

25 *Everything Is Beginning to Collapse*

I didn't feel like criticizing the cat-people any more; criticism won't turn a lump of stone into an exquisite piece of sculpture. Anything that I could possibly forgive them, I fully excused; and those things that were past all excuse, I blamed on their unlucky environment.

I went to wait for Young Scorpion, still hoping to go to the front with him to see things for myself. I was almost totally ignorant of the international situation that obtained among the various Martian states. I asked Revery, but all that she knew was that such-and-such a country's face powder was much whiter and finer than the Cat Country product. She answered every question that I had with a negative shake of her pretty little head. And after each of my questions, she in turn would ask, "Why isn't he here yet?" It was an effective counterattack, for that question was one that I couldn't answer either. All I could do was offer a silent prayer on behalf of all the women of Mars that there would never be another war.

After we had waited for a whole day, he still hadn't

come back. Revery was beside herself. The officials had all evacuated the city and the streets were no longer as lively as usual, though quite a few people still came to see Hawk's head. There was no way of getting any news. You couldn't ask anybody, for no one knew anything about national affairs, despite the fact that *national* was one of the most frequently used words in Felinese: reverie leaves were the "national" food; Hawk had been a "national" villain; the stinking mud in the ditch had been called "national" mud.

I felt like going out for a look at the foreign enclave, but at the same time I was afraid that Young Scorpion might return while I was out. Revery stuck to me like glue, and kept saying, "Don't you think we'd better run away too? Everyone else is gone; even the other girls have gone!" I merely shook my head, for I couldn't think of a suitable reply.

After we had spent another day in waiting, he came home. The expression of happy boredom that I was used to seeing on his face had completely disappeared. Revery was so happy that she couldn't speak, but merely stared at him through tear-filled eyes. I let him catch his breath before I asked: "How are things going?"

"It's hopeless," he sighed.

Revery looked at me, looked at him, and then gathered together enough strength to force out a question that she had wanted to ask for some time but hadn't dared. "Are you still going to leave?"

Without looking at her, Young Scorpion shook his head.

I didn't dare press the issue, just in case Young Scorpion was lying. What would be the point of wringing the truth out of him only to hurt Revery? Of course, even if I did press him, there was no guarantee that I'd be able to tell whether or not he was trying to hoodwink her.

After a good rest, he said that he was going to see his father. Revery didn't say anything, but one could somehow sense that she was determined to go with him. Apparently Young Scorpion sensed it too, for he seemed thrown for a loss as to what to do, and his very uneasiness gave away more than half his secret. I decided that perhaps I should help him pull the wool over Revery's eyes, but the expression in those eyes made me shrink back. Young Scorpion was still pacing about when Revery, unable to contain herself any longer, said: "I'm going anywhere that you do!" Her tears followed the words and Young Scorpion lowered his head.

After a long pause he raised his head and said, "Perhaps it will be just as well."

It was my turn: "I'll tag along too." Of course, my motives were quite different from Revery's.

We walked westward, but all the people we met on the way were headed east. Even the soldiers were marching eastward.

"Why is the army moving to the east when the enemy is on the western front?" I asked without thinking.

"Because there's peace and safety to the east!" Young Scorpion replied with ill-concealed anger.

We ran into quite a few scholars. Divided into a traditional and a modern group, they too were proceeding toward the east. The traditional scholars came first and seemed in unusually high spirits. A few of the old school came over and greeted Young Scorpion: "We're going east to see the Emperor. We're going to hold an academic conclave before the throne. 'Saving the country,' of course, is everybody's business, but it takes scholars to come up with real ideas about what to do! Scholars! Do any of you know how many soldiers are at the front? Do you think that the enemy will occupy Cat City? For if it looks as though he will, then, of course, we shall have to advise His Highness to remove a bit more to the east. There's no question about it. And to think that at a time like this His Glorious Majesty has still not forgotten his scholars! And in return, his glorious scholars will wear themselves out in loyal service to His Glorious Highness!" Young Scorpion didn't make a sound, but the traditional scholars, brimming over with "glory" because they had been summoned by the Emperor, were apparently unaware of anything amiss in his silence.

They had no more than gone away, when Young Scorpion was surrounded by another delegation, this one from the group of young scholars. They seemed exceedingly depressed, as if each of them had just lost a close relative. "Help us! Help us, Great Sir! Why has the Emperor convened an academic conclave and yet left us out? Can our scholarship be one whit inferior to that older group of dogs? Can our reputations be any lower than those of that group of beasts? We simply must attend that conclave! If we don't, who will consider us as scholars any more? Great Sir, we implore you as a personal favor to use your prestige to have us included in that conclave!" As before, Young Scorpion remained stonily silent. The young scholars became frantic: "If, Great Sir, you are unwilling to help us, then do not blame us if we start criticizing the government so that every man's honor will be whittled away without exception!" Young Scorpion grabbed Revery by the hand and went on his way, leaving the young scholars loudly weeping their outcast fate.

Some more troops approached us. Around his neck, each of the soldiers sported a necklace made of red cord. I had never seen this kind of army before, but I hadn't the heart to ask Young Scorpion about it, for I knew that the scholars still had him seething with anger. However, he guessed what I was thinking, and suddenly roared with mad laughter. "You're wondering what kind of an army this is aren't you? This is our National Shareskyism Corps. This kind of army has in the past been organized in other countries too; they all wear red cords about their necks to symbolize their affiliation. But in other countries, the Shareskyism Corps has always been composed of chauvinists whose minds have been filled with thoughts of country to the complete exclusion of any personal aim, every man an ardent and hidebound follower of Shareskyism. But as you see, our Red Cord Corps is moving out to an area of peace and safety just like everyone else. You see, they're too patriotic. After all, their corps belongs to the nation, and to allow the nation's armed forces to be destroyed out of any personal consideration would be clearly unpatriotic. Besides, if they were killed by the enemy, how could they be patriotic any more? You have to be sharp to follow their reasoning!" Once more Young Scorpion burst into gales of mad laughter, and for a moment I feared that he had really lost his senses.

I didn't dare say anything more, but simply continued marching ahead, observing the Red Corps out of the corner of my eye. In the middle of the corps there was a man who was being carried by ten or so soldiers; the cord around his neck was unusually thick. Young Scorpion took a look at him and said to me in a low voice, "He's the commander of the Red Cord Corps. His ambition is to snatch all political authority into his own two hands. Then he can become a dictator and make Cat Country strong, just the way that kind of thing has been done in other countries. He hasn't yet attained complete authority, but he is more powerful than anyone else—or perhaps I should say 'crafty.' For instance, right now it looks as though he's retreating to defend the capital, but what he's really doing is moving toward the capital to finish off the Emperor and thus realize at last his own ambitious plans. I'm sure of it!"

"Well, perhaps it will be to the best interests of Cat Country anyway," I observed.

"I'd agree with you that you can attain political power through craftiness, but I'm not sure that you can make the country strong that way. The most important thing to that man is his personal ambitions; the concept of 'country' doesn't even exist in his ambitious mind. Those who really love their country spill their blood against its enemies."

I began to realize that the arrival of enemy soldiers was going to be the fuse to set off a civil war. The passing mass of red cords began to blur before my eyes and then it suddenly turned into an inglorious sea of red blood in which soldiers were floundering about.

We were already well out of Cat City, and for some reason or other that I couldn't quite put my finger on, I had the feeling that I should never see it again. Before we had gone much farther, we ran into a rather singular group of Cat People. They were all very tall and unusually stupid looking. Each of them grasped a blade of grass in his hand. Revery, who hadn't spoken for a long time, suddenly said: "Thank goodness! The Great Mystics from the West have come!"

"What in the hell are you talking about?" I had never before seen Young Scorpion angry with Revery, but now he was obviously furious. Revery immediately changed her tune.

"I don't really believe in them, Scorpion."

I knew that if I threw in a question I could deflect some of the anger that he was preparing to heap on Revery. "What Great Mystics?" I asked.

Young Scorpion did not react immediately. Then instead of answering, he asked a question of me: "What would you say the greatest weakness of the cat-people is?"

That was really a hard one, and I began to ponder it.

Young Scorpion answered it himself: "Mixed-up!" I knew that he didn't mean me.

We continued walking for a bit and then he said, "You see, my friend, our fatal weakness is being always mixed-up. Among all of our people you cannot find a single one who fully understands anything. That's why we are always imitating others: it makes us seem less mixed-up and a casual observer might even be misled into believing that the imitation was the real thing or that we really did know and understand a lot. That's why we sometimes pretend to understand something new even when we don't.

"And yet, as you can well see by observing Revery's

reaction to these Mystics, whenever catastrophe is imminent, we will toss to one side all of the new terms we've memorized, and returning to old ways, we will reach for the most absurd and confused of concepts—concepts which lie stored in the deepest cellars of our spirits—and haul them out again. You see, we are empty to begin with, and as soon as we panic we expose our emptiness and begin calling for mama just like little children. For instance, as soon as the followers of Everybody Shareskyism panic, they burn incense and pray to Uncle Karl the Great, blithely oblivious to the fact that their Uncle Karl was one of the greatest enemies of superstition who ever lived. When our revolutionaries panic, then they begin the transport of the Great Mystics from the West wholesale, people who are much more mixed-up then they are mystical, a muddle-headed crew who only know how to walk around carrying stalks of grass. No one has any understanding of problems, and then when the point arrives where a problem must be solved immediately, they call in the Great Mystics. This is the very reason that we are certain to perish; we are all muddle-headed and confused. Neither economics, nor education, nor military affairs is really enough to extinguish a nation, but when every last one of its people is muddle-headed and confused—that is enough to destroy the race. For no one on our entire planet will treat as people, creatures who are as stupid and confused as beasts. This time our defeat is a foregone conclusion, and after our defeat, wait and see if the enemy doesn't slaughter every last one of us precisely because they don't regard us as people to begin with. Thus when they do kill us, it will seem to them much more like slaughtering animals than killing people; it will be a slaughter that will elicit absolutely no response from any other country, for no one ever gets all that worked-up over the butchering of animals. People are always cruel to those whom they don't respect. Generally, people don't respect other people who are hopelessly confused; they will often exterminate such creatures without a second thought. You wait and see if my words aren't borne out."

I really felt like going back to see what the Great Mystics from the West were up to, but I couldn't bring myself to desert Young Scorpion and Revery.

We rested for a while in a village. What I mean by "village" is simply a place where there were the ruins of a few collapsed houses, but no people.

"When I was little," Young Scorpion began and one could tell from the tone of his voice that he was reminiscing over the sweets of childhood, "this was a large village. And that was not too many years ago; and now, there's not so much as a single shadow! The destruction of an entire people can come about very easily!" He seemed to be talking to himself, and in order to spare him further pain I refrained from asking him how it was that this village had been destroyed.

Besides, I could almost answer it myself—revolution. War follows in the wake of every revolution; but it is the victorious ones who are helpless. Understanding only how to tear things down, they lack the imagination and ardor necessary to build things up again. And the only result of the revolution is to increase the number of soldiers in arms and the number of corrupt officials preying upon the common people. In this kind of situation the common people will go hungry whether they work or not. And so it had probably been with this deserted village. The villagers had no doubt begun to run into the cities or had joined the army for a few reverie leaves a month. This one dies and that one becomes a refugee and before you know it, the village is emptied clean as a barrel. To carry on a revolution without the knowledge necessary for its success—what a terribly dangerous thing that is! Nothing would save the cat-people unless they, themselves, realized that revolution was nothing but a noose about their necks.

I was just in the midst of this train of thought when Revery suddenly jumped up: "Look over there!"

Off to the west a great cloud of grey dust rose high into the sky as though some terrible and unnatural wind had suddenly stirred it up.

Young Scorpion's lips were visibly trembling as he said: "They're falling back in full rout!"

26 *The Last Gasp of a Dying State*

"You two had better go hide." Although Young Scorpion's tone was calm, he was obviously worried; I had never before seen such an intense expression in his eyes. "Our soldiers don't show much aggressiveness as they approach the front, but in retreat they run wild. You really ought to hide."

Still gazing toward the front lines, he said, "Friend, I place Revery in your hands!" Still not turning around, he extended one hand behind his back to feel whether Revery was still there or not. Revery took his hand and said with a tremble: "We'll die together!"

I was totally at a loss as to what to do. Should I take Revery away with me, or stay there and die with them. I wasn't afraid of dying, but I would have to consider what kind of death would be more worthwhile. I knew that if several hundred soldiers attacked me, then with only a single revolver to rely on I should be overwhelmed. However, I couldn't afford to waste too much time weighing the pros and cons of things; and so I grabbed one of them in each hand and ran toward a dilapidated old house behind the village. I really can't say what I had in mind. My plan—I really shouldn't call it a plan because I had no time to weigh things carefully—was nothing more than a flash of intuition. According to my intuition, there was only one course of action open: the three of us would hide until the main body of the army was past. Then I would foray out, capture one of the stragglers and thus determine the situation at the front. Then we'd be able to decide what to do on the basis of sound intelligence. If, unfortunately, we were discovered by the main body of troops—and there was no guarantee that they wouldn't bivouac in our area—then I would simply put up as much resistance as I could with my revolver; the rest, I would leave to heaven.

Before we had gone very far, Young Scorpion stopped and refused to go on. He seemed to have his reasons, but I didn't have the time to examine them; for if he didn't come, then obviously I had no hopes of Revery's going with me. I was once more at a loss. The dust that we had seen to the west was moving ominously closer. I had great respect for the speed and sight of the cat-people; and I knew that if the soldiers got much closer, there would be no more opportunity to hide.

"You're not going to die in their hands! I won't permit it!" There was urgency in my voice as I tried to pull them toward the dilapidated old house, but Young Scorpion still wouldn't budge.

"It's all over! There's no point in your dying too. Let Revery do whatever she chooses. I release you from all responsibility." Young Scorpion sounded quite determined. In strength, however, I knew that he was no match for me. I grabbed him around the waist and, half hugging half pushing, forced him toward safety. Since he wasn't the rugged type to begin with, he didn't put up a struggle. Revery, of course, had no choice but to follow. Thus I won out and before long we were all hidden safely away in a dilapidated little house back of the village.

I piled broken bricks into a wall that shielded us from view, and then peeked out through the cracks to see what was going on. Revery sat beside me and held Young Scorpion's hand.

Before long, the main body of troops came our way. It moved forward looking like a tornado whose vortex was a chaotic mass of debris. And from within the cone of this furry tornado, there issued forth one confused roar after another. Then the sound of the roar died suddenly away, the way that the sound of a wave does after just having broken on the beach. I held my breath waiting for the roar to suddenly build up again, but it didn't. When the cone of the cat-tornado was past and the mass had thinned out a bit, I was able to make out individual soldiers. They didn't even have the wooden clubs that I was used to seeing them carry back in the reverie forest. Their eyes were glued to their toes, as they ran desperately forward as though they were scared out of their wits. Their weird appearance made my blood run cold. An army without the whinnying of horses, without banners, without swords or guns, without rank or file—just a huge chaos of naked cats scurrying madly across the hot sands, each of them apparently pushed to the verge of madness by fright, hurtling forward for his very life. A group of, a field of, an entire horizon of, a whole planet of madmen! I had never before seen such a thing! Had they maintained some semblance of order I shouldn't have been nearly so frightened, but they were a pure random chaos!

I began wondering what point there was in Young Scorpion's coming at all this way just to see a defeated army in rout. Were these crazed soldiers running back to settle accounts with his father? That would be logical enough, but why shouldn't Young Scorpion hide from them rather than going out to meet them? I couldn't figure it out, and my confusion and curiosity made me bold: I decided to venture out of our hideout and capture one of the enemy soldiers. However, on second thought I realized that if I did venture out, I would be spotted immediately; for except for a few dilapidated houses, there wasn't a single tree or obstacle behind which I might take cover.

I waited some more, and finally the flow of soldiers dribbled away to almost nothing. However, those soldiers who were hindmost were also running the fastest. They were, no doubt, especially terrified because they had fallen behind the main body of troops and were doing their very best to catch up. It would be pointless for me to try to overtake one of them. They were simply running too fast for me. I decided that I'd have to come up with some other plan.

All right, then. Why not try my skill with my revolver? I knew that if I wounded one of them, those behind would run right past him without giving him a second glance, and those in front of him wouldn't so much as turn their heads when they heard the report of my revolver. But how could I guarantee that I should be sufficiently skillful to hit just one of them, and sufficiently accurate to wound him just enough to enable me to capture him alive? Moreover, even if I were able to hit him in a non-vital spot, would I have the heart to interrogate a man with a slug in him? Never having been a military officer, I seemed to lack the requisite touch of cruelty for such a task. I concluded that my plan was something less than honorable.

There were hardly any soldiers going by now and I realized that if I procrastinated any longer, there wouldn't be a single one left. I decided to go out and seize one bodily. At any rate there were so few of them left now that, at the worst, only a few of them would be able to gang up on me and my chances would still be pretty good. It was now or never. I pulled out my revolver and rushed out.

Things are never as easy as we think they should be in the abstract, nor are they as difficult either. If the stragglers had bolted upon seeing me, then it was a foregone conclusion that I could chase them the livelong day without catching a single one. But one of them, upon spotting me, actually froze like a frog surprised by a water snake. The rest of it was easy. I threw him across my shoulders like a shawl and carried him back to our hideout the way one brings a pig home from market. He neither cried out nor struggled. He was probably so tired and terrified that he was as good as half dead anyway. I put him down in our dilapidated hideout, but it was a long time before he opened his eyes. He took one look at Young Scorpion, and one would have thought that someone had just jabbed him with a pin. He glared so furiously at my young friend that it was obvious that he wanted to get up and spring upon him like a tiger. With me beside him, however, it seemed that he had nerve enough to get angry but not enough to act.

Young Scorpion didn't seem to be the least bit interested in him; he merely sat holding Revery by the hand with a blank expression on his face. I knew that if I used a soft approach in interrogating this prisoner, I might well get nothing out of him. I'd have to intimidate him, and when I had him scared enough, I'd ask how the army was defeated.

My captive quickly seemed to have forgotten everything and went blank. And then after a long while, he seemed to have thought of something: "It's all his fault!" He pointed at Young Scorpion and the latter smiled.

"Speak!" I ordered him.

"It's all his fault!" The soldier repeated his statement. I knew how verbose and roundabout cat-people can be and so I waited patiently until he had worked off some of his anger.

"None of us wanted to go to war, but *he* tricked us into going to fight. The enemy was even prepared to give us National Souls, but he wouldn't let us take them! The only thing *he* was good for was controlling us and keeping us from what *we* wanted to do. The Red Cord Corps and a number of other units all took the foreigners' National Souls and retreated in perfect safety. We were the only ones left for the enemy to give a good beating to, and believe me they did! We are his father's personal troops, but rather than looking after our welfare, Young Scorpion there led us straight to the execution ground. It seemed that as long as there was one of us left alive, he'd still want that lone individual to die like a well-behaved little soldier! His father was already planning to pull us out. But *that* one! *He* wouldn't go along with it. The other troops retreated in perfect safety; they weren't wounded and would be in good shape for looting when they got back to the rear. But *us!* We don't even have a single club left now. How are we to go on living?" He seemed caught up in his own eloquence and neither Young Scorpion nor myself said anything. We just listened. At least I listened, for Young Scorpion was perhaps so caught up in his own grief that he wasn't paying attention. I, on the other hand, was definitely fascinated by everything the soldier had to say. I just hoped that he would go on and on, the more the better.

"Our land, homes, and families," he continued, "have all been taken away by you. Old Scorpion does *this* to us today and you do *that* to us tomorrow. The number of officials increases every day and the poverty of the people increases apace. You thieve and cheat us until there's nothing left for us but to join the army. And then once you have us in the army, you force us to help you thieve from others just like ourselves. And the ruling class always takes the lion's share of the loot. You let us have a tiny bit of it only for fear that we won't go on helping you if you don't. We *can't* work, for you make soldiers of our parents so that we had to grow up in the army, knowing nothing but soldiering. If we weren't soldiers, we wouldn't be able to make a living in any other line!" He stopped to catch his breath and I took advantage of the opportunity to ask him a question.

"Since you know that they're no good, why don't you simply kill them and take over everything yourselves?"

The soldier rolled his eyes away. At first I thought

that it was because he didn't understand my words, but then I realized that he was thinking. After a while, he asked, "You mean we ought to revolt?"

I nodded my head. I hadn't thought that a simple soldier would be familiar with the term "revolution," for I had, for the moment, forgotten about the great number of revolutions the cat-people had already gone through.

"There's no point in talking about that. We don't believe in it any more. There'd be some pleasure in killing them for revenge, but revolution's a waste of time. Every time there's a revolution, we common folk just lose something else. The revolutionaries are all bad. Take that time when they were going to split up all the land and property, for instance. Everyone thought it was a great idea. But in the end each man only got a tiny bit of land, not even enough to plant a dozen reverie trees on. And as a result, we went hungry whether we worked the land or not.

"The ruling group couldn't come up with any way of solving our economic problems, especially the younger ones—all they were good for was coming up with plans, but they never paid any attention to whether our stomachs were empty or not. Any plan that isn't directed at filling the bellies of the common people is a joke. We don't believe anything they say any more. But since we don't have any way out ourselves, we simply serve as soldiers to anyone who gives us reverie leaves. And now they won't even let us be soldiers anymore! There's no point in revolting, but killing them would be sweet. We'll kill every last one of them! In having us go to war against the foreigners, *they* tried to kill us. But if we were all dead, who would there be to eat their reverie leaves and serve them as soldiers? They collect reverie leaves by the pile and wives by the dozen but now they won't even give us a scrap of their leaves. Instead, they send us out to make war against the foreigners and kill or be killed!"

"And now you've come back especially to kill him?" I pointed at Young Scorpion.

"That's exactly the reason! He orders us out to die at the front and won't even allow us to accept the foreigners' National Souls!"

"What are you going to do after you've killed him?" I asked.

He was silent.

Young Scorpion was the first clear-headed person that I met during my Martian experience, and yet this soldier and his comrades hated him to the very marrow of his bones. Of course, it wasn't my place to, nor did I have the time to, explain to this soldier that Young Scorpion was not the man he should hate. He had mistakenly taken Young Scorpion as representative of the official class, and since he couldn't put his hands on the whole of officialdom, had decided to take his revenge on Young Scorpion. This revealed to me one of the real reasons for the debilitation of Cat Country: those with a little intelligence were forever leading their compatriots to revolt before they had secured a firm knowledge of the real workings and power structure of their own society. Then, while seeking to solve the political and economic problems of the Cat Country, these well-intentioned and self-appointed leaders would themselves be swept up in the whirlwind of the very problems they had set out to solve.

The common people, having gone through a series of revolutions, had, to be sure, cultivated a class consciousness. But they were still in such a state of abysmal ignorance that their class consciousness was limited to realizing that they were being swindled as a group, but not being able to do anything about it. The upper classes were confused; and the common people were confused. Above and below, they were equally confused! This was the fatal weakness in the body politic of the cat-people! Suffering from such weakness, even though they were shocked by the prospect of the imminent extinction of their whole race, even *that* kind of shock still wasn't enough to make them grit their teeth, stand up and fight back.

What was I to do with this soldier? That was a problem. If I let him go, he might well run off to get help and then come back to finish off Young Scorpion. And if we kept him with us, he certainly wouldn't be the most congenial of companions. Besides, where would we go?

It was already late in the day and we'd have to make up our minds what we were going to do. Young Scorpion's expression indicated that he was only hoping for a quick death; I knew that this would be to do him no favor, but from the point of view of my own feelings, I couldn't do otherwise. Where were we to go? Going back east to Cat City would be dangerous. And the west? That would be to jump into the maw of death, for it was quite likely that the enemy was advancing in our direction at this very moment. After long deliberation, it seemed to me that seeking refuge in the foreign enclave was the only course of action that was really open to us.

Young Scorpion shook his head at the suggestion. I should have known. He would rather die than lose face by seeking refuge with the foreigners. He told me to release the soldier. "Let him go wherever he wants to!" I had to admit that that was the only thing we really could do with the soldier, and so I released him.

The sky gradually darkened. It grew unusually and fearfully dark. And all was silence. There was no one in the immediate vicinity. And yet we knew that in the distance, there were defeated troops behind us, and enemy soldiers before us. It was a silence like that on a desert island just before the sudden fury of a storm. And the quieter that it got the more nervous we became.

Of course, if Cat Country were wiped out, I could still go someplace else. But I was heart-broken with thoughts of my friend, Young Scorpion. To spend the eve of the extinction of a whole nation in a small lonely room—what a melancholy prospect! By now I had even learned to like Revery so that I couldn't bring myself to leave her either.

Only when a state is on the verge of extinction does one comprehend what a weighty relationship exists between an individual and his nationality. Of course, this had nothing to do with me personally, but I had to consider things from Scorpion and Revery's point of view so that I might be able to enter into their hearts and shoulder part of the load of grief that was there. There was nothing that I could say by way of comfort, for the destruction of the country was due to the stupidity of an entire people. What was the point in trying to comfort one or two individuals? The "death of a state" is not the catharsis of a tragedy; nor is it a poet's metaphor for righteousness; it is a cold and ugly fact; it is the steel logic of history. How can one explain away a fact, no matter how many emotional phrases one uses? I was actually listening to the last gasp of a dying state! My two friends, of course, heard it even more clearly than I did. In their hearts they were, no doubt, cursing the bitters of the past and reminiscing over its sweets. Now reliving the past was all they had, for there was no future, and their present had nothing to offer except the gradual fulfillment of the greatest disgrace to which creatures can be subjected—annihilation.

The sky was as black as usual, and the stars were as bright as ever. The environment was peaceful, and yet on this eve of the demise of an entire nation, one simply couldn't close one's eyes. I knew that they were awake, and they knew that I wasn't sleeping either. Yet none of us said anything. Our tongues seemed to be tied by the cords of doom. From this time on, neither people nor country would be permitted to speak again. The culture of another country had become dumb. Her last dream had been a song of freedom that had come too late. Now she would never wake again. Her soul could only go to hell, for her record in life was nothing but a dark and dirty spot on the pages of history.

27 *Farewell to Mars*

It must have been about daylight when I finally dozed off. By the time that I was conscious of the two loud reports, it was already too late—the bodies of my two friends were lying in pools of blood on the floor not two feet away from me. My revolver was next to Young Scorpion.

It would be impossible to describe what I felt at the time. My mind was a total blank and I was only conscious of a generalized pain. I felt the unflinching stare of my lively friends' eyes fixed upon me. "Lively?" For a moment my brain was unable to make the transition and I couldn't imagine two such lively friends as actually being dead. They both seemed to be staring at me, but there was no expression in their eyes.

They seemed to have grasped hold of some enigmatic and secret affirmation that they challenged me to guess. I stared at them until my eyes began to ache; their deathly gaze was still fixed upon me. It was as though they had given me a very difficult riddle to guess, but my mind was a total blank. Standing before them and unable to think of any way of bringing them back from the dead, I was painfully aware of the fragility and helplessness of life. I shed not a single tear; except for the fact that I was standing and they were lying on the floor, we were equally wooden.

Without thinking, I knelt down and felt them; they were still warm. Everything was the same, except the lack of a friendly response. All that was left of them now was that tiny fraction of their lives that still survived in my memory; the rest had died with them. Death is perhaps not without its tranquil beauty.

Revery was the more pitiable of the two. Beautiful girls were not meant to live in dying states. I felt that my heart would shatter. The sisters, wives, and mothers of a people have to pay for its sins as well as anyone else. If I were God, I'd surely regret having made women for such a spineless people. Knowing Young Scorpion made me pity Revery all the more. It seemed that while there may have been a logic behind Young Scorpion's death, Revery at least should have been spared. But perhaps it was idle to argue the rights and wrongs of dying with one's country; for like it or not, an individual's nation and people control his very existence, and when the nation or people perish, so does the individual. And besides, when that dreadful day arrives, who could be so wooden and soulless as not to want to perish with his state or people?

I began loving Young Scorpion and Revery all the more for having consciously chosen to accompany Cat Country to oblivion. I longed to call them back to life just long enough to tell them that they, at least, were pure, and that their souls were still their own. I longed to wake them up and take them back to Earth with me so that they might enjoy all those pleasures that life ought to hold. Fantasy is useless, but my only other alternative was grief; and yet no matter what direction my fantasy took, Revery and Scorpion remained woodenly stretched out on the floor, seeming to have already forgotten that I had once been their good friend. Now they would never be able to appreciate the intensity of pain that their fates had occasioned in my heart. It was as though life and death were separated from each other by a long series of skies piled one on top of the other. On one side, everything was life; on the other, death. And the two sides seemed separated by an infinite unknown. To me Scorpion and Reverie now stood in the same relationship as flowers or birds: although I might be able to explain to the world something of what it felt like to be a flower or a bird, still I would never be able to make one of them speak for itself. The silence of death is as absolute a fact as the inarticulateness of flowers. I didn't know what to do. My friends had already made their final decision but I was unable to decide anymore, for I no longer felt that life had any meaning.

I sat woodenly watching over them until the sun was up. I could see their forms more and more clearly, but was less and less clear as to what I should do next. The light struck Revery's face. She was still as beautiful and lovable as ever, but as silent and immobile as a piece of stone. Young Scorpion's head was nested in the corner of the wall, and his face still gave one the impression of boredom, as though even death had not cured him of his pessimism. There were absolutely no signs of fear on Revery's face.

I couldn't guard them anymore. For I suddenly realized that if I watched over them much longer, I would go out of my mind. Should I leave them? The thought of this possibility caused those tears that I had not yet shed to fall like rain. Alone on this vast planet, where was I to go? It was much more painful to have to give up two friends now and go off wandering alone, than it had been to leave Earth on my voyage to Mars in the first place. The loneliness of being a stranger in a foreign land is always difficult to bear at best; but how much more painful it would be since my departure from Cat Country had been caused by the death of two good friends! Their death would pursue me wherever I went. After crying for I don't know how long, I clasped them in my arms and sobbed out: "Revery, Young Scorpion, goodbye!"

I didn't have the time to worry about burying them. I felt that if I wasted another second, I should never be able to leave. Gritting my teeth, I picked up my revolver, and ran out. After I was some distance from the dilapidated little house, I turned and looked back. I decided not to go back; even though their corpses would rot, I could not go back. Then I began castigating myself. What a bad-luck-piece I was! The friend who had come with me from Earth had died here, and now I had to see my two Martian friends end like this. I ought never to make another friend!

Where would I go? Back to Cat City, of course; that was my only home. I didn't see anyone along the way. Everything was shrouded in death. The sky was grey, and several soldiers lay stretched out along the grey-yellow road, white-tailed hawks devouring the bodies. The scavengers flew up and down like graceful dancers, punctuating their movements with shrill shrieks. Revery's smile was suddenly before my eyes, and Young Scorpion's favorite words and phrases began to echo in my ears. I started running! They were still pursuing me.

My heart was beating furiously as I neared Cat City. Was it from hope or fear? I couldn't have said. There was no one around when I arrived. On the street, one here another there, lay the bodies of several women, mute reminders that the soldiers had come through. "The flowers have all run away!" It was almost as though I heard Revery's voice in my ear telling me of the fate of the rest of Young Scorpion's women. Yes, they must have indeed run off; otherwise, they would have been killed by the soldiers and I would have discovered their bodies among the others. I didn't have time to look things over too carefully, but just kept on running straight ahead until I reached the spot where Hawk's head was displayed. He was still there guarding the empty city! The flesh on the head had already been completely pecked away by the birds, and now he had become the soul of this dead city! Next I went to Young Scorpion's place. There was nothing there. Even the walls had been pushed in in two places. I wanted something, no matter how small, as a souvenir of Young Scorpion, but the soldiers had not left any of his possessions. There was nothing left, even brick and stone of the place was enough to move me to tears. I just had to leave.

I went off to the east, for I knew that the refugees must have fled in that direction. I turned around for a last look—a dead city standing alone in a vast expanse of grey. I went toward Old Scorpion's reverie forest, for this was the route that I was most familiar with. The little village that I remembered from the last time I had passed through was completely empty now—another mute reminder of the passage of soldiers.

There was no one in the reverie forest when I arrived. I sat under a tree and rested for a while, and then I felt that I'd just have to go on. Loneliness forced me to keep moving. I went down to the sandy beach where I had so often bathed. Through the mists I saw a man walking toward me from the west. I guessed that perhaps a turning point in the struggle had arrived so that the people were now returning to Cat City. Every little while another person appeared. Gradually I made out that they were rich people accompanied by soldiers. As I sat resting and watching on the bank of the river, more and more people began to appear. The people who had soldiers under them seemed to be racing each other as if there were some reward to be gained once they had reached their goal.

It went on like this for a while, and then before one realized what was happening, the soldiers started fighting over the road. The rich people started giving instructions to their troops, and the whole thing took on the aspect of a formal battle, leaving me even more bewildered than before. Furthermore, when the cat-people fought it was never very easy to distinguish between victor and vanquished. They simply set upon each other with wooden clubs, but it was only very seldom that one of them would be knocked down, for they spent much more time in circling around each other than they did in swinging their clubs. A ducks B, and B ducks A so that unless A or B becomes careless, there is little chance of one of the clubs finding its mark. As time dragged on, they still circled each other in an increasingly chaotic mass. Moreover, the distance between opponents grew greater and greater. One of the groups, however, seemed to be moving forward at the same time that it was circling. Their leader probably wanted to take advantage of the confusion to move his troops forward a bit and thus gain an edge on his competitors so that he would be closer to his goal when the battle was all over. As this group neared the river, I recognized their leader: Old Scorpion! I should have known—for Old Scorpion was, after all, the master strategist of Cat Country. Before long, he had circled his troops around until they were all up front. And just as I had anticipated, when they were all clear of the melee, they bolted off toward Cat City.

My opportunity had arrived. I took off toward Old Scorpion like an arrow and actually succeeded in catching up with him. He seemed very pleased to meet me, but at the same time he didn't seem too anxious to talk to me. He was too busy galloping forward toward Cat City. Panting for all I was worth, I ran beside him and asked him what he was up to.

"Follow me! Please follow me!" In the most sincere and imploring of tones, he panted out: "The enemy is approaching Cat City. Perhaps they've already gone through. I'm not sure!"

I was most pleased with his words, for I thought that he and his men were probably rushing to the defense of Cat City now that they were utterly convinced that there was no alternative but to fight. And yet I couldn't help wondering why, if they were all uniting to meet the enemy, they had staged a civil war along the way? There must be something more to it. I told Old Scorpion that unless he told me what he was up to, I wouldn't go with him.

He seemed unwilling to let the cat out of the bag, but at the same time he desperately wanted my help. Since he was familiar with my disposition, he had no choice but to tell me the truth.

"We're going to surrender. Whoever gets to Cat City first will have the honor of turning it over to the enemy, and you can be sure that there'll be no shortage of official positions for whoever gets to do that!"

I pointed toward the city and said, "Go right ahead, but I'll be damned if I have any time to waste on helping you to surrender!" Not taking the time to waste a second sentence on him, I turned around and headed back toward the reverie forest.

The soldiers to the rear, having apparently profited by Old Scorpion's example, also began jockeying forward as they fought. Among them I recognized the leader of the Red Cord Corps. An exceedingly thick red cord still tied about his neck, he was struggling forward with phenomenal energy in order to be the first to surrender.

Just at that point, all activity came to a sudden standstill up front. I turned around and saw that the enemy had arrived, and were in direct confrontation with Old Scorpion. Now that really did capture my interest, for I wanted to see exactly how he would surrender; I ran toward Old Scorpion's troops.

All of the leaders behind me dashed forward too. The leader of the Red Cord Corps was especially fast and even got ahead of Old Scorpion to kneel at the feet of the enemy. Then, one after another, all the leaders knelt down in submission. It reminded me very much of a group of filial sons and duteous grandsons kneeling before a coffin in an extended family back home in the old days.

This was the first time that I had seen the enemy army. In stature, most of them were a bit shorter than the cat-people, and judging from their facial expressions, they weren't too bright. They all looked mean and vicious. Since I knew nothing of their history or national character, I had no real basis upon which to judge them, but my first impression was that they were stupid, mean and vicious. Each of them carried a short stick that looked as though it were made of steel, but I couldn't see clearly enough to tell what these sticks were intended for.

When all of the cat-leaders were kneeling, at a signal from one of the short enemy who was obviously an officer, a row of soldiers sprang forward with great dexterity from the rear of the enemy ranks. They tapped the cat-leaders on the heads with their short clubs. The latter immediately lowered their heads, shivered, and then collapsed lifeless on the ground. Were the clubs electrified? I couldn't tell. The cat-soldiers to the rear, upon seeing their surrendered leaders all killed, let out a cry. It was a cry that sounded as though it had come from ten million roosters each of which had felt the cold steel of the butcher's knife against his neck. They ran to the rear almost faster, it seemed, then the sound of the cry that they had just issued. A great number of them lost their footing in the press and were trampled to death. The enemy did not even bother to pursue them.

They merely kicked aside the bodies of the leaders they had just killed and continued advancing.

I thought of what Young Scorpion had said: "The enemy won't be satisfied until they have killed every last one of us!"

But I still cherished one last scrap of hope for the cat-people. The circumstances were, in a way, now favorable for their salvation, for they had never before faced the situation in which they now found themselves: they would be murdered whether they resisted or not. Could that situation fail to stir them to a united resistance? If they banded together in resistance, I thought it unlikely that the enemy would be able to destroy them. I, myself, am a pacifist, but my reading of history has taught me that war is sometimes the only way to self-preservation. When there is no other way out, it becomes the duty of every individual to go to the front and, if need be, die. Chauvinism is a despicable thing, but self-preservation is a duty of nature.

I began to convince myself that after suffering this latest horror, the cat-people would certainly be shocked into putting their backs to the wall and fighting until the last man. And if they actually did so, I didn't think the enemy would necessarily be able to defeat them. I began to follow the enemy army. I noticed that as they advanced, they were finishing off those cat-soldiers who were too wounded to get away. One touch of that short club and it was all over. As far as I could see, these short enemy soldiers were not people of high cultural accomplishments, though perhaps they were ever so slightly in advance of the cat-people. If nothing else, they had one thing over the cat-people—a sense of national consciousness. Of course, national consciousness is only an enlargement of individual selfishness, but after all it *is* an *enlargement.* The cat-people, on the other hand, had never been aware of anything beyond their petty individual existences.

Fortunately, when I had set out for the front with Young Scorpion, I had taken along a supply of reverie leaves; otherwise, I certainly would have starved, for begging food of the enemy was unthinkable. I followed the main body of the short enemy troops at a distance. I didn't dare get too close to them, for they might well have captured me as a spy. They continued marching until they came to the spot where my aircraft had crashed. Then they fell out for a rest. I kept an eye on them from a distance. The space ship seemed to have aroused their interest. That was another point of difference between them and the cat-people: at least *they* had cultivated the habit of being curious about new things. I thought once more of my childhood friend; his unburied bones were doubtless being trampled to splinters by the enemy host!

After they had rested for a while, a group of them began digging, working with amazing rapidity. In appearance they were stupid and clumsy, but when they had made up their minds to do something, apparently they set right to it with no sign of hesitation or sloth. Nor was there anything slipshod about the way they approached their task. Before long they had completed digging a deep, broad pit. A bit later, a group of cat-people appeared from the east. Several of the short enemy soldiers were behind them, driving them forward like a flock of sheep. When they neared the pit, the soldiers who had been resting after the dig, all stood up and surrounded them. The enemy crowded the cat-people into the pit. The shrieks and cries of the cat-people were enough to shatter a heart made of steel, but the hearts of the enemy must have been even harder than that, for they went right on prodding the cat-people into the pit with their steel clubs.

Among the cat-people were men, women, and even mothers clasping babies to their breasts. The pain which such a sight occasioned in me defies all description, and yet there was absolutely nothing that I could do to save them. I closed my eyes, but I shall always remember those heart-rending shrieks. I can hear them even now. Suddenly the screaming died away, and when I opened my eyes again, I saw those short little enemy beasts busily throwing earth into the hole. The cat-people buried alive! This then was their punishment for failing to make themselves strong. I didn't know upon what object I ought to vent my hatred. And yet I had learned something from all of this, for whatever consolation that it was worth. People who don't consider themselves as people will not be treated as people by others. The unchecked selfish desires of each individual are enough to cause countless of his compatriots to suffer the barbarous punishment of being buried alive!

If I were to describe everything that I saw that day, I would weep myself blind, for those short enemy soldiers were the cruelest people whom I had ever known. The destruction of Cat Country was now complete; I even doubt that very many of their flies were left.

Toward the end, I actually saw a few cat-people try

to resist, but even then they could only manage to band together in groups of three or five at the most. On the very brink of death, they still didn't understand the need for co-operation. Later on, on a small mountain I ran into ten or so cat-people who had escaped. It was the only spot that had not yet been occupied by the enemy soldiers. But before three days were out, even this group of refugees had begun fighting each other so that over half of them were already dead. Before the enemy troops had yet arrived in the area, the group was down to two; they must have been the last two survivors of all of Cat Country. And by the time the enemy arrived, these two were locked in mortal combat. Rather than killing them, the enemy soldiers locked them in a large wooden cage where they continued their struggle until they had bitten each other to death. Thus the cat-people themselves completed their own destruction.

* * *

After living on Mars for another half year, I encountered a French exploration aircraft and thus was able to return alive to my own great, glorious, and free China.

NOVELS OF LAO SHE AVAILABLE IN ENGLISH TRANSLATION

Rickshaw Boy. A translation of *Lo-t'o Hsiang-tzu,* by Evan King. New York: Reynal and Hitchcock, 1945.

Divorce. A translation of *Li Hun* by Evan King. St. Petersburg, King Publications, 1948.

The Quest for Love of Lao Lee. A translation of *Li Hun,* by Helena Kuo. New York: Reynal and Hitchcock, 1948.

Heavensent. A translation of *Niu T'ien-tz'u Chuan,* by Ida Pruitt (?). London: J. M. Dent & Sons, 1951.

The Yellow Storm. An abridged translation of *Ssu-shih T'ung-t'ang,* by Ida Pruitt. New York: Harcourt, Brace & Co., 1951.

The Drum Singers. Translated by Helena Kuo. New York: Harcourt, Brace & Co., 1952. The Chinese version of this wartime novel has never appeared.

Cat City. An abridged translation of *Mao-ch'eng Chi,* by James Dew. Center for Chinese Studies, Occasional Paper No. 3. Ann Arbor: University of Michigan, 1964.